Stepping Stones, Scissors & Sex

Melissa Sorrentino

Published by Independent Author, 2020.

Copyright & Disclaimer

This book is a work of fiction. Any resemblance to actual persons, living or dead or actual events is coincidental. Names, characters, businesses, organizations, places, events and incidents are products of the author's imagination or are used fictitiously.

For anyone still becoming.

If this story makes you laugh, ache, or stay up too late,

please leave a quick review.

Thank you.

PREFACE

Yes, this is a work of fiction for entertainment. So, anyone who knows me, don't get any funny ideas! Really, any use of famous names, brands or locations is purely fictional and used with artistic license to indicate and set a tone for the period of the novel, which is circa mid-nineties with a few flashbacks to earlier eras.

Since I had one of the first text phones, you can trust my expertise on the nineties. I had AOL dial-up and a sweet, sweet Kyocera Palm Pilot flip phone. Pretty rad.

All characters are complete invention and not necessarily based on anyone's real life nor circumstances. However, I have spent much time in the locations herein and did my own personal stint auditioning in Detroit, Chicago, and primarily in Hollywood pounding the pavement as an actress for a couple of decades. I spent at least half my income on thick boxes of black and white headshots printed upon litho cardstock and at least half my time cutting actual paper résumés into 8x10s and stapling them to the back.

Meanwhile, I wrote this book in the wee hours, often after late-night improv shows while living in the 213, a crummy ghetto apartment in Westlake, LA not far from infamous MacArthur Park.

Please enjoy setting your own life aside for a while, as I did while writing it, to read and experience the adventures and misadventures in this lighthearted, fun, moving and uplifting story!

With Appreciation,
The Author

Chapter 1

HONEYMOON
Amber scanned the Fijian horizon for some sign of sunshine in the monochrome of gray. A last long drag on her cigarette and she chucked it into the shallow surf, quietly brooding. A cool wave lapped it into the ocean's morning silence. Fish slept, rocks slept, sand slept, and her spirit too had fallen into a dull, blank coma. An experience that seemed peacefully liberating fourteen days ago suddenly appeared as glum as her old single apartment in Downtown Detroit.

Pushing a tendril of mousy hair back into its sloppy ponytail, Amber couldn't believe she could be bored of Paradise so quickly. Two weeks into a fresh marriage and she already hated herself. She hated her redundantly ridiculous life. She hated the thought of being here for yet one more long, supposedly exotic week, trying to pretend she wouldn't have to leave.

The Fijians had it right. A lone fisherman stood knee-deep twenty meters into the beginnings of a sunrise, casting out into the Pacific, as if solitude came by second nature. Amber wished she could be him, a content soul simply pacified by a calm image of a fish on a hook. Marriage felt like a deep hook within her, and she felt its choke tightening in her throat.

She remembered being young, vibrant and giving a shit. Maybe that was less memory than fantasy. Amber couldn't remember any particular moments of satisfaction. Not today. If only she could swim out and never stop until the mighty ocean helped her disappear. If only she could feel the peace of this morning instead of dreading breakfast which would be in less than fifteen minutes. If only her life could be like the kava ceremony she'd witnessed last night, with old familiar friends circling a single goal: enjoying the moment.

AMBER WALKED DOWN THE imported Italian marble aisle as if in a dream. Her dress felt like a soft white cloud. Her smile wide, like the wings of an airplane. Every atom of her lovely body felt like soaring. She caught a glimpse of her own bronze flesh as she turned and grinned for a nearby camera. One swing of her head went left, then one right to lock eyes with Uncle Brian (crying, by the way) and straight forward. There stood Mr. Right and Wonderful, a.k.a. Aaron Spinnaker, a.k.a. Steel Fingers Wildboy. Steel couldn't have looked sexier than he did today. His tight long black pants flared slightly over expensive lizard boots. His wiry build looked straight and tall under a velvet Sergeant Pepper tailcoat covering his impeccably tailored white linen wide-collared shirt.

Steely, as Amber called him, was a rock star in every sense of the word. A steady diet of fast motorcycles, whiskey from the bottle, and stunningly rich exotic friends kept his expression perpetually beaming. Amber loved the way he could make her laugh.

He cracked her up as irreverently as ever when he proposed, screaming over his concert crowd's din as he rode onstage upon an African elephant's back.

"You marry me?" He asked, pointing at her and himself.

"What?!" Amber had mouthed from her spot in the front row.

Cupping his hands around his mouth, Aaron yelled as he rode closer to the lip of the stage, "I said, will you marry me or what, you little smartass?"

"What the fuck...?"

Aaron dismounted the giant beast with help from two rather tall pleather-clad females and rushed over to the edge. A bouncer tossed Amber up as Aaron scooped her onto the lip of the apron. "I asked you to be Mrs. Wildboy," he screamed directly into her ear. She felt her long gold earring pressing into the side of her neck.

"Mrs. Steel-Fingers?" She had returned sarcastically.

"Mrs. Aaron Spinnaker," He looked deep into her green eyes. Amber felt her lip curling into a smile. She hated her natural smile. Too gummy. Secretly, she hoped no one was snapping any pictures at the moment. A kiss served as her reply, and seconds later, Aaron had become Steel Fingers Wildboy again, several yards away, owning the heck out of his electric guitar. Amber floated backstage, escorted by a huge skinhead bouncer, and drank several glasses of champagne until the evening's images bubbled into a noisy blur.

AMBER SHOOK HERSELF into reality. The beach was still uninhabited besides herself and the lone fisherman who had become a small silhouette against a hazy backdrop of twinkling water ripples. *I have to get out of here.*

A moment later, she had lost one sandal but still found herself running toward the thatch-roofed open-air lobby of their resort. It had begun to softly rain, which Amber noted as a sign. Around two more bends, she'd be able to catch the concierge before Aaron showed up for breakfast buffet service.

Amber took note that ahead on her trail, a final pass through the resort's green hilly grounds would take her adjacent to their assigned private buré bungalow six, so she ducked down beneath its window and crawled low, past two wet tropical flower plots on her way. Her light cotton batik skirt soaked up brown mud on both knees, but she didn't care. She was getting the hell out of here.

Rounding one more railing to turn into the front desk area, Amber took a close call as Aaron almost saw her. He stumbled tiredly onto the dining balcony. She zipped around one last pillar and hunched to fast-walk a final stretch behind a long low wall divider adorned with geometric Fijian woven mats. A fuzzy-haired woman with a wide white smile greeted her.

"Bula, Mrs. Spinnaker. You have found yourself in the rain this morning," she let out a hearty laugh. Amber looked a total mess.

"Yes. I have to hurry to catch the next flight from Nadi," She replied, avoiding eye contact. Something about Fijians made her hate lying to them. "There's a, uh, family emergency and I need to return to the United States. Please tell your driver I will need a ride into the city right away."

"I am sorry that I did not know this," said the woman, scratching her head with the back of a pen. "No one told me you had received a message."

"It was on my email," Amber lied again, looking down at her single rain-soaked sandal.

"I will let Sanji know right away."

Amber waited on one of the lobby deck's wide wicker chairs, kicking her lone sandal off to hide it under her seat. *Fijians do everything barefoot, so why not?* She clasped her small shoulder purse on her lap, glad she had decided to bring her wallet and identification with her this morning as she crept out of the buré under the protection of Steely's loud smoker's snore. No point letting the anticipation drag on all day, frantically searching for exit routes with new heavy-petting husband in tow.

It seemed an age before Sanji pulled up in his clunky white van the resort staff used for everything. Amber jumped in, lying that her luggage was all set to be shipped by her husband. She spent the entire forty-minute drive staring out a rattling window as gossamer sheets of rain washed the palm-lined landscape. Sanji played a Shania Twain CD and sang along with it most of the way, tapping the steering wheel with one hand. His shiny silver digital watch made a faint jingling sound to the beat.

Chapter 2

D ETROIT
Apartment 14's door creaked open to a familiar musty smell, carrying a puff of stale warmth toward Amber's face as she stepped inside. Two locks, one chain, and she turned toward the empty room. The carpet still showed dents where her few furniture pieces had been, now donated to Purple Heart. There had been no need to keep her self-assembled cheap collection rounded up from Ikea, Target and a local garage sale when she had moved out of her uncle's house a few years ago. At least her electricity was still on, Amber noted. She hadn't yet told her landlady she had moved out last month, and Aaron had pre-paid rent through August as a gift for her last birthday.

"WHAT DO YOU WANT?" Steely asked, lifting another fresh beer bottle to his lips. "Anything. You want to move in with me? A tattoo of my face on your little arse, what?"

Amber laughed, stroking his forearm where two tight veins bulged out of his smooth white skin. She loved his Irish brogue and didn't think it would ever cease to charm her. Thoughts of waking up next to Steel, having a cup of coffee on his West Coast oceanfront home's rear porch filled her mind. Cautiously, she chose her next words.

"Aaron. The only man I'll move in with is going to be my husband."

Steely grabbed her biceps and pulled her in close to his face. He smelled of thick cigar tobacco and cologne. A long kiss told her that his feelings were serious, but he chose not to respond to the marriage hint for the time being.

It was all for the best, as Amber really wasn't ready to say yes yet. She still had a chance to make it on her own. She could finish up the Equity play she was in, and move herself to Hollywood. Since high school, she had wished to play hard, suffer hard, and win big eventually. On her own terms. Knowing Steely would be out there waiting for her on the Southwest Coast with an on-call limo driver and a swimming pool only fueled her incentive to stay the course for now.

"Fine then, you play hardball. I'll keep your ass in that rank apartment until you move to L.A. with me."

"With-?" Amber searched his face. Steely cut her off with a wave of his silver ringed hand. "Until you move to L.A. *on your own*." He answered, already halfway into their next kiss.

A TEAR IN THE HEAVY plastic beige curtain revealed that dusk had begun to fall. Amber stepped past the curtain and onto Apartment 14's tiny wooden balcony, lighting up a cigarette from her purse. Watching the sun go down gave a simple pleasure for several minutes as she tried to calm a hyper-anxious feeling in her stomach. Deciding the feeling was hunger, she headed out for an egg sandwich from Dino's across the street.

Ninety minutes later, glad to have shared a pot of decaf with Dino's wife and co-restaurateur, Sharon, Amber headed back home for the night. The carpet felt scratchy but oddly welcome as she lay down in the center of the empty room's 17' by 19' floor. Amber watched as shadows from a nearby tree fluttered across the hole in her balcony curtain, blinking slowly until sleep came over her like the blanket she didn't have.

NICK THE BARTENDER had just finished an obnoxiously fast and stubbly-rough round of oral sex when he began climbing up Amber's abdomen one sticky kiss at a time. She knew he would be devouring her mouth soon, just as anxiously as he had tried to please her down below. Or at least tried to impress he was talented at pleasing her. Not so much. Four wet-placed kisses later and she found herself annoyed that Nick had paused to rivet her already sore nipple a few more times on his way up.

Amber liked the dizzy feeling Nick's living room provided, with a red bulb in the bedside lamp and a wildly contemporary mural painted on his ceiling. She let the overhead paint colors blend together as her eyes closed slightly and she focused only on the hazy flavor of gin and lime still lingering on her tongue. Feigning tremendous pleasure, Amber had begged Nick to give it to her now. If he didn't get it over with, she knew she would fall asleep any minute. He pumped into her like a starved woodpecker seeking the last termite of spring. Sex did bring a certain amount of freedom, but sex with Nick tonight seemed more like a necessary chore.

Gripping her hips now, Nick's face showed the telltale signals he was ready to finish. His eyebrows merged together and he bit his lip in a hilarious white-man's overbite. Amber almost laughed, but then his eyes flashed a devilish look that appeared more scary than funny. Slam, slam, wiggle and done. Amber rolled to her side and grabbed her Kools from the nightstand.

Nick had a goofy phone shaped like red lips and a clock that looked like it came from a Disney souvenir shop. Its silver bells reminded her of panda ears above the pot-bellied shape of the black and white timer. Four-twenty-seven in the morning. Amber had to be nuts to stay up so late with their own goddamn bartender. Nick was harmless company; never serious anyway, with both nipples pierced and a tattoo of wrought-iron filigree entwined with rose blossoms cuffing his left wrist.

They had finished closing Chazzy's Saloon around two o'clock when Nick lined up shots of lemon-drops for the cocktail girls. This ritual seemed to repeat every night of their five-day workweek. Amber liked Nick's warm scent as he leaned in to smell her hair after her third shot. She was sure it must reek of smoke and hairspray. He glanced down her low-cut white T-shirt and touched the tiny angel-shaped tattoo on her left breast.

"Hmm, you have inked yourself," Nick chuckled at his own wit. Amber wrapped her own hand tightly around his decorated wrist. Flirting, she rubbed it seductively as she whispered, "Your tat reminds me of Westminster Abbey." Still sober enough to catch herself laying it on a bit thick, Amber wanted the attention tonight. The other three girls had worked at Chazzy's forever, but a new girl like her always took a while to get comfortable. When they clocked out, Amber wasted no time climbing the narrow stairs behind the bar up to Nick's flat. She imagined this initiation probably repeating for each waitress during her first few weeks at Chazzy's Saloon.

"I like you," Nick cooed, taking her hand to help her up the last step.

"I like this job," Amber lied.

Moments later, Nick was pouring her a second gin and tonic from a small bottle and Amber found her hands unbuckling his canvas army-green belt.

Now she found herself too tired to sleep, enjoying the tiny lift buzzing from her smoke. Nick returned from the bathroom, took a puff from her and promptly fell asleep. Amber found her lacy things, shook her ass back into her miniskirt and tall boots, and headed for the door. Just before exiting, she made one last glance toward the nightstand table, grabbed the last third left of Nick's gin bottle and took off.

Chapter 3

MALIBU
Steely carried her over the threshold twice: once at his Malibu home and once on the way into bungalow six on Maravu. The first time Amber felt the thrill of wifedom. She glanced around the beachfront home and soaked in its hardwood floors, mirrored walls and tall narrow Cape Cod style windows. A fireplace blazed at the flick of a hidden switch in Steely's lofty travertine mantle. A maid named Cindra had brought them each a two-hand-sized Cuervo margarita and hastened to a shy exit. The night sky opened through a giant open view, promising an endless universe of expansive opportunity. Amber sighed into Aaron's lap seated on his faux lambswool fireplace throw and fell into a deep sleep.

Morning brought scones with creamy butter, fresh-squeezed orange juice and espresso so smooth she could hardly feel it pour down her throat. Aaron had awakened early to finish some last-minute arrangements at the studio and Amber found herself accompanied only by loud early Malibu surf and a quiet maid. She watched Cindra clear breakfast, wipe expansive granite countertops and collect a garbage bag from its hidden under-counter basket. Amber stepped back in through the patio door to refill her coffee mug when the answering machine destroyed her.

"Hey, yeah, Steel-Fingers, it's A.J." The voice belonged to Aaron's manager, she knew, "I showed those pictures of your little girlfriend to Kyle and it's a no-go, man. She's too chubby for one, and her vibe is so *Midwest*," he practically sneered, "The best he'll do is set up a meeting with a commercial agent. She can't pass as a teenager with that rack, and way too short for any model stuff. Seriously, man, I can't keep plugging these bitches for you. Get her on a diet and maybe we'll talk." Beep, click and out.

Amber noticed her hand had found its way to her belly, slightly distended from breakfast and a late period. For a moment she and Cindra locked eyes before the statuesque blonde maid briskly left the kitchen.

"*Bitch?*" Amber shouted at her husband, who had yet to look up from opening his mail. "Apparently you haven't told anyone that I'm your *wife*?"

Steely opened another envelope as though it contained the answers to the meaning of life. He unfolded the paper inside. Amber could tell it was a credit-card pre-approval form, junk mail. She slammed a large wooden planter containing Japanese orchids and pussy willows from its pedestal. Steely did not flinch, but headed upstairs to his office and gently closed the door with a click.

He found her outside later, sweating from a furious run along the beach, just as she plunked down on his home's redwood rear stairs. Amber stared at the sand stuck to her feet, fighting tears as her heart began to soften at Steely's touch. He pulled her into his chest, promising that her career would launch to a great start as soon as they returned from their honeymoon. They had only three hours left to gather their luggage and grab dinner on the way to LAX.

"You'll adore the islands," he reassured her, quietly whispering in her ear, "It's paradise."

Chapter 4

D ETROIT
Only three ladies remained in the gray-carpeted waiting room. Amber tried to calm her nerves, knowing there wasn't enough time to sneak one last cigarette before they would call her name. She noticed her headshot was getting damp on the edge where her sweaty hand clutched its margin.

Inside the audition room, two men and a tall tart woman sat behind a large brown table. They had a big bowl of M&Ms mixed with individually wrapped Starbursts to share between them. The woman held a venti Coffee Bean cup, from which she seemed to keep drinking what appeared to be the last swallow.

Amber held the script sides in her left hand and didn't know what to do with her right. She decided to shove it in the front pocket of her dark purple blazer to give the appearance of confidently planting still. The lines were stupid, and the three-chip digital camera on a tripod looked cheaper than the one she and Mr. Spinnaker had used for their trip to Fiji.

Feeling like an ass, the five-and-a-half-foot actress attempted to give a shit about Ford's upcoming stock options. Detroit auditions were almost always devoted to the auto industry. At least if she booked this, Amber knew no one would ever see her suck ass in an in-house training video. She would be six hundred dollars wealthier and could afford a one-way coach flight back to Hollywood on her own bank account. Finishing a final gesture to the crappy little camera, Amber smiled as the three corporates whispered.

Scary Coffee Woman took yet another worthless swig from her cup and muttered an annoyed "Thank you," without looking away from her contemporaries. Neither of them glanced in her direction either. Dejected, Amber slothed off toward her bus stop. Time to serve more booze to lonely urban losers again.

FOUR MONTHS IN MICHIGAN qualified for what Amber called Sweater Weather. Today, a V-necked navy shirt over a black camisole top kept her warm enough to sit outside on a stone bench at Kensington State Park and enjoy the quiet buzzing of some nearby bees pollinating a group of yellow daffodils. Her hangovers had become a comfort zone for these early morning nature calls.

No matter what life rains down, Amber's mother wrote once, *find some sunshine in a garden.* She closed her eyes and tried to hear her mother's voice in the wind. Tucking one loose end of her brown hair behind one ear, Amber knew she couldn't remember how Mom had sounded. She died when Amber was three, and Amber never really understood the painful and complicated story behind it all.

When Amber was around ten, she had found a journal that had belonged to her mother in an old box with broken teacups and a few scratched, coverless record albums in Uncle Brian's basement. Brian hadn't saved much of his sister's memoirs, and Amber knew he probably had not even known about this box. One corner was worn away by either years of moisture damage or rat gnawing. She imagined a family of rats sniffing around down here, just like the mice in her favorite book at the time, The Littles. Ten-year-old orphans took stories about happy mice families very seriously. There might have been a Dad Rat, a Mom Rat and several rambunctious little Rat Children scurrying around down there for years, calling Uncle Brian's basement their home while little Amber slept upstairs in her silver daybed. Amber sat on a dusty piano bench and placed the journal in her lap.

The cover featured a frame around an actual fabric inset embroidered with a chubby owl in classic seventies colors of burnt umber, mustard yellow and brick red. The owl's eyes had tiny knots for pupils that stuck out past the level of the journal's surface. Amber ran her hand over it and pictured her mother's delicate long fingers embroidering it. Dad would have been around still then, too, and they would have been sipping red wine or eating popcorn from a wooden bowl together. The record spinning would have been Judy Collins, and maybe the song Both Sides Now would play.

Each entry contained fragment sentences and doodles. Mrs. Paige had not dated nor organized her thoughts. Her writing looked almost like artwork, scrolling and long with no regard to the faint line guides on each page. Allison Paige did not love rules.

I hear the baby crying. He has an earache and I think: IS THIS THE FIRST PAIN HE WILL ENDURE?

She had written next, beside a blue-penned doodle of two apples and a flower:

Will he be happy? I love this boy more than even my darling Steven. HOW CAN I NOT BURST OPEN AND FLY OUT OF MY BODY?

Amber turned toward later entries. Some pages had none of the flamboyant scrolls in their margins. The writing looked lighter here, small and on the lines:

This man doesn't know how
To hurt like a lover.
He looks at me and I am not there.
He feels me and I am not moved.

My heart is gone under.
Underground is my heart.
The earth shelters the dead
From sorrow again but I am not moved.

I wait to feel anything tomorrow
When he and I can touch again.
I wait for comfort from the earth.
While near this man I am not moved.

I long for earth to be my cover
Who shelters me from this mother fucker.

The ten-year-old slammed the book closed and hid it in her shirt as she stole away upstairs, passing where Uncle Brian slept on the couch. MTV's nighttime veejay's voice cut through the white noise like a gentle hand through fog.

Now the park bees were becoming antsy, landing on a half-eaten blueberry muffin Amber had set down on the bench beside her. If she'd brought her cigarettes, the smoke might scare them off. A cigarette would have tasted perfect right now.

Amber leaned her head back and closed her eyes, leaving the muffin where it sat, covered with a small family of excited insects.

Chapter 5

CHICAGO

Aaron's familiar ring tone jarred Amber awake. It was only midnight for him on the West Coast, but she needed some beauty-sleep for an audition tomorrow at ten. A minute later a single beep woke her again. Each following minute another beep reminded her to check a message. Amber rolled off the pull-out couch. Not an easy feat, considering it dipped down in a deep valley where the supporting center crossbar had been busted in half. She pulled down her gray tank to cover the top of her panties, just in case John's creepy brother was still up. Crossing the living room into the apartment's paint-chipped foyer, Amber snatched her cell phone off the sideboard and clicked it off. Faint snorts from behind closed doors told her that John and Paul were each asleep in their own rooms for once.

John usually worked days and Paul worked nights at the Daily Grill, so Amber rarely had the unfortunate pleasure of dealing with both Italian brothers at the same time. She learned within weeks of staying with them that one Italian plus one Italian did not equal two Italians, but rather it summed into a room full of loudness escalating to near-constant fever pitch.

John's love-making wasn't much different, but hey, they weren't a couple, so who cared? He got a friend-with-benefits, and her benefit included one free bed to sleep on until she could find a place of her own. She could kick herself at the thought of her little old Detroit apartment 14 just sitting there, paid up for one more whole month.

Flopping on the squeaky thin mattress, Amber checked her latest message from Steely. Of course, he said all the same things he had been saying in messages for the last several weeks. Where the hell was she? Was she coming back? And if she was, then she should hurry up because his balls could only handle so much blue.

Steely's accent made even the stupidest phrases sound intelligent. She tried to convince herself that in Ireland he probably sounded half-American and maybe even obnoxious to everyday folk. Good God, he kept a monstrous Escalade parked in his Irish father's garage, which he had shipped there as soon as he became chummy with some of A.J.'s rapper clientele. How pretentious he must appear to his old playground buddies there!

She chuckled to herself, challenging her mind to scan for negatives about him. Trying not to remember how their trip to his homeland for Valentine's Day had become a turning point in their relationship, leading to a fairytale princess destination wedding in the stunning Chiesa Italiana di San Pietro in Clerkenwell. Aaron had seen Amber's face when she saw a wedding magazine shot of the location. One squeal and a smile, and he made it happen, stat. She'd never been to England, Ireland, all that Europe! Stones, bridges, trees. All blurry surreal memories which seemed to belong to some other person.

Only a handful of Aaron's closest family and friends had attended the ceremony. One guest from her side. Then Steely's father had insisted Uncle Brian accompany him home and stay on in Ireland the following week, drinking warm beer while his guest's newlywed niece enjoyed warm weather in the South Pacific.

These snapshots of kindness and romantic fantasy were hard to shake. Amber couldn't sleep again. Why did he have to call her when she actually had a decent audition at CBS in the morning?

She lit up and took a few puffs, staring at her own distorted reflection in John's 19-inch television screen. *I am a firebreather. They will book me tomorrow because I am dangerously hot.* She checked herself out as she lowered her smoke out of the TV's frame. Her face looked clownish and her shoulders sloped. She flashed a smile. Yuck. Crushing the smoke into an overflowing orange glass ashtray, Amber laid back down to fight with her eyelids for several minutes.

Sitting up, she decided to get tired another way. She ran a comb through her long wavy hair until it snagged at the bottom. *Good enough.* She took a swig of warm gin from a bottle next to her couch-bed and padded her way down the creaky wooden hallway toward John's room.

———— ⟡ ————

AMBER NORMALLY WOULD have resented schlepping twenty-one blocks back to Johnny's place in Chicago's humid July heat. Over her forearm, she carried a folded black suit coat from the audition she'd just left. Its synthetic fabric seemed to emit its own heat. A pale peach tank top clung damply to her, especially on the left side where a microfiber messenger bag rested against the curve of her waist. It bumped jauntily against her with each light step. Sweeps of hair clung to the back of her neck, but she didn't care.

A homeless older man gave a dirty sneer as she passed his real-estate claim of one sidewalk bench and a medium-sized box. He seemed sincere enough so Amber graced the fellow with a healthy grin.

"I wanna suck the juice outta those melons!" He called out after her.

"Thank you very much," she replied politely.

Even the fruit cart man seemed genuine as she paid for a banana with three quarters. "Here you go," she offered, "Exact change."

The man placed the coins in his apron pocket and without looking up from behind his baseball cap visor muttered, "Wish I was that banana."

"Ha, I heard that," Amber surprised herself by actually continuing the exchange. The man quickly refocused his attention on a businessman who bought two bananas and a can of orange juice.

"You must be hungry," she said to the guy as they both headed in the same direction.

"You must be looking for a date," He shook his head, lifting a ringed left hand. "Sorry, honey, not interested."

Amber stepped up her speed and dug her MP3-player out of her bag. A moment later, the Red Hot Chili Peppers serenaded her for the rest of the walk home.

AN ELECTRIC SOUNDING rendition of the Hallelujah chorus interrupted Amber and Paul as they strategically ignored each other over a dinner of macaroni and cheese with turkey hot dogs. Watching Paul lap up the orange goop as if he were the family cat, Amber flipped open her phone and held it to one ear. Paul drank a hefty gulp of Coke and went back at his bowl. The line sounded like her agent's assistant, Carol Ann.

"Hey, what's up," Amber asked, shoving a small enough bite in her mouth so she'd have finished swallowing by the time her turn came to speak again.

Paul watched his bowl emptying in front of him. The news from his end sounded positive. Grouchy-bitch Amber just might take a night off from her constant moaning about how bad her life sucked. Maybe he wouldn't even get awakened later by another late-night pathetic plea for his brother's sexual attentions and her even more pathetic attempts at sounding like she was having multiple orgasms. Paul hoped for her sake that her acting fared better at auditions.

He was sorry that he ever pointed the chick out at Denny's a little over a month ago. She looked so thoughtful there alone at a smoking table, puffing away while she sipped a hot chocolate and stared out the window. It was difficult, too, not to notice her curvy figure beneath a barely buttoned yellow blouse. Her hair was up in a clip with enough stragglers falling down to show it was long enough to be sexy. She didn't seem to have much makeup on, but her lips had a natural rosy color. His brother John hadn't seen her as they walked to their table because he was busy ranting about his most recent break-up. Apparently, John had really thought that his latest "one" was "the one" and now was re-thinking dating in general ever again, etcetera ad nauseam.

Now Paul spent another brotherless dinner hour at home. John obviously couldn't be bothered with the likes of Amber on a Thursday night while his new "the one" had this evening available. This latest girl, Paul knew John hadn't banged yet. And he could afford to wait for it, too, with Miss bouncy-chest paying rent with her vagina.

Looking up, Paul thought Amber looked almost sweet again, like that first encounter. Her eyes brightened since the phone call, and she hummed low between bites and sips. He didn't recognize the tune, an upbeat melody from Jesus Christ Superstar. Paul cleared his paper plate into the garbage under the sink and put his glass on the counter. Opening the fridge to refresh his beverage, he looked toward Amber. She was speaking.

"Don't you dare take the last of that pop, it's mine."

"I don't see your name on it."

"Eat me, Fuckhead." Amber said and carried her plate into the other room.

JOHNNY DUCKED AS AN orange ashtray careened by his head, smashing into the edge of a picture frame on the wall behind him. Turning to check its damage, sharp fingernails digging into his hair caught him off guard.

Amber stood in the door frame, mouth agape watching this blonde lollipop of a girl beat the crap out of her host and sometimes booty-caller. Tonight had been one, and Amber didn't understand why Jennifer would even care when she walked in on the two roommates making out against Johnny's hallway wall. They had only dated a few weeks, so what was this young lady's problem?

Johnny tried reasoning with the spitfire. "Let's talk this out," "I didn't realize we were going to the next level," "It didn't mean anything" type of thing. Amber lit up a smoke and watched from the puffy recliner seat to get the best view. It took several minutes before John turned to her, mumbling something about her not helping.

"Hey, you're the one who decided to go for Miss Teen USA here," she gestured toward the red-faced eighteen-year-old.

"Shut up, this doesn't concern you," said the girl through clenched teeth.

"Seems to me it doesn't concern you either. Now would the two of you please get out of my room, I have to change for a callback." Amber turned toward her makeshift bedroom area surrounding the living room's pull-out couch. She pulled one hanger off a wooden dowel straddling an end table and the arm of a sofa, which served as her closet. The suit coat still looked pressed enough, and would just have to do.

The next moment took Amber and Johnny by such surprise; they almost didn't react for one full ten count. Jennifer had marched up behind Amber, pulled a pair of scissors from her pocket and lopped off Amber's entire ponytail right at the nape of her neck. Shocked, Johnny reached for the scissors from Jennifer's small pale hand when the disgruntled gal lunged forward and shoved the scissors into his belly.

"Holy crap!" After screaming, Amber thanked God to see Paul come in from around the kitchen corner, grabbing Jennifer from behind. He wrapped one hand around her waist and secured the wrist of the weapon-bearing hand with the other.

Johnny writhed on the floor while Amber's shaking hands dialed 911 and Paul wrestled Jennifer into the puffy nearby armchair. A bloody pair of scissors now rested between them, leaving a small red smudge on beige carpeting.

Chapter 6

Sleeping on the subway could be a challenge, especially when a woman alone had her knapsack handles laced through her legs to keep anyone from snatching all of her earthly belongings. The smell could keep you awake if you weren't used to it, too. Amber had become accustomed to this kind of nap. Sleeping on the subway, albeit a risk, still beat sleeping outside on a rainy September night.

Aaron always smelled like cologne, Amber repeated to herself with her last moment of consciousness as she drifted off. Only the stifling warmth of morning crowds would wake her four hours later.

A round-faced brunette girl stared at her as Amber blinked open her eyes to the morning. The smell of her own damp coat contrasted with a clean ray of sunshine streaming through scratched windowpanes of the public vehicle. The girl's mother caught Amber's eye and promptly scooped up her four-year-old to find a clear standing spot on the opposite side of the car.

Her hair practically knotted into dreadlocks and smudgy kohl-liner beneath each eye made Amber look like a sad Cirque-du-Soleil character living in a surreal time and place. Befitting her freakish looks, her days and nights had become a blur of cigarette butts and garbage cans, drunken make-outs for a night indoors and a shower, and snobbish casting assistants telling her she wasn't the right "type."

Unless the "type" was "homeless degenerate." Amber knew her one still almost-clean outfit of white T-top, black bra straps and jeans were unlikely candidates for booking a position. Her suit coat looked patchworked with spots of brown dirt and sidewalk dust.

She didn't regret giving Paul and Johnny the last three hundred bucks she'd managed to make, but she never could have anticipated the windfall of events that followed Johnny's hospital stay.

She booked a recurring role on a local soap. Amber would play the long-lost sister of a principal character. The principal character, Jax, had recently turned evil villain, and Amber's character would save the day by accepting custody of Jax's rejected one-year-old blind son. If the audience fans responded to Amber's heroics, she could be looking at a three-season contract to boot.

Christ, she couldn't wait to get on set for the first day of her shoot. Kinko's served as her office, faxing the upcoming script to her. Poor belly-stabbed Johnny's hospital room served as her rehearsal room, where the unenthused and aggravated patient read lines with her, occasionally asking for another sip of water from a Styrofoam cup with a bendy straw.

One afternoon, two days before the shoot, a phone call ruined everything. Paul answered his cell to the glorious announcement that their parents would be moving and donating their home for the boys to oversee in their absence. With Johnny's health condition, a new rent-free house answered their redundant Catholic prayers. The boys were moving to Philadelphia.

Paul made it obvious that he wouldn't mind seeing her move on with no continued ties to his household. She had until the next month to find a new home or come up with enough money to sublet the boys' apartment. No problem, she'd be well-off as soon as CBS cut her first check!

A trip to the ATM gave Amber the power to take over the Chicago two-bedroom apartment's modest security fee, and the next day she gladly helped Paul carry boxes down a brown-carpeted hallway into a waiting elevator.

An early morning call on the set brought with it bagels, omelets and a glasses-clad assistant escorting Amber to her dressing room. "Amber Paige" was written in red marker on a ripped half-piece of loose-leaf paper and taped to the door. It might as well have been a pink and black star on the Hollywood Walk of Fame to her. Drinking fresh-squeezed grapefruit juice while a tall goatee-wearing stylist back-combed the crown of her hair kept Amber busy until her agent came in. Amber expected her agent's assistant to deliver her first week's day-player contract. But when Kevin, her agent himself came soberly to the set, closing the dressing room door behind him, Amber knew the news would hurt.

The moments that followed spun in a nauseous wave around her, like gnarled hair clumps surrounding a bathtub drain just before they disappear with a sucking sound. The actor playing Jax had successfully renewed his contract, his managers talking the writers out of the entire blind-kid storyline and into some new idea that would introduce his softer side at the child's funeral next week. Amber had been tossed a bone by getting to have three lines in a hotel with Jax's character, as Woman In Elevator. She would ask if Jax had experienced a bad day, he would answer in the affirmative, she would say that every cloud had a silver lining, he would nod, she would arrive at her floor and say goodbye to him with a smile. Then the doors would close as the camera steadicammed into Jax's eyes which would tear up, exhibiting the villain's first sign of humanity.

Then came the legal fees attached to pressing charges against the crazy petite Jennifer. Her frivolous suit against Amber and the boys would prove nothing other than Jennifer's own mental instability, but Johnny's parents had secured a team of lawyers that weren't cheap. Amber wanted no more to do with the nightmare, so she carefully placed a check for three hundred dollars into an envelope addressed to their new Philly house. On the outside of it, she scrawled a note mentioning its post-date so she could safely cash her CBS day-rate check on time to keep the funds from bouncing.

Now she bounced on a subway rail, thoughts consumed with where she might find some breakfast booze today since being forced awake by the sun and its public and an adorable little girl.

Chapter 7

Cops take an earnest oath to help people when they swear into the force. Officer Bryant had done so seven years ago, dreaming of children needing protection from abusive parents and frail old ladies needing their purses retrieved from muggers. Bad guys abound in the Windy City, from street corner drug sales to late-night looting through broken store windows. Tonight, the breeze blew in another vagrant trying to get away with delinquent nonsense.

A trashy whore sat on a curb; her legs wide open as if inviting whatever john would be cheap enough to donate five bucks to her cause. Red lipstick smudged across her lips matched that on the back of her hand. The woman had obviously puked recently and was now almost passed out right there near a public metro station. Lying down, Amber watched the night sky spiral into a drunken soup. Closing her eyes, she gave in to a swirling feeling of falling upward. Officer Bryant kicked the sleeping hooker hard in her ankle.

She blinked sluggishly. "What's up?"

Grasping the woman's thin upper-arm in a bruising vice grip, the policeman hoisted her to her feet in one motion. She fell forward, and he stabilized her with his other hand.

Amber felt a gloved palm against her right breast. She batted the arm down. "What the fuck?"

Falling forward again, Amber kicked one boot-clad leg in front of herself to keep from falling over. She bent into a deep lunge, which made her laugh through a sickening groaning sound.

The cop held fast her arm and looked down into the girl's face. He could tell she wasn't as ugly as she appeared underneath all the drunken squalor. Telling her she can't sleep out here, the officer tried to help her remain standing, but every time he let go, she would tumble down. Finally, he leaned her against the sill of a storeroom window.

"I suppose there isn't anyone I can call for you?" he asked, already turning to walk away.

"Yeah, come here," Amber said. The officer stood over her, trying to make out what she mumbled when she reached around his neck and pulled him into her face for a deep rough kiss.

Bryant tossed her down, sickened by the puke-alcohol flavor of the woman's mouth. As he hurried away, the officer adjusted his shirt where it tucked into his belt. Amber watched him stop, turn his head and spit. He wiped his mouth and returned to his patrol car before driving off.

Amber stared at the gray stone beside her. It looked rough and felt cold. The sky above her seemed huge and empty. Even the overhead yellow railway reminded her somehow of an old ghost town. *I am a ghost,* she thought, enjoying the unstable feeling of turning her head quickly from left to right.

Losing her grasp on the sill, Amber slid down to the sidewalk with a crack to her tailbone. She let the momentum bring her all the way down, resting her head in some dirty water that had collected in the crevice between the sidewalk and the storefront. A roach marched across her view. It looked giant, silhouetted against a faint street lamp's haze. Eyes closing, Amber waited for a wave of nausea to pass. She spat up a few tablespoons without moving and did not remember falling asleep.

Chapter 8

B RIAN
The lettuce had run out and now Brian had several mouthfuls left of feta cheese saturated with Greek dressing. He thought he had carefully rationed just enough cheese per lettuce bite, but now he just stared quietly into a large bowl of fat soaking in fat juice. He could practically feel his Dockers getting tighter. He sopped up some dressing in the last inch of pita bread and popped it in his mouth. Chew, chew, chew. It wasn't going down. Pita bread tastes awful when it's cold. The lard in it coagulates. A drink of ice water and Brian finally got the bite down.

He stared into the remaining feta cheese mound as if it were Mount Kilimanjaro. Two huge forkfuls ought to do it. It tasted like solid butter smearing between his teeth.

Dino glanced over from his favorite spot behind the counter, leaning into a corner next to his cash register. Brian caught his eye and swallowed fast. He put a ten-dollar bill on the counter, nodded at the proprietor, and walked to the bathroom.

Six minutes later, after he rinsed the vomit from his mouth, Brian headed out the side exit next to a couple of pay phones. He was not ready for Dino to recognize him.

SHARON HAD THE THICK naturally curly kind of hair that wouldn't stay put all night. Junior Prom was over and Brian noticed she pulled out all her bobby pins and let her hair tangle like little snakes in the wind through the open window. He wished she would close the window so he could hear Frank

Sinatra on the radio. AM stations didn't come in clearly, but he thought prom night should be accompanied by Old Blue Eyes. Rat Pack Gents. Somebody in a tux with a red pocket flower.

Junior Prom should be perfect, magical, and dripping with class. Brian hated the clinking mess of bobby pins in the cup holder. Sharon obviously didn't know how to treat a rented classic Jaguar. Also, he hated the watch she always wore. It had a silver face and a gold band. Sharon bragged that it went with everything. Brian thought it went with nothing. Particularly not with a formal dress!

Sharon looked at him, licking her lips a little and trying to be sexy. She put on some strawberry-flavored lip gloss with its roll-on applicator and placed the makeup back in her rhinestone-trimmed ivory satin handbag. Brian's vision of two fat losers doing it on prom night made his stomach churn. Mostly because one of the fat losers would be him.

Pulling up to Sharon's driveway, Brian knew she must be disappointed. To avoid deeply hurting his best friend, he would pull her close, kiss her on the lips hard and say something Bogartesque, like "Thanks for the lovely party, kid." Yes, that was exactly what he would say.

Sharon turned toward him the moment she heard the engine turn off. Grabbing his lapels, she practically shoved her whole tongue down his mouth. Brian could taste waxy artificial strawberry mingled with garlic croutons from a dinner salad they had been served three hours ago. Barely catching his bearings, he suddenly felt something hot and clammy in his pants. She had wedged her hand into his trousers and reached deep into Brian's crotch! He wasn't hard. In fact, if it was possible to get softer, that's what happened. Holding position with almost no response, Brian tried to count to ten before pushing the spitfire off of him. He got to eight.

"Thanks for..." His classic line escaped him. Brian muttered a quick goodnight and turned toward the leather-wrapped steering wheel until a very awkward and teetering redhead in puffy turquoise tulle left the vehicle. Placing the car in gear, Brian turned up the Sinatra-only radio station for his ride home. "Luck be a lady, I'm the guy that you came in with. Luck be a lady tonight." He sang along until the radio transmission faded into static, then rode the rest of the way in silence.

A SKINNY WAITRESS WITH short hair cleared the soup bowl from Brian's seat at the counter. She refilled his coffee as he asked for the check.

"On the house," she nodded toward Dino, leaning against his corner.

"Last night you left too much money," Dino called over to him, "The salad was only four ninety-nine."

Brian nodded, avoiding eye contact. If Dino recognized him now, he would never get to the bathroom in time. But he had already begun to come over, tossing a towel over his shoulder. The dark-haired man put out a hand to his new regular customer. "Name's Dino. I own this joint."

Brian nodded. Jesus, the man would think he was mute if he didn't say something soon.

"So, now you know my life. What do you do?" Dino still had perfect white teeth. "Obviously you're not an accountant." Dino still had an easy, healthy laugh.

"IT" Brian managed. He ignored his growling belly.

"What's it?" Dino laughed again. "Just kidding. I know that's computers something. I'm Greek. Not an idiot."

Brian noticed a few smile lines around the handsome man's eyes. Dino also had acquired a couple of gray hairs on each temple. They looked great.

Brian managed to chuckle a little. If he left now, he might still get to the toilet in time. He pulled out his brown tri-fold wallet.

Dino put up a hand. "No, I'm serious. If you're going to be one of my regulars, you'll have to save your money to come again soon." This guy could be in a Marlboro ad.

Brian laughed as he slid off the green counter stool. Putting his wallet away, he pretended not to see Dino's arm extended for a handshake. A sweaty palm was not the kind of reunion he had planned. "Okay, then. See you soon."

In the bathroom, Brian's gag reflex took three tries. He could tell by the result that more than half the lemon rice soup would make it into his intestines. On his jog home, he circled the block two extra times.

FAT KIDS HATED GYM class and Brian was no exception. The first day had to be the worst. Looking around, he noticed Sharon talking to some pretty girls. Summer had been good to her. She wore shorts and even had a light brown tan between the freckles on her face.

Last year, she and Brian planned their schedules together, choosing to get gym out of the way during first period so they wouldn't have to dread it all day. Without her, Brian contemplated suicide all summer but chose instead to find comfort in ice cream milkshakes and potato chips. Catching her eye the first day made his cheeks burn. Sharon could always guess his weight to the pound. Now she stood with the shapely girls, checking out boys as they volleyed for attention.

Two tall boys walked up to the group of young ladies. Brian thought they must be brothers with their thick brown hair and similar deep dark eyes. Their biceps flexed as they folded their arms, trying to look laid-back in front of the gals.

Brian wondered what it must be like for new kids to move into a school district at the beginning of senior year. He felt as if he wouldn't make it through the day without Sharon's friendship. No one had talked to him or even made eye contact as he put his jacket in his locker this morning. And here were two new guys already getting play from the chicas. One of them turned and Brian could see dark hair on his chest where his white polo shirt opened in a V shape. He rubbed his own chest where exactly four light strawberry blonde curls had shown up this summer.

Mr. Crayhill blew his ridiculous silver whistle and gestured for the students to collect around him next to a bin of basketballs. Brian sighed, trying not to let his thighs rub together as he crossed the floor to join the rest of the class.

"NO KIDDING, YOU WENT to Macon?" Dino smelled like fresh soap as he tossed a casual arm around Brian's back. "I barely remember anything about that place, except I met my wife there. We only stayed for like a year before my parents got transferred to North Carolina. Then my brother and I got our own place."

"Is your brother here now? I don't think I've ever seen him come in," Brian sipped his black coffee slowly. This is the most Dino spoke to him since he started coming into the restaurant a few weeks earlier.

"No. He ended up in Portland, where we spent most of high school. He left a girl back there when we moved here." Dino winked. He could beat George Clooney in a charm competition.

"Then you ended up leaving a girl here that you came back to marry?" Brian looked at the man's wedding ring. It shined in nice contrast with the tan hardworking finger that displayed it.

"That's right," Dino rose to make a new pot of coffee. "You haven't met Sharon yet."

"You married Sharon Isaacson?!" Brian practically yelled it.

Dino stopped pouring water into the top of the coffeemaker. "You knew her?"

Brian felt like he fell into a deep echoing well. The room spun. He suddenly noticed that the diner's fluorescent lighting flickered slightly, very fast. Had it always done that? He knew he couldn't avoid telling Dino he was the obese loner from his high school gym class. The guy who wouldn't undress in front of anyone and got teased every morning for changing his clothes inside a bathroom stall.

But *Sharon?* Years later, she still knew more about him than anyone else probably ever did. Even his niece who had lived with him probably knew Brian less intimately. He took a slow breath and held out his arms on both sides.

"I'm Brian Darity." Brian puffed up his cheeks and made a waddling motion on his barstool back and forth.

Just then a lovely woman entered the restaurant, jingling the bell on the front door as she sprung in. She removed a denim fisherman-style floppy hat and shook out her long red hair. Turning her sinew-thin body on her heel, she saw a funny man puffing out his cheeks and stamping his feet on either side of the barstool he sat upon. Her husband shook his head, looking confused. The silly customer turned to look at her right in the eye.

She gasped, dropping her hat to the floor. "Brian goddamn Darity! You look absolutely amazing!"

———— ❧ ————

Chapter 9

Stan Shane stared at his computer monitor. "You have performed an illegal operation and will be shut down," said several ominous-looking rectangles in the center of his screen. The window covered an almost finished Excel spreadsheet full of client names, addresses, and various statistics. Stan had been working on it since before lunch, and if that sucker bleeped off, he would surely have to stay late re-entering all the data. Screw that.

Stan lifted the phone to his right ear just above a silver ring in its lobe. Perfect opportunity to call cutie IT guy from the second floor. Hopefully, that blonde Brian doll with the chic round glasses would be his knight in shining armor this time, instead of Oliver, geek extraordinaire who whistled and spit a little every time he pronounced a word with an "S" in it.

Six minutes later, Stan returned from the break room with two fresh mugs of coffee. He didn't know if Brian took cream or sugar, but asking him would be the ideal ice-breaker for further conversation.

Stan had a difficult time finding companionship at work with other men. The other administrative assistants were all women, who loved him of course, while the sales department, which was predominantly men, was a bunch of competitive butch types. It wasn't as if Stan looked for a date. His boyfriend of three years and he had built a strong relationship based on trust and mutual attraction. But a little workplace flirting or at least some warm conversation with another gentleman would be nice.

Stan rounded the last corner to his cubicle, careful not to spill any coffee. Looking up from the two mugs in hand, his heart sank a little.

"I fished your error meshage, Shtan," Oliver looked up from where he knelt next to Stan's CPU on the floor. "And I notished you need a new network cable down here—oh, ish that for me?"

Stan sighed as he handed the IT specialist a mug.

Oliver frowned at the brown liquid. "I take cream and sugar," he said.

"You know where it is." Stan avoided eye contact as he sat down and set his own mug next to his keyboard. He immediately clicked the floppy disk icon on the spreadsheet's menu bar.

"I'll shend Brian up with the cable before five," Oliver mumbled as he made his exit.

Stan smiled as he took a sip, looking forward to Brian crawling under his desk later. With a little nudge, Stan pushed his computer tower deeper into the cubicle corner beneath him.

SHARON'S COTTON-CANDY pink nails sported the only remaining tell that this otherwise chic thirtysomething had ever been the chubby giggle-box Brian remembered from his youth. The sun peeked in through the Coffee Bean's window at just the right angle to give away tiny immature sparkles beneath her pastel varnish. Otherwise, in her black Bebe T-shirt and silver hoop earrings, Sharon Isaacson had most definitely grown up.

"So, was it during college that you lost the weight, Brian? It must have been a while ago because you're wearing it so well," Sharon remembered her own loose skin at the start of her senior year in high school. Dropping forty-six pounds in one summer could do that. Mercifully, by the next bikini season it had tightened up. She took another sip of her skinny vanilla latte and leaned back, once again taking in her old friend's new physique. *Good for him*, she thought, *better late than never.* "Stop doing that, you're making me self-conscious," Brian genuinely hated the compliment. Sharon was thin. Sharon was gorgeous. Sharon had sex with Dino, probably passionately and often. Brian wanted to turn invisible.

"What!? You look mah-valous!" she impersonated Billy Crystal a little too loudly.

Brian squished an inch lower in his wooden chair and glanced around. "Well thanks, but let's talk about you." *And Dino.*

Sharon chatted adoringly about their little house and its cursed patch of front lawn that always seemed to be in the shade. No matter what time of day. So they couldn't grow more than low ground-covering myrtle, and even those weren't thriving. She made some kind of crack about her uterus being similar which made Brian's gag reflex kick in for a moment and then, thank God, started talking about Dino and his incredible super-power for needing only four hours of sleep each night.

"And he never ever gets sick, I swear it!" She chuckled, shaking her head the way only wives can about husbands, "If only we could put that in a bottle and market it..." Her chatting continued.

Brian liked the sound of her voice, and he wondered how he had gone so long without hearing its light chime. He thought of their late-night gab sessions behind the library in middle school. He remembered once in grade school, how he had asked her to trade him two of his regular stickers for one of her puffies. She had given him the sticker outright without even accepting his trades in return. He thought of the way they used to roll down the hill behind First Presbyterian until the sky turned robin's egg blue, then race home as fast as they could to see who could call the other first. She usually beat him.

And here she was, beating him again. She was living the dream while his life felt like a coma.

"I BROUGHT YOU A DONUT. Do you like peanuts or sprinkles?" Stan stood over Brian, noticing the flex of his glutes.

"Neither thanks."

Stan glanced at his midsection, hating the way his sweater didn't hang right at the bottom. "I hate you," he laughed and sat down to eat them both himself.

Brian cursed Microsoft for printing its product keycodes on the backs of their computers. If it were stamped in big letters and numbers across the front, he wouldn't be forced to bend over in front of every sleazeball that worked in the office. Stan was the worst one. And that periwinkle sweater made him even more pale and rat-looking than usual today. *I guess the one good thing about being down here is that I don't have to look at his ugly bald head.*

"So," Rat Stan frothed on from behind his face full of donut, "I bet everyone you know loves it that you're a total computer genius, huh?"

Brian waited to see if the pause would end before he was forced to answer. A conversation would ensue at any sign of weakness toward Rat Stan; he just knew it. Brian stayed silent.

"Yup," Stan continued, "I almost went into computer training, but then I met my boyfriend, and I thought, what the hell, I'll let him be the brains of the establishment. I'll just be the brawn—" a pause for laughter proved unavailing. "No, seriously, I've always been skin and bones." Another lame laugh pause. "Except for this little paunch I've got going here that makes me look P-to-the-G!" More laughing, followed by the telltale sucking sound of picking sprinkles out of teeth.

Why are these cords so tangled up back here? I'm going to have to unhook all this stuff before I can read the sticker. Oh good, I think it's there behind the metal casing for the cooling fan...

"If I were a woman, I swear people would ask me when I was due. Good thing I'm a dude!'

Good thing I'm almost done...

"So, does your partner totally love it that you are so handy with computers?"

Brian stood up and brushed the wrinkles out of his Dockers.

"I think that's so handy—"

"Stan—" Brian felt his cheeks growing red and he carefully chose his next words. Stan looked innocent enough, but that last exchange had gone too far. This was the first time he had come so close to actually hitting on him.

Brian knew as soon as he came back from referencing the key code downstairs, he would have to spend at least another hour up here overseeing a data backup and network update for this darned PC. There was no getting out of it now. Ugh.

"Stan," Brian stammered, lowering his voice.

Suddenly the rat's face softened, and Stan placed a sympathetic hand on the back of his own. "What is it, sweetie?"

Brian's heart melted a little. Stan's eyes were deep blue, not pink as he had somehow always pictured them.

"Um, let's just lay off the 'partner' word, okay?" Brian's bowels dropped as he almost came out for the first time to a coworker in the office of all people. And Rat Stan to boot! He remembered suddenly where he was and to whom he was talking, "I'm not married," he spit out, hoping that would suffice.

"Oh, good!" Stan cooed.

With rapid-fire determination, his next words shot out like a whispering Tommy gun. "And I'm not gay, either!"

With that, Brian was gone.

Stan Shane blinked two wide blue eyes at the blank floor where cutie IT guy from the second floor had just stood. Could it be possible? No way. He grabbed the peanut-covered cake donut without looking away from the spot on the floor.

"Fucking shame," he mumbled through crumbs to himself, shrugging. Turning toward his PC, he put one shoe up on top of it and sighed. "Well, that is just sad," Rat Stan said right out loud. "That is seriously, seriously, pathetically sad."

Chapter 10

A ARON
Nothing complements warm bourbon like the spicy aftertaste of clove cigarettes. Aaron sucked down another mouthful, thankful that he could afford smooth booze and satin sheets. Cream-colored satin sheets made even his pale chest look peachy in the dim lighting of scented candlelight. The earthy scent was carefully chosen by his maid to mask the odor of pot, upon his request. Any concierge worth knowing wouldn't care one bit that Steely and his boys had pretty much saturated the fabrics of their suite with sweet pungent hash, but Aaron was feeling his advancing age now, and couldn't get his Mum's voice out of his head these days. She'd told him time and again to always wear clean underwear "just in case you get in an accident." So, Aaron could be sure she wouldn't have approved of his leaving a cloud of reeking reefer behind wherever he traveled on tour. Nor would she approve of the foggy blur he left behind made up of all the sweat-scented women he fucked at each destination. Luckily, he eased his conscience by writing that up to "public relations."

This one looked fourteen as she slept beside him. More and more these days women in their early twenties looked so helplessly young to him. Were they eating differently than when he had been twenty? Drinking more bottled water, perhaps? No, Aaron had to admit his perception was either a sign of his own getting older or a sign he longed to take care of someone. Regardless of what it meant, he seemed to cope with the new perspective by screwing as many as he could lure up to his room each city. The libido had slowed down such that he usually spent each night with only one at a time and often enjoyed waking up beside them even more than shagging them to his own exhaustion the night before. He knew they expected rock star cock and rock star bull, and he planned to deliver it every time. Thank goodness his balls kept up, he chuckled to himself, lighting up another smoke.

He glanced at last night's conquest as she turned over, the sheet falling softly open to reveal one round full breast. Aaron longed to grab it and squeeze it but after glancing at her relaxed smooth eyelids, he didn't dare disturb her. What sweet innocence this young vixen held as she slept! Aaron remembered her dark red lipstick last night wrapped around his... *Oh, man, better not think of that right now,* he thought. *Baseball, baseball,* isn't that what his old friend A.J. had joked about? Aaron hadn't played a game of baseball in his life. No crack of the bat, no cheering fans in bleachers. Glass smashing. That was the sound of his youth. Better fodder for songwriting, he'd always reckoned. As a boy back in Ireland, he did recall pitching rocks into school and church windows during the twilight hours of summertime, but no bases were involved.

Thinking of bases, Aaron's mind went back to that exposed smooth melon only inches away from where he leaned against the headboard. The nipple was softly waiting for him to tease. He smoked again, wondering how a man his age with so many women around him could continually be surprised by the awesome beauty of a perfect titty. There might be a song in there somewhere. Tits were timeless, though, and Aaron felt himself growing excited again just thinking about how she had used them against him last night. Quite literally.

A small shiver went up his spine which he shook off quickly accompanied by another swig from his rocks glass. No rocks in the way, just one last inch of brown liquid warmed his throat as it went down. Man, he couldn't stop thinking about how much he didn't want to leave this little girl tomorrow. Something about her drove him into a dizziness he hadn't felt since he was her age.

She even slept cool, all laid back, with no weird expression on her face. No mouth hanging open like most girls' did by the time morning light streamed in through morning windows. He liked that. A woman he liked during the day already, a day which had barely begun. He loved that. He shook her awake.

"What the f-"

Aaron held a finger to her mouth. "Don't talk like a sailor, cookie. I want to tell you somethin."

The girl blinked a few times, obviously unsure of her surroundings. Aaron ignored the unsurprised expression behind her adjusting eyes, which told him she was not new to waking up in unknown places. Beds, particularly.

A flashback of last night's moaning sounds chimed into his head for a moment. Yeah, she was good. She was good because she enjoyed it; something rare in his experience. Sure, girls wanted to enjoy it. They even tried hard to enjoy it. Once in a while he caught glimpses of unguarded pleasure in a young woman's face, but usually it faded as soon as he spoke or did anything at all to try to make them comfortable.

He caressed her hair and let the girl blink back to sleep again. Aaron wanted women to be comfortable around him. He wanted them to think of him as a gentleman. A sexy rogue, yes, but nonetheless a gentleman. His mum's voice returned to his mind, saying, "Remember I raised a gentleman, Aaron. Never mind that your pop was a lousy arse. You aren't going to be one." He chuckled, remembering her stubby index finger waving at him.

Regardless of Mum's good advice, his quest to find a girl who would let him be a gentleman came up wanting time and again. They were groupies, and they wanted to show off their abilities to serve him. No matter how much he'd hope a woman would get lost in his chivalry, inevitably Aaron would do something that reminded her who he was.

He was famous and he was a rock star. There was no way to feign a normal life. That deer-in-headlights look would often flash across even the coolest chicks, forever keeping him from true connection with any lover. Sure, there were aloof bitches he could call who were unfazed by his fame. Unfortunately, those ones often proved equally unfazed by romance in general.

Worldly numbness never attracted him. He feared that he would attain that flat affect, an undesirable quality, himself one day if no red-blooded woman stepped in soon. But to give one of them his name? No, thank you. His name? Good God, what was he thinking? Aaron became suddenly aware that he hadn't taken his eyes off this sleeping girl for a moment since he woke up, and now he was edging toward marital thoughts? He lifted the empty glass to his lips and washed the thought from his head with a mouthful of air.

Glass bottom hit end table with a thump. He noticed the girl barely stir beneath those wrinkle-free eyelids. Gorgeous eyelashes. So soft. So pretty. *Run*, he told himself.

But there he sat, rubbing one foot quietly against the other beneath the sheets. She looked innocent enough, so he let his mind continue to wander. Alas, whatever fantasies he allowed himself to indulge, he would always know she was far from virginal. She just spent the night with a rock star she barely knew, for the love of Pete.

Meditating on the obviously well-practiced methods she demonstrated last night, he didn't wish Amber was a virgin one bit. That would be a total waste of inborn skill, he figured. Where had she learned that slow yet enticingly forceful kiss thing? Aaron didn't want to know, but he suddenly found his face coming down on her mouth like a hawk seizing prey. Such a hot little mouth. Damn!

She bolted up and went straight for her clothes on the floor, pulling up her vinyl black skirt without bothering to hunt the floor for any underwear.

Aaron pointed a thumb toward the bedpost where he'd hung her bra and panties last night. She shrugged off the advice and began buttoning up his white shirt over her round white breasts, bra free. He could see her chest poking through the fabric. There was no way he was letting her out of here looking like that.

In a moment, Aaron found himself next to her, beside her, smelling her messy brown hair, kissing her soft neck around the delicate chain of her necklace. "I want you," he whispered, knowing it was cheesy as fucking hell.

AMBER

He's kinda corny, but that accent! Amber found herself on that bed once again, pulling up the hem of her skirt.

Chapter 11

BRIAN—DETROIT

Brian never drank. He drank coffee, sure, and plenty, due to its diuretic qualities. Sometimes if he thought his ankles looked even slightly puffier than the day before, he'd even risk being late for work just to stop off for a venti brew with an extra kick of espresso shot. Then he'd have the whole thing down before sliding his pass into the parking garage entry gate. Once inside, he'd gladly urinate as much as possible before the usual ten a.m. morning meeting. On those bloaty days, by Brian's lunch break, he'd check to see how deeply his sock elastic had marked his ankles and rarely be disappointed.

Tonight, though, Brian did not drink an eight-inch dark hot beverage out of a paper cup. He sat at a grungy-looking sports bar and attempted to drink as butchly as possible out of a green Heineken bottle. Yes, right out of the bottle. How the hell most guys could pull off one quick gulp after another without even once accidentally chipping a tooth was beyond his understanding, that's for sure. But Brian knew his options were slim tonight. He'd either risk the pain of glass tapping tooth enamel or be forced to summon the very scary-looking Latino bartender with a dandy request for a glass to drink from.

Okay, so the bartender was more Latina than Latino, but he was sure she could kick his ass with one quick back-kick of her black platform boot. Brian guessed the little barkeep would actually barely stand the height of his collarbone if she took off those giant Goth things. However, fact was, there she stood behind that counter glaring at him, boots most definitely secured to her sinewy tan legs.

"You gay?" She suddenly asked, after staring at least two holes into him.

Brian's Heineken banged into his upper lip as he coughed a shocked, "Excuse me?"

Gia stepped over to plant right across from him. She bent over and leaned two pointy elbows on the bar, her shrunken gray menswear vest opening to reveal a tattoo of an eagle across the top of her breasts. Brian thought it was an eagle anyway; much of the animal's ink was drawn beneath a line even Gia drew as showing too much skin. She smelled like sweet alcohol and vanilla perfume. It was nice, actually.

Gia looked Brian dead in the face. She could see she'd scared him and felt kinda bad about it. Poor guy, she thought. Whoops. He obviously wasn't even out yet. Yet? Maybe this dude never would. He was however wearing a blue button-up shirt with the faintest pale pink stripes. Maybe her gaydar was faulty tonight? One too many black Russians, maybe. Nah, he seemed totally repressed. And maybe depressed. Poor guy, she thought.

But Gia was bored.

"I was asking do you want me to give you a blowjob in the bathroom? It's slow tonight and I'm a little drunk already."

Brian felt a lump of beer-flavored vomit forming at the top of his esophagus. "Ew," he wanted to say. Instead, he looked around for a friendly face to lock eyes with for a moment. The closest he received back were two green lights from behind the eyes of a skeleton face on the pinball machine. When Brian spun his head back toward Gia, he felt the room spin a little. Geez, was he a lightweight. Two and a quarter beers and he was already buzzed. What the heck.

"Sure," he couldn't believe he heard himself say. "If it's free." Brian laughed to himself. Wow, I'm witty when I'm drunk, he thought.

In what seemed like the next moment, Brian watched Gia wash her mouth out in the grubby little bathroom sink. She made her way back over to him and patted him on the shoulder. The two made their way back to the main room of the bar as Gia mumbled a low, "Oh shit," upon seeing two frustrated-looking customers waiting.

Brian found a high two-top in a corner near the bathroom hallway. He didn't feel so good.

By the time Gia returned to sit across from him, Brian was holding his stomach and to his own disgust, actually groaning a little right out loud. She pushed a bowl of pretzel sticks and tiny Melba toasts toward him.

"You okay?" She looked softer and quite sweet to him suddenly.

"Just a stomachache," Brian groaned. He popped a couple of snacks into his mouth and chewed for a moment before his mouth was inundated with the vinegary flavor of Worcestershire. Immediately he dashed back into the bathroom to empty what little contents there were in his mouth and stomach.

When he came back, Gia was busy helping an attractive couple at a table near the dartboard. Brian pulled his keys out of his pocket and planned to head ASAP toward his BMW.

Even from behind, he would recognize Dino and Sharon anywhere. As Dino suddenly turned toward his direction, Brian spun to sit at the nearest seat with his back to them. An uncharacteristic slouch served as his disguise. It seemed to work.

GIA PUSHED A DARK COIL of hair behind her ear as she rushed over to sit down across from Brian at the corner table. There was no way she'd let this tipsy pasty guy drive home yet. She wondered if he'd ever been to a bar before tonight.

Brian set his keys on the table and let himself flop around on his seat cushion, angling his back toward the couple from the diner as much as possible. He actually felt a lot closer to normal now and had to admit it was nicer to chat with a friendly face than drive home drunk.

"Thanks," he said sincerely, once they got initial introductions behind them.

"Part of the job," Gia replied. "I know a lightweight when I see one, Mr. Sloppy Three-Beers."

Great, Brian had a nickname now. "Please, just call me Mr. STB when we're in public." More wit! He was pleased with himself.

Gia laughed. "Just so long as I don't screw up and say Mr. STD!" She pushed a new drink at him from where she had placed it on the table. This one was in a mug and hot.

"Thanks again." He said, taking a sip of coffee. He appreciated the hot drink as much as the warm banter.

"It's not decaf, so you can drive home in a little bit if you want to."

They sat quietly for a moment, each remembering their own POV of what had just taken place in the bathroom earlier. Brian pondered that he had gotten excited enough to go through with it. Gia wondered if maybe he was bi. She didn't care. He was nice and she hadn't had a civilized conversation with anyone close to decent in a long while. Finally, one of them spoke. It was Brian.

"Yes."

"What?"

"Yes," he said. "The answer to your question is yes." He looked down into his coffee, hoping he was actually fast asleep in his own bed and this whole evening was actually some weird dream.

"How do you know the question I was thinking? What if I was thinking 'I wonder if he's a psycho killer?' Are you a psychotic killer?"

"Do I look like a psychotic killer?" Brian leaned back to reveal how his striped button-down shirt was tucked neatly into a brown GAP belt at his waist.

"Well," Gia checked him out. All she could think was, *Gay As The Day Is Long*. But he was nice, and she was done hurting his feelings. He really did seem genuine. "Actually, you look like some kind of accountant, or a computer genius or something." She raised a finger and shook it, chuckling, "But I watch a lot of Law & Order and that's what the psycho killers usually look like."

Brian liked the thought that maybe someone out there guessed there was more to him than face value. He did have secrets, he thought guiltily, but not the kind that hurt other people.

"You pegged me." He said, pausing for emphasis and putting out his wrists, "Cuff me. I'm a natural-born computer geek."

"Oh! I win!" Gia put out a hand to high-five his. The geek left her hangin'. Yes, he was definitely as nerdy as he looked.

"No, seriously, though. I meant the answer to your question earlier." Brian's bowels dropped. He absolutely positively could not believe his own ears when he heard himself. Or his own mouth for saying it. Or for saying this: "I mean when you asked if I was gay."

Brian's cheeks burned hot. He felt suddenly dizzy and reached into his pocket for his keys. Where were his keys? Where was Dino? His eyes darted around. He located Sharon standing behind two other women near the bar, holding some cash and waiting for a cocktail server's attention. He saw his keys three inches in front of himself on the table.

Gia was floored. It was like she was the coming out beacon of the universe. She could no longer remember how many perfect strangers had come out to her. Obviously, this guy was about to lose his shit. She shoved more pretzels his way, not sure what else she could do. Jesus, he looked like he was about to cry. She put out a hand to pat his wrist and wanted to hug him right now. Poor little guy.

Glancing toward the bar, she could see her boss Nick looking her way. Then he glanced at his watch. She still had ten minutes left of her break, cocksucker. But hugging a customer right now? That would probably not be cool. Instead, she offered her condolences.

"Fuck me, are you ok?"

Brian stared at this nice little tough Latina lady who had just performed oral sex on him not more than an hour ago. He could tell she was trying to be nice. Suddenly, his chest opened up as if he were inhaling for the first time. He observed his own heart rate as it returned to normal. More normal than it had been in a long, long time. Brian felt tears well up in his eyes and surprised himself to discover they were not forming out of sadness.

Gia patted his wrist. She pressed her lips together. "Wait, then why did you—"

Just then she was cut off by a man's voice from right next to them.

"Hey, Brian," said Dino.

"Fancy meeting you here!" Sharon chimed in.

Fancy? Gia thought. *You have no idea.*

Chapter 12

It didn't take Brian long to determine Gia wasn't normal. Being an in-the-closet bulimic wasn't all that "normal" either, Brian knew, but at least he looked normal. Gia's tattoo for starters was not only huge but also the way her brassieres fit caused the bird of prey to practically take flight. Brian watched as passersby watched her, sandwiched vertically between a green park bench and a self-created canopy of cigarette smoke. He figured people must have been wondering what the two were doing there together on a Wednesday afternoon. They must think I'm a white-collar recreational drug user and she's my supplier, he thought. Had he been, he'd never buy from her. She'd rip him off with one hand tied behind her back, and that same lit cigarette in the other.

"So, after that I was always thinking I'd have to live on the streets again, like any second I'd go to an ATM and it would say sorry bitch, the jig is up! then like a big fist would come out of the screen and punch me in the face and I'd wake up all sweaty and covered in my own piss on a bench somewhere." Gia cracked herself up. Her giggle was surprisingly girlish.

"Oh, you mean like this one?" Brian felt comfortable with her, like she was some kind of guardian angel to him lately.

"Uh, yeah, except all sweaty and covered in my own piss I said. Are you even listening to me right now?"

Yes, of course he was listening, but Brian thrilled to see another opportunity to be witty. Usually, he'd edit himself before saying something that could be misconstrued as impolite, but somehow he was sure Gia could take it. "Oh, I see," He braved, "You mean in your nightmare you would be even more sweaty and urine-smelling than you are right now." Ha! Take that, Miss Toughness!

Gia slugged Brian in the arm so hard that he almost fell off the bench. He let out a muffled ouch and immediately rubbed his outer biceps. Even though it hurt, Brian actually enjoyed the human contact a little. It was something.

"Jesus, you're skinny! I'm sorry, man, are you okay?"

"I prefer the term bony actually." Brian continued to rub his arm, noting how flabby it actually felt to him. Dinner tonight would be beef broth followed by a few reps on his rowing machine.

"Fine. You're fucking bony then, Mr. STD."

"So, now that I know your life story, and you're the only one on earth who knows that I'm gay, does this make us best friends now?" Brian asked.

Gia held out a pinky with her hand that still held the remaining nub of her smoke. She nodded somewhat seriously, "Besties."

Chapter 13

The only sound worse than waking up to a car alarm beneath your apartment is the sound of your own phone ringing because that means you have to actually get up out of bed. Supposedly there were people in this world capable of letting a phone ring and ring, or worse yet, letting the caller get a machine and then screening them. The former of these options would imply that you weren't home, which created a problem for Brian because he was always home. The latter would... Brian had no time to suppose anymore. He couldn't allow for the possibility that someone might get mad at him, especially not his rental manager, who was frankly the only person who knew where he lived besides his niece who lived either in Chicago or somewhere in Hollywood, he was never sure where. Who else even had his home number, he wondered? Someone from work?

Brian in his half-asleep stupor forgot he had given his number out just that afternoon. He glanced at the clock, which read 3:40 am. Belay that. Yesterday afternoon. He now knew who it would be.

"Hello, Bestie," Brian's cute salutation was ill-received.

"Please don't fucking joke with me right now." Gia's voice was slightly slurred.

"I'm sorry, Gia, what's going on? Are you alright?"

"No, I am not alright. I am so not all right. Can you come pick me up?"

"From—"

"From the bar. I'm at work and I totally just—you know that asshole dickhead Nick? The one who's always on my ass about trying to get me to split tips and never lets me chill out on my breaks, or like basically ever, oh my God I cannot believe this—"

Brian had to cut her off. Gia was talking a mile a minute. "Yes, I know who you mean, the guy with the eyeliner, right?"

"That's not eyeliner, you friggin' WASP, he's Indian."

"Oh, sorry. Anyway, he's kind of good-looking—"

"No, I'm sorry. But Brian, forget that right now because I am seriously, seriously fucked. Can you please come and get me?"

BRIAN WATCHED GIA DRINK three consecutive glasses of water before she seemed ready to talk. The clock on his oven read 4:56 and his anxiety about getting to work on time began to escalate. He skipped the idea of getting any more sleep than the few hours he'd already had and pulled out a small frypan and four eggs from the refrigerator. Gia nodded as she finished her last gulp of water. "You got any toast?"

"No, sorry. It doesn't go down well."

"What?"

"Never mind," Brian cracked the eggs into a bowl for scrambling. "Stop avoiding it and just tell me what happened."

"Okay," Gia said. She took a deep breath and dispensed a half glass more water from Brian's refrigerator door before she began. She never touched it until she finished: "Okay, so you know that guy I work for is a real asshole and he always has been and probably always—" she choked for a moment and continued, "Well, tonight I cannot believe it but for some fucked up reason after we broke down all the bottles—during which he's all being the usual prick to me. You know, asking did I drink any of this while he holds up a Chianti bottle and shit all like I'm some big-time wop or something—"

"You're Italian?" Brian interrupted.

Gia stopped for a second to stare at him. "Yeah, what the fuck did you think I was?"

"Well, I guess I assumed you were L—"

"A lezzy? Fuck you!" Gia stood up and clomped around the kitchen floor with her gigantic boots.

"I didn't say you were a Lesbian, geez. That's not a nationality, Gia. I was going to say Latina."

Gia unfolded her arms and returned to her stool next to the island countertop. "Okay. Anyway, am I gonna finish or are you gonna keep interrupting me?"

Brian wasn't sure how to deal with her personality yet, so he opted to gently nod and finish cooking them some breakfast.

"So Nick's being the usual dick to me when all of a sudden he gets all nice and says he's only rude to me because I seem smart or some bullshit and something about how he only fucks chicks who are dumber than him 'cause he thinks he's got a complex or some crap about how his brother is a doctor and blah, blah, next thing you know I'm giving him a handjob behind the counter and he's got his hands all up my skirt and we're going at it and the whole time I'm thinking, God this guy is like the biggest asshole ever, but you know I have a soft spot for guys when they seem pathetic."

Brian turned around to give her a look before going back to scoop the eggs onto two Noritake plates.

"So, we're getting all into it and I'm thinking to myself that Nick's probably gay because slutty guys always end up being big old faggots."

Another look from Brian. Gia continued, unscathed, "So I'm thinkin' not only are slutty guys always gay but so are prudey ones, like actually if you think about it, anyone who has any kind of extreme sexual behavior one way or the other, I'm thinkin', chances are they're gay." Gia shoveled eggs in her mouth between sentences.

Brian realized he couldn't eat eggs without being sure he'd get a chance to off them before work. He pushed his plate forward and rested his elbows on the counter next to her. "Go on."

"So by now he's inside me, you know, and I don't know where he is except by the look on his face—he's not with me at all, if you know what I'm sayin'—but that's okay, see, cause I'm obviously nowhere near him either, except that physically he's inside me but, you know, whatever. So now I start thinking that maybe I'm too slutty, and I laugh to myself, right out loud a little, and he stops and he's all like 'what the fuck?' you know cause I laughed and I just go, 'oh, no, Nick, it's great' so he would go back to what he was doing, you know, and leave me alone. In my head, I mean, which he does at this point. I'm thinking for a second, this is my boss, you know, I mean if he doesn't like me, he just tells Mrs. C and boom." She clapped her hands and held them open like a

Vegas dealer. Brian's blank eyes just looked at her. "Mrs. Chazawhatever—that's his Mom, who owns the place—And boom, I'm fired," Gia repeats the hand clap thing for emphasis again. "Ya know I do need this job, right?"

Realizing her pause was long, Brian blurted out, "Of course. Right. Yes. You need your job. I mean everybody needs their job, of course." The stove clock now read 5:16. His alarm would ring soon. "Go on."

Gia picked up her glass of water and without drinking out of it, placed it back down. Her silver bracelets clinked together.

"So first of all, I'm there thinking, oh shit, I'm fucking my boss, then I think to myself, No, actually he's fucking me—"

"You think a lot when you're having intercourse, I'm noticing," Brian attempted to lighten the mood. Ill-received again.

"That is not my point, Brian."

"Well, you did say *faggot* earlier," Brian said quietly.

"Sorry. Ok. I wasn't talking about you, though."

"I know. But it's rude. So touché."

"Oh my God, can we not speak French right now, please?" She exhaled a few times, apparently trying to calm herself down. "I really am sorry. I should not have said that. But I have to tell you, so I'm... God, where was I?"

"He's fucking you."

"Oh, yeah."

"And you're thinking about stuff."

"Yes. So, I think this, that I'm not fucking him but he's fucking me like I just said, and then, oh my God, you're right I guess I am really rude! So, I do something so fucking dumb. I can't believe how dumb I am." Gia seemed lost for a minute, seeing something clearly in her mind.

"So, what did you do?"

"I laughed. Again. Right out loud. The guy's got his dick inside me. He's obviously having a good time and there I go and laugh. He's fucking me and I'm thinking about wordplay. Like that I'm *fucked*, get it?" She didn't even pause to see if Brian did get it. "So, this time he gets a little handsy on me. Pushes on my hips pretty hard with, you know like the heels of his hands, right here? He kind of shoves me off for a second but then pulls me in real close. I mean like, ouch-your-dick-is-in-my-throat close, you know?"

"Not really,"

"I'm saying like he shoves himself into me real hard, like *shoves*! And he looks me dead in the face and says 'what the fuck is so funny?' and I'm like 'I swear to God, Nick' and I tell him some bullshit like I didn't expect he'd be so sexy and that I'd worked with him so long, blah, blah, blah. It's embarrassing even now to tell you this, the shit I was saying. So, Thank God—and it's a good thing I don't believe in God—" she paused for a long time, staring at some memory Brian couldn't see.

"It's okay, tell me."

"So, Thank... Well, thank goodness this shuts him up and he keeps going. Only now he's like extra hard, you know? Like it turned him on a little when he got mad or something and I'm thinking, shit, shit, shit, right?"

"Right. You're thinking 'shit' because he's your manager. Totally appropriate at this point."

Brian visualized his own manager, who probably wouldn't even notice if Brian was late today. Typically, Brian arrived before most of his managers showed up anyway. He liked the quiet, and he liked to finish off any last-minute breakfast drive-through into a toilet stall before starting the day. His stomachache growled, a comforting feeling. She *thinks I'm bony*, he thought, watching Gia get more animated as she spoke.

"So, where was I? Yeah, so he's still going at it and I'm hoping it doesn't take him much longer and my mind wanders back to the whole maybe he's gay thing, and I remember what I was thinking or starting to think of before I laughed which was about myself being such a slut and all—" She hesitated, but her Bestie offered no oh-you're-not-a-slut protest.

"And I think suddenly, it's like this aha moment and I suddenly get this visual of being at a dance club—I mean we're talking a hundred years ago—like maybe even I was in high school before my mom even kicked me out or anything, and I'm at this—no, fuck me, Dude, I think it was a school dance," she grabbed Brian's forearm, not looking at him at all, "It was totally at a school dance and I was super fucked up on some kamikaze poison crap we drank beforehand, and this chick—oh my God, totally this chick, Terry something. Oh my God, I can't believe... I mean I thought I forgot her name... This really cool chick, like a total badass... I'm like, why is she even here? She's on the dance floor and she totally puts her hand around the back of my head and shoves her tongue in my mouth! Oh my God, I totally remember this now, she grabs me in the middle of the cafeteria right there and in the middle of this totally spinning and packed dance crowd of kids all shoved together and I'm French-kissing the fuck out of this older girl, Terry oh my God, her last name started with an E or something, we're totally making out to the end of Purple Rain. And I swear to you, Brian, that was like the biggest boner I ever got in my life." Gia left a huge pause Brian could only fill with nodding slowly. Her restart was sudden, "So, I have this kind of like vague flashback while Nick is having his way just totally fucking the shit out of my—Oh my God—and there I am just completely remembering the taste of this girl's mouth, like grape Bubble Yum, and how unbelievably soft she was!"

Brian, who hadn't breathed through most of her last several sentences, finally took a deep gulp of air.

Gia continued, "So I think, holy shit I wonder if I'm a fucking lesbian! And I think of you for like a half-second, and I picture the two of us the other day, so full of shit, you know, trying to fit in, you know, like to make the world think we're normal as if that's gonna change everything and make us normal so I suck you off in the bathroom? And I look at Nick and his ears are pierced, you know? I mean both of them, and I'm like 'what's that supposed to mean?' so then it just gets worse because like I'm not sure, you know? I mean this is not something you figure out while you're in the middle of faking that you're having a good time fucking your manager just because you don't wanna get fired, right?"

"Right," Brian replied quietly, having a hard time catching a full breath.

Suddenly Gia broke down crying. She slammed down her fist on the counter and knocked over the half-full glass of water. On its side, the glass was now more than half-empty. Brian mopped up the water with a dishtowel and sat down next to this new woman in his life, surprised how his heart was breaking so much over her troubles. Last time he checked in with himself, his best friend was his TiVo remote.

As quickly as she had started, Gia stopped crying, cold. She sat up poker straight and with a robotically calm voice, she said a sentence Brian did not expect to hear from his new best friend.

"This time when I laughed again, he slapped me, so I killed him."

Chapter 14

A ARON
Steely squinted into the din of the crowd before him. He knew better than to look at the rail full of lights above them, but somehow during the first few minutes of every concert, he couldn't help himself. A quick glance sent a surge of bright pain past his corneas, into his optic nerve and planted with a familiar zing into a particular spot at the back of his skull. Now he could play.

It's a sickness.
Oh God, it's a sickness
I got. For you.

He'd performed this song so many times he could do it in his sleep. Glad he chose an easy one to open with, Aaron Spinnaker let his mind wander to the last time he'd seen Amber. He and his new wife had fallen asleep on a hammock in front of buré six in Maravu Resort. She had rested her head in the crook of his arm. He'd never felt so protective of another being in his life as he did that moment. He remembered stroking her hair, twisting a long strand around his index finger and nodding off.

Next morning, she was gone.

I never knew a pain
To touch me this way
I never knew sickness
Till I met you—

Where the hell had she gone, and why? Steely thought they'd had the perfect wedding. They were just wrapping up what he thought had been the perfect honeymoon. Wasn't that what all young cute girls wanted, a dream wedding in a huge historic cathedral with a gorgeously rich rock star groom like himself? He started to get angry and channeled it into his closing guitar solo. His crowd went apeshit, and he stuck his landing by flicking his pick in their direction. Some young girl would probably bring it to school tomorrow to show off to her friends. She'd keep it in the back pocket of her skinny jeans all day where it would get warm next to her little bum, then put it under her pillow as she went to sleep. Who am I kidding, he thought, I'm a middle-aged jilted husband with a hot little wife wandering the streets somewhere? More likely his pick would end up on the floor stuck in a chewed-up piece of gum.

As the vamp to his second song came up, Steely became overwhelmed. He couldn't remember which song was next. The drums pounded snare, snare, bass and cymbals, but none of it sounded familiar. He had a catch in his throat. With his tongue, he tried to feel if there was a hair in his mouth. Somehow he had to get his throat to relax, so he walked from one side of the stage to the other. His band members sensed something was wrong because Steely wasn't even high-stepping his knees. He just walked around, facing the floor as if he were a forty-year-old taking a stroll to get his morning paper. A few more minutes of this and the audience would not be impressed.

Dave took over the reins with the first few lines of *Stay Now Honey Then Go*. As the other musicians followed, Steely made his way stage-left, behind a stack of amps and into the wing. He found the mirror always set up for him and opened his mouth. Their backstage assistant Chloe had made her way to him to ask what was wrong.

"Nothing, love, just something in my throat. Lint or something—" She already held out a bottle of water for him.

Steely took a swig, which set off a cascade of coughing. Chloe looked left and right until she found a bottle of whiskey to hand him. Aaron grabbed it and tried to down a few drops between coughs.

"Tissue!" He could tell that Dave's song was putting the audience to sleep by now. Fucking bummer after they'd had such a great start. Now he'd have to get the energy up doubly when he stepped back out there.

Coughing into the tissue, Aaron noted a few drops of blood had landed among the phlegm. Before Chloe could see it, he crumpled the Kleenex and dropped it on the floor. Grabbing a few tissues to shove in his shirt pocket, Aaron shook his head to become Steel Fingers Wildboy once again.

Just before high-stepping back out there, Steely fisted his booze bottle and took a hefty guzzle. Philadelphia would not be disappointed tonight.

Chapter 15

B RIAN
Since Gia'd already finished his tiny stash of two hotel minibar bottles of Bailey's Irish Cream, Brian found himself out of ideas to console her.

"Oh my God, I'm like that hideous woman with nappy hair from that movie. I'm a dyke, I think. I'm a dyke psycho-killer," Her hands shook as she tried to smooth her hair back.

Brian felt pretty sure he'd never seen whatever movie Gia spoke about. He excused himself to make a phone call. He didn't even need to fake the authentic scratchy sound in his voice, so he didn't think anyone would question him.

To be honest, only on a good day might someone even notice he was gone. Maybe the whole network would crash today, and the upstairs office would frantically search their phone lists for his extension. If they even knew his name. Was he exaggerating? He wished he knew how invisible he actually was, and how invisible he might only imagine himself to be. Meantime, Gia seemed to need him today and he thrilled at the idea of being useful in the flesh, rather than just the virtual.

Time to get practical. Brian helped Gia onto his chocolate-leather sofa and put a fuzzy afghan across her lap. He took a deep breath.

"Gia?"

She seemed a little calmer now.

"You're going to need to tell me what happened. How it happened and what happened after."

"What? I told you what happened. I told you—" instead of hyperventilating, she had begun to breathe deep and slow. Brian waited as she drew a long deliberate inhale.

"Okay. I told you I laughed again when I started thinking of you and me and us being gay and somehow never able to admit it and I felt so relieved. All I could think about was, number one, that I wanted to call you and tell you; and number two, that Nick was probably gay, too and there we were right then, each of us pretending that we liked doing it with each other. I mean he was getting pretty dramatic about driving me, ya know? Like he was on film or something. And I'm like, Jesus, get it over with already, you're not in a contest. And I chuckled...and... He slaps me." She tilted her head so Brian could see her cheek was in fact red on one side. Her hair had hidden it earlier, but Brian noticed now that the mark actually looked like it might even develop into a bruise by tomorrow.

"I don't really know what happened then because I just lost it. I mean, you might not know to look at me, but I got a real fucking temper, and when it's on, it's fucking on, ya know? So, before I know it, my hand goes around behind his neck and I'm yanking his shirt collar kind of over his head. He just grabs my hips and it's like he's thinking he's gonna keep on fuckin' between my legs. So, I'm like, hell no. We don't talk or anything, it's kind of quiet actually, except you can hear us each kind of grunting and snorting—like animals, like a couple of retarded fucking animals, I know."

Brian put his hand on her shoulder. Using "retarded" was so not PC, but he kept it to himself.

Gia took a moment to watch whatever was going on in her head. "So, then he's starting to look like he's gonna come! And I get so pissed off, I mean like I've been so pissed off once I yanked a chunk of my own hair right out of my own head just because I missed the bus, but this was like...I mean I was seeing red, I mean like literally, everything was red, and worst of all, Nick's ugly I'm-coming face. So hideous, he looked like the Devil. I swear to God he looked just like the Devil in his face. So I can't say I didn't know what I was doing, because I know exactly where the knife is that we use to cut the lemons and limes up for garnish, ya know, and boom, I couldn't believe how quick I reached it because it was totally on the counter behind him and I must've literally like climbed right over his back, but boom! I had that knife and I stuck it right in his belly. I think I was aiming lower, I was so pissed, but then something of my right mind took over and was like, 'No, Gia, you are not going to chop this guy's dick off' and thank God I didn't, except that what I did was even worse." Now the tears came. Two steady streams poured in parallel lines down her smooth cheeks.

Brian tried to picture Nick convulsing on the floor, blood squirting all over the place. He'd never seen something like that before; he didn't even like violent television shows.

"All right, now we're past that. I think that was the hard part, so tell me what next."

Gia threw her hands up, "What next? What, then I called you!"

"So, you had me come pick you up while Nick was still lying on the floor? Was he still breathing? Was he bleeding to death? Gia, why aren't you covered in blood?"

She looked down at her jean shorts, black and white striped tights and yellow T-shirt. The T-shirt had a white teddy bear on it, flipping up his furry little middle finger. She looked down at her hands, front and back.

"Gia, why don't you have any blood on you?"

She looked back up at him. "Maybe when you get stabbed in the stomach you don't bleed that much."

Brian put one hand on each thigh and stared straight ahead for a moment. In a flash he stood up and headed toward the door, grabbing his key fob from a silver tray next to the front door.

"Where are you going?"

"To see if he's even dead."

Gia pulled her knees up to her chest. "Let me know when you get back," she said, leaned into the arm of the sofa and closed her eyes.

Chapter 16

A MBER
On a still night sometimes the city of Detroit could feel like a movie set. Amber stumbled her way along the edge of a curb, pretending to take a DUI test by touching her nose alternately with each hand. She would pass tonight. Too bad she didn't have a car.

Chazzy's neon sign was still on, and Amber thought for a moment about stopping in to get her paycheck. Most of her money came in cash tips there, but a measly hundred-buck check or so wouldn't hurt this week. Two lousy auditions. And one for a play, to boot. It was never a good sign when the sign-in gal handed her a couple pages of script and said, "This job pays a small stipend per week, is that okay?" Amber had nodded. The only thing worse than a "stipend" was a "small stipend." Whatever. It had been an opportunity for a job that did not involve spilling beer all over her hands all night and getting dry-humped by sweaty jeans crotches, so she'd tried out.

The last thing Amber would do was give up. She would make her own way, buy herself her very own car, drive back to L.A. and show Aaron she was more than his groupie. None of his friends could insult her then. She'd be a wealthy woman with or without him. And a successful one, too. Aaron was to be icing, not her cake. Or maybe she didn't need any icing. Maybe she didn't even need a cake. Good Lord, maybe she just needed a good night's sleep.

These thoughts gave pause as Amber noticed the back light was still lit underneath the side entrance to Chazzy's. They did have to fix that door; a full-grown rat could crawl right under it, and probably often did.

Amber headed quietly up the gravel path toward the side door. The last thing she wanted was to run into one of her fellow waitresses who likely had just finished a walk of shame up to Nick's apartment, as she herself had done a few times. She listened at the door.

After a few faint shuffles, the door came flying open. Nick stumbled out, doubled over.

"You don't look so good, Nick. What happened, did she say no?" Amber chuckled to herself only a moment when she realized something seemed awry. Nick fell to the ground in front of her on his back. When she bent over him, she realized the bottom of his shirt was saturated with blood. "Oh my God!"

"Call somebody, k?" Nick looked up at her with puppy-dog eyes. For a weasel, Nick sure had beautiful eyes. That was probably why he got so much play from the waitstaff. That, and the fact that by the end of the night most of them were always drunk, horny, bored and depressed. Amber looked at his face, suddenly realizing how young Nick looked. He couldn't be older than twenty-seven or twenty-eight, she thought.

"Oh, honey, I don't have my purse. You're going to have to try to get up and walk to my place with me."

Nick's brow crumpled, "Why the hell don't you have your purse? Who the hell goes out without a purse?"

"I only live two blocks that way," she pointed to her left, behind the bar, "I always go out for a walk before I go to sleep."

Nick's eyes started closing. Amber wondered if he was starting to die, when he whispered, "That's pretty dumb."

BRIAN PULLED INTO THE same parking space he had used when picking up Gia earlier that night. The sunrise had begun, giving the wee hours a surreal quality. Beauty glowing over a possible murder scene. Brian didn't have time to notice the irony.

Outside, the city still slept, mostly. A couple of trucks turned at the corner, delivering restaurant supplies and inventory to local merchants. Brian looked around before approaching the front door to the bar. He could hear the faint buzz of the pink neon sign in front. Brian's stomach sank at the thought that no one had been able to click off the bright "Chazzy's" sign last night after closing. Definitely not a good sign. Brian didn't have time to notice the pun.

About to push on the front door's metal plate handle, Brian thought again. Fingerprints. Did he watch too much TV, or was his hesitation legitimate? He decided he'd better be safe than sorry and pulled out a handkerchief from his pocket. Sometimes it paid to be preppy.

He tried the door and it opened. Heart rate increasing, he stepped inside and let his eyes adjust for a moment before letting the door close completely behind him.

The bar looked neat except for two beer bottles on it, one tipped over a small wet circle of spillage, the other empty. Brian hoofed over to the bar, looking for that little swinging part he could lift and step under. Once found, he moved a few white towels off of it before lifting and stepping into the bartender area.

The floor squeaked a little under his loafers as Brian tiptoed around the area, searching for clues. The biggest clue he noticed right away: no Nick in sight. Brian's eyes had finally adjusted to the dim light when he found the knife Gia must have told him about. It lay at an angle across a narrow stainless-steel shelf just below the bar level. Brian didn't want to touch it so he leaned in close to inspect the blade. Sure enough, there was a decent blob of blood on the sharp serrated part. On the shelf surface beside it, he saw what appeared to be three smeared blood marks shaped a lot like a man's knuckles or fingertips. Nick must've pulled the knife out and set it here before leaving. Brian saw no blood drips or smears on the floor, and judging from the size of the knife blade, he didn't expect to find any. The murder weapon in question had a skinny blade less than two inches long.

Chances were Nick would probably need some stitches and an opportunity to tell off his assailant in person. Brian left quickly, found his car and drove home.

AMBER RAN TO THE PARKING lot toward the car that had pulled into Chazzy's parking area. A black BMW usually indicated trouble, so when she got closer, she hesitated a moment before asking for help. In Amber's experience, a black BMW that clean-looking belonged to either an arrogant tax guy, a pervy salesman or some white-collar, high-functioning alcoholic. Pulling into Chazzy's? Probably the latter.

Then she saw him. Uncle Brian had told her once that she should call him if she ever made it back into town, but somehow with no new résumé credits besides ditching Fiji, cocktail waiting and occasional one-night-stands, she hadn't had the heart to tell him what she'd done since seeing him in Europe. Best he imagined her and Steely holding hands and making newlywed eyes at one another than the truth.

What was the truth, anyway, she wondered? If she didn't even know what the hell she was doing, Amber sure as hell couldn't explain it to Uncle Clean and Perfect. God bless Uncle Brian, but he sure could make her feel like she should scrub her fingernails better. He'd look at her with that sad, "whatever happened to my poor sister's daughter" look in his eyes, and she'd be back to square one with no job and a gin & tonic for breakfast.

As things stood now, Amber had drawn a proud line at 5 pm for alcohol. Happy Hour, like the rest of the normal world. That wasn't so bad, was it? And she even had an audition later this week. Sure, it was for a murder-mystery dinner theater show that paid fifty bucks per night, but it was something. She wasn't going to check herself against the standards Uncle Brian set for himself, with his Martha Stewart kitchen and fresh-pressed pants. Alas, just by thinking about it, she already had.

Amber ducked back around the side of the building as she watched Brian come out of his car. When Nick mumbled something to her from the ground, she didn't even turn toward him as she hissed a loud "shhhh!" Brian looked the same as ever, albeit a little tired. His shirt was tucked neatly into his belted pants and his cuffs grazed his shoes at perfectly tailored length. He wore his hair a little shorter than the last time she'd seen him, probably a fresh cut. The weird thing, though, was that he walked right up to the door, took out a handkerchief and stepped inside! What the heck was that about?

She sneaked around the front, dying to peek inside, but Amber knew she could never crack open the door in this light without giving herself away. She dashed back around the side door again and stepped in through there, stopping for a moment to quiet Nick with a quick reassurance. He had sat down for a rest against a concrete block but now pondered curling into a ball on the ground. Not yet.

"There's a car here and I'm gonna see if I can get you some help," she lied.

Nick nodded and closed his eyes. He rested his head on his forearms.

Once inside, Amber couldn't see much. She couldn't think what her uncle was doing here? Was he lost? Was he working on something? No idea. More importantly, she couldn't think how she would possibly explain why her uncle was suddenly bumping into her on an early morning in a creepy bar with a dude whose stomach was bleeding just outside the door.

Maybe next week she would just call him for lunch.

Brian didn't make enough noise for Amber to tell if he had left yet or not. She waited in the hallway by Chazzy's bathrooms until she heard the door shut. Then she quickly stepped out behind him and tucked herself against the recessed wall of the entryway. It was one of those half-in, half-out setups. A vestibule between last night's booze and the rest of the world's morning.

Pine board paneling snagged the cutoff edge of her sweat shorts. The day's oncoming sunlight brought out a rustic smell from the wood.

Suddenly Brian took one last glance toward the building. Amber leaned quickly, smacking her backside against a door hinge.

One elbow over her face, as if to shield the sun, concealed his niece enough for Brian to overlook her as he bolted by. She hoped the shadow hid her entirely and did not move a muscle as she listened to his engine fire up. Amber fought back a tear as she watched his profile, glasses reflecting the morning sun, as Uncle Brian's car rolled across a gravelly dip and made a left turn out of Chazzy's parking lot. He used his blinker, of course.

Amber didn't have time to ponder what Brian had been doing there, because Nick bellowed from behind her.

SEVERAL MINUTES BEFORE a bull bursts its way from his pen into the fighting ring, it spends some time huffing, puffing and generally indulging in a very pissed off mood from the pokes and jibes of those hired to piss it off. The animal shifts its weight back and forth between massive front hooves, kicks up dirt and lowers its head in preparation to ram anything soon to get in his way.

Mrs. Chazhatri burst into the emergency room in a similar fashion today. Huge gold hoops tapped her neck as she bullied her way past an old couple and a preteen on crutches. Her silhouette filled the entire two-door opening from teased up hair to stilettos, top to bottom, and from giant black purse to four-carat diamond ring, measured side-to-side. Even the triage receptionist, a take-no-shit and leave-no-prisoners hard-ass found herself ill-equipped to deal with such a force so early in the day.

"My son," barked the Chazhatri woman, tossing aside the sign-in sheet and placing both deep tan claws onto the countertop.

Dissatisfied with this half-moment which had not yet yielded a response, she snatched the sign-in clipboard and, while staring down at it, walked toward a pair of large beige doors that led further into the hospital. She found her son's name, tossed the clipboard onto a nearby silver cart and slammed a diamond-adorned fist into a large square button on the wall. Two giant doors swished open, Mrs. Chazhatri catwalked in, and the doors swung shut. Just before the doors rejoined on another, a last predatory call could be heard through the crack. "My Nicky!"

Amber hunched lower into her waiting room chair and pondered what she could say to the owner of the bar where she worked, about her recently-stabbed bar manager son. Nothing, she resolved. Not a fucking thing. Amber rose, smoothed down her riding-up sweat shorts and got the hell out of there.

Chapter 17

B RIAN—DETROIT
Brian spoke emphatically, "No, you can't stay here."

Gia served him another scoop of Mackinac Island cherry-rum ice cream.

"You can't butter me up with ice cream," Brian assured her. "I don't respond to calories."

"Aw, come on, Brian. You saved my life last night. We're so officially Besties now, there's no denying it. Fucking live a little. Your place is like a frickin' morgue."

"Excuse me?"

"Look at this!" she pounded on the doors of his refrigerator, stepped to her right a few feet and gave a light kick to his oven door. Then she opened his bread drawer, which was also stainless steel on the surface and gave it a tap with her acrylic fingernails. "A fricking morgue!"

"Well, there are no bodies in there," he smirked. "Yet."

"Ha ha, you're hilarious. I'm serious! It's depressing in here," Gia exhaled with exasperation, "You might as well lie down in a drawer," she stuck out her tongue to the side and faked a dead person. Then she added a mimed noose rope with one hand for further emphasis.

Brian did not appreciate the reference. He had ordered this kitchen from The Great Indoors, which happened to be one of his favorite stores.

He felt the ice cream beginning to curdle in his stomach and excused himself for a few minutes.

Gia stood next to the door, yelling all the while. "You're like a ghost, man. You don't do diddly jack, you told me that, so what the hell could it hurt to have a roommate for a while? I gotta lay low so Mrs. Chazhatri doesn't hide my fucking ass, and I got my last three paychecks in there I still haven't picked up. Come on, a few weeks just to get my shit together, and I'll go. Besides, you need me so much more than I need you, anyways!"

Brian shoved his finger down his throat and emptied his stomach as quietly as he could. His face sweat from it a little, but he was almost certain Gia hadn't heard him over her own blabbing. He rinsed his face off with water and squirted a tiny bit of paste on his toothbrush.

Gia's whining got more ridiculous. She panted and scratched at the door. "Do you like puppies, Brian?" She scratched some more. Brian chuckled a little, head shaking side to side. He spat and rinsed off his brush. "Maybe you're more of a cat person?" Gia started to meow and whine. He could hear her rubbing her back against the door. Hopefully it was her back.

The door burst open. "Fine! But I'm going to regret this!"

Gia jumped up and down like a little kid. She grabbed Brian and hugged him hard.

"You want a blowjob?" she asked.

They both laughed their way back into the kitchen for some coffee.

Chapter 18

A ARON—LOS ANGELES

Doctors have this look they get when they have dire news for you. It isn't quite sympathy, because that would seem weak. It's more like pity. Aaron waited for the whitecoat to look up from his papers.

"The biopsy shows advanced cirrhosis, Mr. Spinnaker. We should get started with a full screen of all possible causes, although given your history of excessive alcohol use, it's likely that we will rule out any other forms of liver disease."

"Like hepatitis?" Aaron's head spun. He needed a drink.

"To be thorough, yes, we'll of course run the gamut of possible causes of liver disease. However, at this stage, the treatment is the same. The course of action would be the same regardless of the cause because the result is the same. Your liver is cirrhotic. In this advanced state, you will need to be listed for transplant as soon as our evaluations are completed."

Aaron put his finger through a hole in the paper he sat upon. He tapped his boot toes together lightly. The floor looked filthy beneath his feet. How many others had sat there today and had similar news? How many had sat their arses on this same spot throughout the years on how many meters of white paper and received better news? His head felt clearer than usual. Sounds slowed. He heard the faint buzz of the fluorescent light above him. Looking up, Steel Fingers Wildboy stared into the white tube above him. Science dictated that the light came from a gas somehow. How *the hell did some bloke figure that out,* he wondered? *Fucking scientists,* he thought, *dry shite fecking squares. Fucking science,* he thought, *goddamn shite.*

AMBER COUNTED THE LAST four quarters from her jar and dropped the silver circles on top of the rest of the cash she'd just counted. Four hundred sixty-two dollars. Enough grocery and booze money to last until she found another job, she was certain.

STAN DUMPED A STACK of file folders onto Brian's desk. He looked around at his neat coworker's area. Four yellow pencils and four black Bic pens stood at-the-ready in a wire mesh cup. A crisp desk calendar from Staples covered the middle of the workspace, noted in block letters here and there with "10 AM MEETING" and "TECH TRAIN 2ND FL @ 3 PM." One object, however, seemed painfully out of place. A coffee cup stood propped on the upper left corner of the calendar pad. It read "Monday." Today was Wednesday.

Stan picked up the multi-line phone and slid out the plastic laminated extension list from the bottom of it.

IT DEPARTMENT...x40

"Hello? Who ish thish?"

Stan noticed that Oliver was on the line, speaking right from the next cubicle over. He huddled low enough to be unseen and placed one finger on the hang-up button. Quietly, he replaced the handset and made his way without being seen, concluding that if cutie-Gap-pants was on vacation, they would have to just chat it up later when Brian got back. *What the heck am I doing anyway?* Stan chided himself silently. It was one thing to flirt a little in the break room, but he shouldn't be going out of his way to swing by the guy's desk now, killing time just because his two o'clock canceled.

I'm so bad, he thought. After all, Stan already had a boyfriend.

"BY THE WAY, IT'S TAN," said Brian, sipping from his black porcelain mug.

"What's tan?" asked Gia, guzzling a huge gulp of milk directly from the carton.

"It's tan your hide. Not hide your ass."

Gia's face said "duh."

"You said Mrs. Chazhatri was going to hide your ass. She'll tan your hide. Your ass would be the hide. Essentially you said she'll ass your ass."

"Whatever," Gia said, opening Brian's stainless-steel refrigerator door. She paused a sec. "Oh, I get it. Like Indians."

"I think you mean Native Americans."

"Jesus Christ."

"I think you mean Jesus *the* Christ. I mean, it's not the guy's last name." Brian held the door open, snatching the carton from her hand to close its top before placing it, label to the front, squarely on the top shelf.

"You're not funny," Gia said, reaching in to angle the carton ever so slightly.

"This will not do, roomie. And... If you don't close it all the way, it'll smell gross." Brian gestured toward the carton.

Gia grabbed his arm, more urgently than Brian thought his teasing had warranted. She looked up at him square in the eyes, without blinking, and spoke about as quietly as an Italian spitfire was capable.

"I don't know how I'm going to thank you." Were her eyes tearing a little? Couldn't be. "You did me a total solid today, and then to let me stay here, on top of it, I just don't know. I mean, I'm not used to people being so fucking, so..."

"...Nice?"

"Yeah. Thank you."

"Generous?"

"That's what I'm saying—"

"Brilliant? Well-dressed?—"

"Shut up, you asshole," She laughed.

"Skinny?"

"I mean it, though. Shit, thanks, Bri." Gia's arm-grab morphed into a soft mellow hug.

Brian felt his insides soften, realizing how tense he must've been for a long time. Gia rocked him a little as she rubbed her hand on his back. He could feel himself relax muscles in his neck and throat until he was pretty sure he actually made a little moaning sound. Gia released him, yet holding onto both forearms. She didn't take her eyes off his. Her face looked... Was it tender? Thoughtful? Was that an expression of empathy, compassion... pity?

Suddenly, on instinct, she shoved Brian around toward the sink, saying, "You don't look so good, honey."

Next thing Brian knew, he was puking clear black liquid down the drain. The coffee was still hot.

"FUCKING, FUCK, FUCK, Aaron. You can't just fucking bail on the rest of the tour, man. Do you have any idea what kind of back-ends I promised—"

"Not my problem, A.J. I'm sorry, but remember what you said? Even if I just didn't *feel* like going on, I was out. Right? Isn't that what you said? I told you I didn't want to add Asia."

"I gave you four fucking weeks Aaron. That's plenty for a honeymoon. Your little wifey is gonna have to just chill and get used to you being gone. You're a rock star for fuck's sake, man. What are you gonna do, start doing yardwork? Follow her around carrying her purse? I mean don't tell me she's unhappy in that huge fucking mansion of yours, right? What do you think, she's gonna cheat on you? You're a rock star, dude. *You* cheat on *her*, man. She's a fucking brunette from the *Midwest*—"

"Watch it, A.J. You want me to hang up?"

Aaron knew A.J. could easily move his opener, Phunkbonne, to headline. Their album had gone top ten between the European and Stateside legs of the tour, and rumors had already leaked they wanted out, to do their own tour. A.J. owned them for at least six more months on paper, though, and he was like a bulldog with a bone about these things. Aaron tapped a pen against the leather inset on his desk, thinking whether he should mention how Phunkbonne had begun to phone in their performances, barely breaking a sweat. But He decided instead that making them look good would probably do more to help his cause.

Aaron sat down on his white sofa, pulling a faux cheetah throw around his bare shoulders and neck. He shuddered occasionally as he tried to bone Phunkbonne up a wee tad between sips of warm tea and motioning for Cindra to bring him more tissues.

"And once you move those fuckers up, I know you have lots of new talent in the wings dying for that opening slot. Hell, it would probably make someone else's *career*. You'll be a Good Samaritan! Then you'll have me, your cake, eat it too and lick the icing." Aaron tapped the mute button as he hacked up some phlegm.

A.J. had to shake his head. He stared at his mute flat screen, which was showing a throwback clip of Barry Sanders in a 42-yard carry against Tampa Bay.

"Man, you couldn't be more needed right now to finish this thing out. Reviews have been off the hook, people are starting to use the word 'legend,' man. Do you know what that means in—"

"Legend? Yeah, I know what that means. It means *old*."

Aaron looked to his right, at his first gold record hanging on the back of his office door. Then a glance out to the turbulent ocean view ahead of him. It rolled like his stomach.

Aaron would never forget how A.J. pulled for him to get his comeback tour rolling after Aaron got out of rehab, years back. He didn't think he'd really needed it, but a very public DUI had kind of forced his hand. Bad press, too. Bloody bad press. Bloody shit time, he recalled. Then, cleaned up and a few more years left of his thirties, Aaron had followed every word of A.J.'s advice to get back to the top plus a few rungs. Best album cover shoot of his career, making the nighttime talk show rounds. Total bad PR delete. The guy had called in plenty of favors.

A.J. was solid, and Aaron knew he was right again about finishing out this tour, putting himself up there at legendary status and making it stick. Steely wished he could do it! But the Aaron side of him knew it would end embarrassingly at best. Probably worse. That second set in Philly nearly knocked him into a coma, and after emergency room doctors had given his belly an ultrasound, they almost didn't let him fly home to run more tests and get the oh-so-joyful verdict from UCLA.

A.J. may be disappointed, but the guy would definitely be okay.

"Do you know what 'legend' means in dollars? I was about to say: dollars."

"Don't you mean yen, A.J.? It's fecking Asia, man. They don't give a shit as long as you give 'em a pale WASP and put 'em in cowboy boots."

"That's racist, dude."

"Yes, I know. You're pissing me off." Aaron poured himself more tea from a white pot. Leaning over made his neck hurt where he had steri-strips applied after one of the tests. It was just a little slit, but ouch.

"So come on, don't you think it's time your lady wakes up to your lifestyle, man? If you want, I'll have someone check up on her, make sure she's being good. I mean, what, she's probably out shopping right now in her glory with your credit card." A.J. twisted the 49ers replica 1985 Super Bowl ring on his left pinkie. He leaned closer to the speakerphone with a little creak of his leather chair. "I got credit cards, too, man. You know what I'm saying?"

Aaron stared at the phone charger with its red slit of a light staring up at him like the Devil. Liar, said the light. Liar, liar pants on fire.

"Even if my only reason was I didn't feel like it, I could get out, that's what you said," Aaron remembered the conversation they'd had on his cell phone. He knew A.J. was just jawing out the usual manager bullshit, but he did in fact say that.

"Whatever, Aaron. I can't talk to you when you're like this." A.J. hung up.

Aaron downed the last inch of his tea and settled against the cushy arm of his sofa. As he drifted off, he remembered distinctly how he'd joked around on the cell phone with his ol' mate manager while he and Amber waited for their 747 at LAX. They'd laughed and made sick jokes about his horny honeymoon plans, practically giddy. He'd stroked his new wife's hair as Amber leaned half-asleep on the new LV duffel he'd surprised her with that morning, all packed with new stuff and ready to go. Amber's white tank top leaned to one side, showing an enticing bit of cleavage above the pink sparkly word "Taken" across her chest. Aaron had worn a black button-down shirt pulled almost closed over the words "Mr. Right" printed across a pale blue T-shirt Amber insisted he put on for their flight.

"We'll get free stuff if you wear it," she'd said. "People always get free stuff on their honeymoons. And everyone's nice to you, too." Aaron pictured her straddling his lap with laughing eyes. She could convince him of anything when she sat on his lap.

CINDRA PULLED MR. SPINNAKER'S slippers off and tucked his feet under his blanket. She pushed the hair off his forehead gently and carefully kissed his eyebrow as the man reminisced himself into a deeper sleep.

She'd never done that before and wondered why she did it now. Walking over toward the panoramic view of the sea, Cindra realized it was because her rock star employer had never seemed so sad, nor so alone, before.

Chapter 19

MICHIGAN
It didn't seem right that a German shepherd should feel more in his element than a human girl hanging around outside a Coffee Bean. His tail gently moving back and forth under a plastic wicker chair, his leash loosely set on top of a wrought-iron table, the dog stared into Amber's eyes without blinking. Amber stared back, pleading for some kind of nonverbal advice. The dog shook his giant dark brown head, eyes fixed on hers, offering nothing.

Through the window, Amber could see the soft glow of incandescent drop lights warming a line of three people as they thought long and hard about which beverage would add just the right touch of perfection to their already perfect lives. Bags of coffee lined mahogany shelves in straight rows. A basket contained exactly one dozen bottles of crystal clear water. Amber shuddered. The dog looked down.

Where was her Uncle Brian anyway? Her watch read 7:43. The message said 7:30, and Amber couldn't remember a time her Uncle had ever been late. For Uncle Brian, on-time was late. Early was on time.

Amber touched the tip of her bleached blonde hair where it jutted out in front of her right ear. Glad she wore a hat, she now wished she also had brought a scarf from home. She bit her lip where the bottom part was chapped until it bled a little. Her phone buzzed.

A text from Mitch, last night's conquest. "Thinkin' bout ur ass," it read. Nice. She turned off her bright pink phone and shoved it in the pocket of her faux lambswool jacket. She rubbed the top of her right shoe against the fishnets on her left calf. Its buckle got stuck. She fussed until she felt a snap where the stocking ripped. Great. A gust of wind sent a chill up her black pleather miniskirt. Fuck this.

As Amber took a step, the dog's owner came out of the Coffee Bean and bumped her hard with the door. The pet stood up, feigning excitement the way old dogs do when they love their owners. He wasn't about to yip around like some pup, but the least he could do is slowly stand and increase tail movement by a few percentage points. Amber cursed under her breath as the door edge cracked against a bony knee.

"Fuck an A, man," she breathed.

"Oh, excuse me," said the dog's owner, Dino, "Barney and I are so sorry. Are you okay?"

Amber looked up into a pair of gorgeous brown eyes, the kind that crinkled permanently after many years spent smiling. His teeth looked impossibly white for someone holding a cup of coffee. Amber couldn't help but smile a little back.

"Oh, that's okay," she said, petting the dog's head. "Barney and I have been hanging out together for the last fifteen minutes." She put her hand gently on Dino's arm, a natural gesture to one who was used to cocktail-waiting. "I probably know him even better than you now. You see, he told me a whole bunch of your secrets."

Dino laughed freely and joined Amber in giving Barney some affection. "Is that right, Buddy? Did you tell this young lady all about me?"

Amber did her best Scooby-Doo impersonation, "I'rr rever tell..." She blushed a little, "Sorry, that was really bad."

Dino laughed again, "That was Shaggy, right?"

"It's really sad because I am supposed to be an actress."

"Really? That's so cool. Anything I would have seen you in?" Dino escorted Amber away from the doorway's line of fire with one well-shaped and great-smelling arm.

There is nothing an out-of-work aspiring actor hates more than the "anything-I-would-have-seen-you-in" question. But this guy was, well...

"Oh, my biggest gig yet was a couple of lines on a soap. Unfortunately, that didn't even cover one month of rent." Why was she talking to this guy? And where the heck was Brian already?

"Ugh, huh?" Dino's brow crinkled as he thought for a moment. "So, I guess you probably wait tables, huh?"

The second least favorite question. Classic. "Actually, I did. But that isn't going so well these days." Amber thought of the dinner she'd just finished in her apartment before walking over here. Beef flavored Ramen noodles. That's why she'd hung outside the Bean instead of going in first. Hopefully, Brian would offer to buy her coffee.

"Hey, let me buy you a cup of joe," Dino said. "You know, to make amends for your broken knee." Amber noticed his wedding band as Dino pushed the door open again with a tan hand.

AT EIGHT O'CLOCK THE Coffee Bean door opened again, letting in a rush of wind and loud laughing. A thin brunette hit her friend with a red handbag one more time before gaining composure to enter a public place. She wore red and white striped tights, gray cut-off shorts and tall black boots.

Amber recognized her as Gia from the bar. Gia was pretty cool for a bartender, but it wasn't like they were friends. The girls at Chazzy's, between taking care of customers and taking care of Nick in ways that helped them take care of their job security, well, they didn't take the best care in getting to know each other. About to duck down in her seat, Amber realized it didn't matter anyway since she hadn't been back to Chazzy's Saloon since dropping that jackass pervert off at the emergency room.

Then in a surreal realization, Amber recognized the friend Gia was smacking around as none other than her Uncle Brian.

BARNEY RESTED HIS HEAD on his front paws, watching red brake lights go by in short parades. A piece of scone lay on the edge of a curb in front of him, still covered with a decent amount of orange icing. He sniffed it in the air as best he could without getting up. The pavement under his body had finally warmed to match his body temperature. Still, that scone might be worth getting up. He sniffed again and closed his eyes for a few moments, considering the plan.

BRIAN SCANNED THE ROOM for his niece as he placed a cardboard sleeve around his cup of black coffee. The place was half full, with a few laptop writers and college kids taking up most of the fluffier seats. He would have thought Amber would've selected a giant cushy chair if she could get one. Right below him, seated with his back pressed against the condiments counter, was a man's head of thick curly dark hair. The man was leaning in toward his date, a blonde slutty-looking woman with a burgundy knit beret on her head. She literally looked like a hooker, but her outfit was so over-the-top that Brian assumed it might be more of a fashion choice. The woman was looking down at her drink with a shy flirty shrug that seemed a little too innocent for her outfit. When she looked up and locked eyes with Brian, he realized the woman was none other than Amber.

CHEWING THE LAST BIT of scone, Barney found his warm spot again and settled in. His tongue tasted all sweet and orangey, and something was sticking to the roof of his mouth that was fun to keep licking. Soon the pavement would warm up even more. He rested his head on his paw and watched the red and white lights fade into a blur as his eyes closed.

"OH MY GOD, IT'S LIKE a friggin' family reunion," Gia said as she scooched her chair into a spot around the tiny round table. She set her hot chocolate down and started sipping before the whipped cream would begin to melt.

"Or a class reunion, right?" said Dino, sitting back down after rising to shake Brian's hand.

"Dino and I went to Macon together," Brian mumbled toward Amber, who had barely moved, trying to take the scene in. So, Uncle Brian had a roommate? And she was this bartender in striped tights and Gene Simmons boots?

The four sat for a moment in classic awkward silence. Brian spoke first. "So, Amber, you cut your hair. It looks—"

"—Very cool," Gia helped him out. She turned toward Amber and touched her fuzzy coat on its arm, "Really, I've always thought your hair kicked ass."

"Yeah, I kind of hate it," Amber admitted, wrapping a small piece around her index finger. "Some crazy chick attacked me and I had to cut it," Amber noticed Dino sit up. When she noticed his expression, he quickly looked away. "I mean, I just got sick of it getting all in the way, I guess."

Long pause with three people at the table wondering what activities Amber did in which long hair would get in the way. Dino visualized grabbing his wife's curly red locks during lovemaking. He crossed his legs. Brian pictured Amber shooting porno flicks; a director yelling, "Your hair is ruining my money shot!" He shuddered. Gia saw herself holding another girl's hair as she puked into a toilet at the bar. She finished off the last of her whipped cream.

"And you're. So. Platinum," Brian couldn't help blurting it out.

Long pause.

Amber leaned back and looked all around. She didn't expect to see her uncle surrounded by this new entourage. The two usually spoke so frankly, albeit often far between. She knew Brian must be pissed at her, and she'd expected his usual careful fishing to get her to answer questions while he led the conversation. This group session would not be so easy.

A TWELVE-YEAR-OLD AMBER walks into her bedroom. Uncle Brian's sitting on her bed reading something. It's a denim-covered book and when he sees her, he tries to shove it under one side of his butt. It's her journal.

"I GOT BETTER TIPS THIS way," Amber explained.

"Oh. I see." Brian wondered for what kind of services Amber was receiving tips.

"I get it, though," Gia turned to Brian. "Why do you think I show half my tits to everybody at Chazzy's?"

"You work at Chazzy's?" Dino tried to normalize the conversation. "We've been there a couple of times."

Brian gestured toward Dino and Amber with his hand, almost coughing, "We, as in you two?"

Dino laughed. "No, remember, we ran into you there—oh yeah," He turned toward Gia, "I remember you there now! My wife and I, Sharon, we play darts sometimes after I close the diner." Dino pointed behind his head with a thumb, in the general direction of his restaurant across the street.

"Oh, yeah!" Amber called out, "You're Sharon's husband! I've talked to her a bunch of times—"

Dino sprung up, practically knocking the table over, "You're Breakfast Girl!"

"You're Dino!" Amber laughed.

"—of Dino's," Amber and Gia both said, nodding in sync.

"But you usually don't dress so-" Dino cut himself off.

"Sleazy?" Brian helped him along. "Whorish?"

Gia laughed and slapped Brian's forearm. His coffee spilled across the table in a clear black river and splattered onto Amber's lap. She jumped up.

"You are being such an asshole!" Amber screamed, silencing the restaurant. She picked up her own coffee and rounded a corner toward the condiment counter. Grabbing napkins, she blotted herself while the whole restaurant watched. She noticed only a few drops on the sleeve of her jacket, which was mostly acrylic. The coffee hadn't been absorbed and didn't leave a mark at all. Her skirt was basically plastic, so she'd left kind of a thin trail of brown drizzle from her chair to this point. She patted the few remaining drops as she stood up, head high. With that, Amber coolly exited the Coffee Bean.

BARNEY RECOGNIZED THE woman's scent as she came from inside the door, bringing a swell of warm air outside with her. He stood up and cranked up the tail wag a couple of notches. Amber walked right past him but stopped at the edge of the curb before stepping down into the street.

She looked both ways and slightly wide in each direction, hoping to glimpse the restaurant interior behind her with peripheral vision. Barney whined a little.

Amber turned around and gave him a quiet, "Shush," as she considered whether or not to actually leave. Instead, she pet his head and sat down at a café table across from his warm spot. She might as well finish her coffee with a friend.

Chapter 20

"And you would not believe how mean he was to his niece. He practically called her a hooker in front of the whole place. Well, actually, I think technically he did call her a slut or a prostitute or something at one point." Dino drank the capful of mouthwash he'd just poured and swished it around.

"I see something about Brian hasn't changed then. I told you he could be just awful sometimes," Sharon put her rings in a crystal dish on her bedstand.

"But he just seems so nice," Dino rinsed the sink where he'd just spit.

"Oh, he is, really. It's just that there are certain things he really is holier-than-thou about. Like after I came back to school having lost all my weight, I think it was the year I met you or around there," Sharon put her clothes into a wicker hamper by the bedroom door. "He just didn't even speak to me. I kept trying to talk to him throughout the year, but he seemed so angry, as if I'd abandoned him or something, I guess."

"Maybe he felt that you had," Dino patted the foot of the bed to invite Barney up. "I mean it wasn't long after that you and I started spending more time together."

Sharon unhooked her bra from the front, letting her breasts free after a long day. She leaned down toward Dino as he reclined against the headboard, "Spending every waking minute together," she said.

"Joined at the hip," Dino pulled her hip bones toward him, delighting in how her beige satin panties stretched across them tightly. A tiny ribbon bow in the center of her waistband seemed to wink at him. He slipped his thumbs under the elastic at the bottom of each side.

Sharon straddled her husband across his waist. "Joined forever," she whispered, leaning down to kiss his mouth.

"Mmm," Dino replied.

Barney rested his head on soft fabric and fell asleep.

AMBER FINISHED WASHING her pleather skirt with a yellow and green kitchen sponge. She draped it across the back of one of her two chairs.

Her phone buzzed in her black microfiber portfolio bag. She did not want to read another text from Mitch. New policy about getting drunk and dry humping at clubs: no-givvy-phone-numbers. Nor did she care to return any calls to Uncle Brian.

From the bag, she pulled out two pages of photocopied paper. The scene she'd cold-read that afternoon for an Equity play stared up at her. She knew she'd totally pooched it as soon as she walked in. The lobby had looked full of attractive bright twenty-somethings who must've all shopped in the same aisle at a Danskin store. Not one person there had anything on other than a leotard, wraparound skirt and legit leather character shoes. A few did have fishnets on like her, and maybe a couple had carefully painted on heavy makeup. But she was the only one who came in looking like a full-blown Cyndi Lauper impersonator. The ad had read, "Lulu—A colorful girl who's seen her share of men." Amber took her hat off and chucked it across the room. It hit the wall and landed on the floor. She put her face into her hands and cried.

Chapter 21

LOS ANGELES—AMBER
There's something about the way light catches dust midair that seems magical when it's streaming in through a slit in a theater blackout curtain. Amber remembered when these things used to inspire her. Plush green velvet on creaky metal theater seats. Red font on stacked ecru playbills with names listed inside. Girls with sloppy hair up in a clip. Guys leaning forward, resting elbows on cross-legged knees. Theater class.

This is what it looked like in the movies, on Inside the Actors' Studio, in still black and white photographs used on Biography.

Amber sat in the second row, unsure if her chest trembled because she was nervous or if the temperature was cold. She had to pee—also a possible false response to nerves. Should she get up and walk across past the two women rehearsing toward the bathroom? Bob Dashen, acting coach and formerly recurring supporting player on a 1970s prime-time episodic television program, had pointed out the unisex bathroom in the back area of the small stage.

"And when you go in there, please please please people, don't flush the toilet until the actors' scene is over, mmkay?" Bob wore a button-up plaid shirt with a solid brown yoke, unbuttoned to the center of his pasty and slightly pinkish chest. Amber could see that his skin was covered with reddish-brown freckles. Did he have makeup on? His face seemed artificially groomed. Something about his... Oh! That was it. Bob Dashen had carefully plucked and gel-smoothed eyebrows.

Amber would have snickered any other time if she wasn't so self-conscious about her own apparel. The other girls in class all seemed to have cashmere (or at least wool blended) sweaters over their loose-fitting tank tops. Some had flowy scarves tied around their necks in fashionable knots even a sailor would need a diagram to duplicate. Amber felt acutely aware of her own boobs practically billowing out the top of her black tank. Hers fit tight, and with the pounds she seemed to keep gaining, coupled with the money she kept not-making, the shirt would continue taking a beating from the inside out.

"Auditors," Bob continued his opening remarks, "Please watch the depth of concentration by your fellow soon-to-be classmates. Notice how nothing deters each from his or her sense of purpose—also known as the what-I-want or through-line motivation of the scene."

Amber's snotty side wanted to raise a hand to ask why a toilet flush should be any different. Shouldn't a real actor be equally undeterred by the sound of water and piss swirling in a bowl?

"And Students, my dearest darlings," pause for expected chuckle from said students, "having auditors here today certainly won't deter you from your purposes—" pronounced like "poiposes" for humor—" Right? Of course, right."

Amber wished she was one of the darling students, not one of the outsiders, the auditors. She longed for that easy way students chimed in with "mmm's" and "un-huhs," nodding their technique-filled heads and widening their glassy, hopeful eyes.

Amber found herself wanting to slam their bobbing little heads together. She visualized the two women on stage suddenly bursting into flames, one redhead exploding off and the blonde one melting like an avalanche of molten skin pouring downward to ruin her rose-colored thin-knit sweater. Her own mouth would not resist pursing into a wicked pucker as she actually tasted bitterness in her mouth. Why did these perfectly groomed Barbie Dolls get to stand up there, all relaxed, while Amber knew she would never even get to know them by their real names?

She would not be returning to class. She would only pretend to have learned something from this "free audit" and return to the trade papers to find another "free audit" to attend next week. Somewhere else next week she'd pretend to be interested in attending some other class and pretend that she'd be part of something, a nodding student sitting in another velvety chair all prepared with last week's scene memorized and ready to receive applause.

Good, Amber thought, as the class applauded to indicate the end of these semi-charmed princesses' scene work. She bolted up and made her way across the stage toward a tiny white room, head down and fully conscious of the heavy way her cheap shoes clunked across the floor.

Inside, several bulk-sized packages of toilet paper lined a white particleboard laminate shelf. An index card with the words, "WOULD YOU WANT SOMEONE TO FLUSH <u>YOUR</u> SCENE DOWN THE TOILET? SHHH!" hand-printed in a red sharpie hung from a shelf at eye level. Another similar sign was taped to the toilet handle: "PUSH HARDER THAN YOU THINK." Everything seemed in place.

Amber sat on the toilet, knees together, not surprised at how little she'd really needed to urinate. Now she just sat here, kind of freezing, yet unable to motivate herself to stand up and go back in there. She looked around some more. The floor had little white squares that buckled and cracked over what seemed like a very old subfloor underneath. How many students had sat here throughout the years, she wondered? How many guys stood facing where she now sat, peeing into this basin? How many girls sat here, mouthing the words to her scene's opening line, a little nervous to show off what she'd rehearsed at home that week? How many of them still worked professionally as actors? Were any of them famous? Did some quit, get married, have babies?

Amber stood up and pulled up her panties underneath the black skirt she never bothered to unzip. There was no mirror, but she could feel that her necklace was crooked and catching a few tiny hairs on the back of her neck.

Suddenly, Amber bolted up. Quietly placing one hand on the large gray door that opened to the outside, she could feel how warm the afternoon sun had gotten in the last couple hours. Pressing the door all the way open, she decided the time had come to get the hell out of there.

HOLLY NOTICED THE BRUNETTE had sat alone most of class with her shoulders hunched over and her head down, hiding her makeup-free face behind a few wavy tendrils of bangs. She'd gone to the bathroom before Holly's scene, and now that she and Charles had gotten notes (more like got reamed for lack of memorization), the audit-girl seemed to have vanished.

Key-fobbing her PT Cruiser doors open, Holly took one last glance around the line of parallel parked cars all the way to Cahuenga Boulevard. A small figure leaned against a gnarly fern tree, smoking a cigarette. Holly tossed her tapestry bag into her passenger seat and locked the door behind her as she headed toward Amber.

Chapter 22

"He was an unexpected villain," said a slender man in his mid-fifties, wearing a light blue hat with some sort of golf emblem on the front.

"You mean he's a guy who usually plays good guys?" asked his lunch companion, whose burgundy shirt rode up in the back, revealing a pale muffin top above khaki shorts.

"No, no, well, he's always the slow-talking guy. Really quiet, pulled together... You know, kind of preppy, maybe?" Slender hat guy sucked a poppy seed from between his teeth before giving up and using his thumbnail.

"Oh, I don't know," the second guy sipped his Arnold Palmer through a black straw. He adjusted his round glasses.

"He was married to Geena Davis, I think."

"Oh! Jeff Goldblum!"

"No, no, in a movie he was married to her."

Glasses guy slumped in disappointment. He was a little younger than his lunch companion and wanted to impress.

Hat guy played a little with his perfectly trimmed salt-and-pepper goatee. He was actually rather handsome. "No, Geena Davis was in this movie with him. Love interest... She had an umbrella." The talker waved in the air as if the elusive actor's name could be grasped out of the California sky. "Blonde. Less hair than you."

The chubbier forty-something rubbed his bushy ruddy-blonde hair. His hairline was mostly intact. Just a little extra forehead these days.

Amber almost didn't notice the waiter waiting with a pitcher of water hovering over the table. Holly was already ordering some kind of whole wheat something sandwich with extra alfalfa sprouts, add avocado. Amber scanned the menu for anything she could order with a single digit to the left of the decimal point.

"Egg bagel," she managed to find on the back page. It was $4.95. For a bagel. Jesus.

"You wanna have it toasted? You wanna cream cheese? Lox?"

Good Lord, Amber wondered, *how much were these bells and whistles going to cost?*

Holly was already busy with her cell phone. It looked like she was just turning it off and on again and again. She brushed her yellow hair out of her eyes several times. It wasn't even windy.

"You wanna it toasted?" the waiter looked around as if someone more important than this customer might walk up any moment to offer him a five-picture movie deal. He looked like a chubby thirty-something-year-old to Amber. Maybe Mexican? His skin had a weird smoothness, though, as much as she could see of it behind his manicured mustache and thimble-sized goatee. Amber thought she recognized a waxiness to his eyebrows, similar to Acting Coach Extraordinaire, Mr. Dashen. "You wanna lox? You need some cream-a-cheese?" His voice trailed off. He was tapping his foot.

Amber enjoyed watching this guy lose his patience. She'd lost hers as well. Locking eyes with Holly, and not looking in the server's direction, Amber quietly spoke, "I've got an idea, why don't you fucking surprise me?"

Holly squirmed. She giggled but squirmed a little.

"Excuse me?" the waiter seemed to wake up. His eyes found Amber's.

"I said why don't you fucking surprise me?" Amber squared her jaw. "I mean, put whipped cream on it, take a dump on it and toast it, I don't really give a shit." She leaned back, holding his stare.

Setting his water pitcher on the edge of their table, the waiter cocked his hip and put one hand on it. He rocked a little with his elbow sticking out, almost clocking Holly in the cheekbone a couple of times. He looked Amber up and down. Her boobs barely rose and fell as she breathed slowly. Finally, Amber softened her face. Suddenly she found herself very nervous and felt her cheeks begin to turn pink.

Holly tapped her nails on the edge of the breadbasket. The waiter picked up his pitcher and walked away.

"That was William Hurt in that?" Burgundy shirt was saying. "Wow, he was scary, then."

"Well, I'm not saying I wouldn't work with him," Golf-hat was saying, "I've heard he gets really intense. But he seemed really normal on the green. And I've directed lots of more charactery character actors than him before!" The two men shared a knowing burst of laughter. The speaker put up a hand, nodding. He rested his thumb and middle finger across the rim of his glass. "Ok, so that time aside, I like character actors."

Amber's ears perked up. *Directed? Did that guy just say "I directed?"*

Holly, too, had noticed the two gentlemen two tables away. She was checking her cell phone again, cheating her face toward them in case they might notice how pretty her red lipstick looked.

Amber's adrenaline had kicked in, and her hands felt sweaty.

"When that guy comes back, I'm ordering a drink."

Holly chuckled a little. "If he comes back."

"Oh, whatever." Amber wondered if Holly was serious.

"Are you hungry, though?" Holly asked.

"I don't know," Amber felt her larynx rise upward. The outside corners of her eyes crinkled.

Holly put her cell phone back into her purse and hung it on the armrest of her wicker-backed chair. She leaned toward this feisty girl from her acting class.

"Are you okay?"

Amber didn't dare look into her eyes. Someone had actually just asked her if she was okay. She could've hugged her. Instead, she pressed the front of one shoe into the back of the other one. She nodded, barely.

Pretty soon the waiter returned, dropping an uncut, obviously untoasted bagel on a white plate in front of Amber. He smiled at the yellow-haired girl as he set her plate down.

"Careful, it's really hot," he said, turning his back a little extra toward Amber's side of the table.

"Thanks," Holly mumbled.

As he turned on his heel and headed toward the two-guy table, Amber called after him. "So, I guess you decided not to take a dump on my bagel, then?"

Both men dropped their utensils. Golf-hat chewed with his mouth hanging open. Burgundy-shirt turned 180 in his seat. Thankfully, a meager few patrons occupied the patio for lunch at 2:20 p.m. One other dude with headphones in his ears worked on a laptop at the far corner table. He looked up a moment before diving back down into his keyboard.

"Choo are a little bitch," the waiter said loudly, still facing the other table.

Holly's mouth hung open.

Amber stood up before she knew it and found herself toe-to-toe with a man who stood only an inch or so taller than her. Two-Guys didn't move.

"What?" Waiter said.

Amber noticed he actually smelled pretty good. His skin looked smooth where the crisp white of his collar opened. She stepped one inch closer to him, almost pressing her bust against his shirt. She had to look up just a little to maintain eye contact.

Quietly, the waiter said, "Jou wanna get me fired?" His hand found its resting place on his cocked hip again. "Because I don' know how much I give a crap about this job anyway."

Two-Guys and Holly inhaled at the same time.

Amber put her hands on Waiter's shoulders and held them there for a moment. "Good," she said finally, "because then I could take your job."

Waiter reached up between her hands on his shoulders, placing his right hand across his body and around Amber's right wrist. She sensed that he knew some kind of self-defense move.

"Choo wanna take your hand offa me?"

"You wanna take your hand off of me?" Amber replied.

The waiter took one more breath before grabbing her wrist considerably harder. Amber anticipated getting flipped next or something. Some karate judo chop action hung eminently in the air, and the audience of three had gained a very confused fourth pair of eyes belonging to that dude at his corner table with a Van Halen guitar riff playing in his ears.

Amber's hand loosened where Waiter gripped it. She stepped back and dropped her left hand off his shoulder. Her right hand stayed suspended by his tight grip. Suddenly, Amber did something she did not expect at all. She burst into tears.

"I'm so sorry, man. I don't know what the hell's wrong with me," she cried.

Carlos put his arms around her where she melted. His hand began to stroke her hair. Amber wept openly as he led her back to her chair and sat her down. Holly came around the table and touched her shoulder. Amber bawled and rocked, gasping between breaths, "You...guys...are...being...so...nice..."

"It's okay," Carlos cooed.

"You're gonna be fine, honey," Holly said. "Maybe after this we'll go get a mani-pedi."

Amber cried loud again, shaking her head. "I can't get a mani-pedi."

Carlos laughed. Two-guys stood up and picked up their bill, also laughing out loud.

"I can't even order a fucking bagel in this town!"

Carlos took her face in both hands and lifted it toward him as he looked down on her, "No, honey. You're wrong. I've been working here a long time and you know how to order a bagel better than anyone I've ever seen."

Amber laughed. The crumpled napkin felt damp in her hands.

Carlos handed her another one.

That is how Amber landed her first waitress job in Los Angeles.

HOLLY KEY-FOBBED OPEN her PT Cruiser as she and her new girlfriend, Amber, headed toward it. A pink tree's flower petals had all but covered the windshield while they'd been inside the restaurant. Holly swept at them with her pink ombre scarf. Amber picked up a blossom and tucked it behind her ear.

"This may just be the best day I've had in a long time," Amber smiled across the silver car's rooftop.

Holly shook her head. "Girl, you must've had some pretty crummy days." She opened the driver's door.

"I look forward to some crummy days," Amber said, "They'll be better than the total motherfucking shit ones."

"Geez, you swear a lot," Holly put her keys in the ignition.

Amber's cheeks flushed. *I didn't always used to be this way,* she thought. Or did she? It was hard to remember. She looked over at her new friend, acutely aware of how petite Holly's hands appeared resting on the steering wheel. Her fingernails looked like little red Skittles. Amber's own hands looked small, too, in her own lap. *Are we really both this small,* she thought?

The girls screamed. Then laughed hysterically. Some guy was standing on the adjacent curb, knocking gently on Amber's window. When they regained their composure enough to open the window, the girls recognized the man with the light blue golf hat.

AARON

His wrist burned where a clear plastic tube lead-line pushed into his skin. White tape pinched and pulled against the hair on his arm when a tender-faced nurse helped him turn onto his left side. He'd been poked at so much for blood tests lately that his wrist seemed to be the only place anyone could get decent access to his veins. Aaron manned up as best he could, wearing a white gown with little blue diamond shapes on it. When he lay on his side, the nurse helped yank on the fabric to cover at least a little of his arse.

His doctor today had long dark hair loosely tied into a braid. He thought for a moment of Amber, wondering where she was, if she'd been in any hospitals lately. Hell, she could be in a hospital too, at this very moment. A few words floated into his head: endoscopic procedure, broken neck, abortion, morgue. He chose instead to think of her jogging along some beach somewhere, or on a movie set living out her dream. Everyone had a right to dream, Aaron thought. Dreams are like fuzzy white clouds with lavender smoke billowing up into a transparent gossamer ribbon reaching up toward the sun.

His anesthetic had kicked in.

Chapter 23

A MBER
Amber's cuticles burned where the nail technician had trimmed them. Now the young girl was buffing at the tips of her nails, working so quickly Amber wondered if she would leave any nail at all left when this thing was over with.

Holly seemed to be in her element. She somehow sat with her hands perfectly relaxed in the deft control of the older technician, who looked like Amber's tech's mother. Or aunt. Who knew? Neither spoke much more than "Eighteen dollar" plus lots of nodding. Yet their bond to each other was undeniable, occasionally laughing in sequence or handing one another an absorbent pad or tissue, on autopilot without even looking at one another.

Amber could barely relax her fingers. The gal had shaken them out over and over, seeming annoyed as she sighed louder with each shake. Apparently, no one in this town had heard of anyone who'd never had a manicure before. Amber wondered how many hands had relaxed here. Probably tons. How many nail virgins had sat in this same chair? Probably none.

Holly couldn't stop gabbing. She went on about her boyfriend, how he'd invited her to live with him but she said no because she didn't want her mother to cut off her trust income. Her dad had been a real estate investor or something. Her boyfriend sounded old. He did all kinds of business stuff. And ran some kind of whale-watching tour company in Long Beach. Holly hated the commute. Amber could barely put together all the information this girl laid out. She felt exhausted but obligated to feign listening. After all, Holly's sugar daddy was the one paying for the manicures. The least she could do is pretend to care.

Amber chose "cool candy" for her nail color, a pale almost-white pink with the slightest lavender iridescence. She noticed Holly chose Skittles strawberry red again. It didn't even seem as if her nails had been chipped before. Was Amber now supposed to get her nails done once a week, like every Tuesday or something? She tried to keep track of all this stuff she was learning about being a California girl.

For a second, while Holly described her boyfriend, Amber saw Aaron in her mind. He'd probably moved on by now, invited some other young girl into his bed and into his life. Someone more like Holly, with a trust fund and blonde hair. Someone with an oversized tapestry bag and a PT Cruiser. Someone who went out of her way to meet a celebrity with a beach house, to mingle with a yacht owner or to date a PR firm president or to hook up with a CEO or CFO or COO or some other acronym-O. Some girl who knew about red carpet events and photo ops, with the right color toenail polish and the right height of strappy heels. Steely would find someone like that, and as soon as Amber contacted him again, he would inquire as to what address his lawyer should forward the divorce papers.

The reverie distracted her, which relaxed Amber's hands finally, and by the time she zoned back in, she'd already acquired four complete cool-candy fingertips.

BURGUNDY POLO SHIRT and blue golf cap were now known as Greg and Garry, respectively.

Amber felt a little drunk. Holly had been getting louder and gigglier for at least a half an hour. Carlos started getting handsy.

"How's your Midori sour?" asked Greg, rolling his almost clear gray eyes toward Garry.

"It's... so sour!" Amber chuckled and placed the half-full rocks glass of green liquid on the bar in front of her knees. Holly picked it up and sipped it.

"Yuck! It's too sweet," she declared, shoving the glass toward Garry's pursed lips.

"Honey, you couldn't pay me enough to drink that," he leaned back on his elbow, purposely brushing his knee against Amber's foot.

"Please do," Amber whined, "It's awful."

"Well, why did you order it then?" Carlos piped up from behind her head, mouth a little too close to her ear. Amber shook her hair into his face to get a little space.

Holly's volume reached maximum level, and now her pitch was rising to a shrill screech, "IT'S BECAUSE OF THE LEPRECHAUNS!"

Amber couldn't help but laugh along. She was more drunk than she realized, and couldn't seem to stop giggling.

Garry laughed as well, feigning annoyance. "You two have got to stop calling them leprechauns. They were little people." A mature eye exchange took place between himself and Greg.

Amber turned to Greg, "Well, then why were they wearing hats?"

Holly laughed, "And playing bagpipes?"

Carlos next, "And sliding down little rainbows into little pots of gold?"

Amber enjoyed the warm laughs between the five, who had become a weird little family over the past few weeks. Greg and Garry were like the parents. Garry was the Mom due to his age and well-practiced gentle and diplomatic mannerisms. Greg, kind of the bumbly Dad figure who never quite caught onto the big picture. Holly could be the teenage daughter, always acting out of hand but easy to keep in check with a slight reminder. Carlos, of course, was the yipping puppy, who sometimes bit but never meant any harm. Amber watched them all as the bar whirled mildly around her in a smooth pool of alcoholic effect. Who was she in this family? The black sheep? The adopted foreign exchange student? She knew what she felt like: the imposter.

Garry put his hand on her shoulder. "You were actually very good today," he said, referring to the commercial shoot he'd kindly booked the three friends on that afternoon.

The set had looked like a big puffy cloud with all sorts of fantasy creatures like a centaur, a unicorn, angels, a dragon, and Carlos as a Greek god in a toga. Holly and Amber had been dressed as tree fairies in short skirts and sparkly wings. Today had been a good day.

Amber remembered Greg approaching her that morning in front of a group of extras. Taking her hand, Garry The Director had announced, "Principals in the foreground, please." Amber could have sworn her costume wings actually took flight for a moment. She floated to her mark; a blue "T" taped onto the floor only about ten feet from the hugest camera she'd ever seen. A makeup girl had hustled over to powder her face and tweak a couple of her eyelashes. She remembered Greg waltzing up to check her work, ever the Art Director on the project. He'd said Garry never had done a single shoot without him since they'd met and bought a house together.

Amber had loved the soft feel of the makeup brush sweeping her cheeks. She'd loved her costume with its little gold gladiator sandals and light green flowy miniskirt. She'd loved Holly for befriending her, and she now loved more than anyone in the entire world at that moment, Mr. Garry Director Holloway, who had booked her on this, her first national commercial for a major soft drink company, and who had presented her first national gorgeous line of dialogue: "Well, I'm refreshed. Aren't you?"

The bar spun like crazy now. Carlos's and Holly's laughs blended together in a giddy duet. Greg began to doze off into his chubby pink hand, one elbow on the edge of the bar. Garry's face got closer and closer to hers. He had lots of wrinkles around his eyes, smearing into deep grooves down his chiseled cheeks. The wrinkles flowed into deep crevices around his mouth, which was coming closer and closer to her face. His tongue was now in her mouth, and hers responded accordingly.

That is how Amber landed her second acting job in Los Angeles.

Chapter 24

A white trailer cast its wide shadow over a grassy area planted with perfect white lilies. Garry gestured with one arm toward the door. Amber climbed four narrow black metal steps and opened it. The first thing she saw inside was a bouquet of yellow roses on a small table. It was flanked by an L-shaped plush banquette seat. Across from the table, a cute mini-kitchen boasted a silver sink and coffeemaker. Past that, a narrow door to a bathroom flashed its own immaculate shiny fixtures. Beyond that, a pretty yellow and white curtain waved hello from the back wall, beckoning entrance into a charming little bedroom.

Amber sat and read the flower card while Garry quietly brewed a pot of coffee. Unlike his confident usual demeanor, the man's eyeline remained low toward the kitchenette area.

Her hair and makeup were already done up, so Amber felt like a bright acrylic painting. As she looked down at her note, she barely recognized the long French-tipped nails which decorated her own hands.

"Thank you for not sleeping with a dirty old bisexual. Respectfully, Your friend, Garry."

Amber felt her eyes tearing up. She waved her hands and looked at the ceiling.

"No, dear!" Garry broke through his morning embarrassment and laughed tenderly, "Not your makeup!" He rummaged through amply pre-stocked drawers until he found her a napkin. It was black and had the letters, "DGA" stamped on it in silver.

Amber touched the corners of it to her eyes. "I'm not gonna bawl, Garry."

"That's Mr. Holloway to you on set, Missy!" He winked. "Professional time, young lady," he put an arm around her shoulders lightly, the way pros know how to lavish affection without leaving a single hair out of place. "Besides, if you show up a mess, Greg will kill us both."

Amber sat up straight. She looked around her trailer; at least hers for the week. Plink! She could swear she felt her expanding heart puff up and break right through her ribs.

"I'M MARRIED!" SHE'D blurted out, practically puking it into Garry's mouth.

"What?!"

"I know, I know, it's the most ridiculous thing, but I'm married. I swear to God, I am." Amber pulled a cigarette from Garry's pack in his parked Jag's cupholder. She put it in her mouth and reached for the dashboard lighter button. She took the cigarette back out of her mouth and gestured with it. "At least I think I am."

Garry sat back in his seat and leaned his wavy dark gray hair against its headrest. He looked over at this emotional young woman waving wildly with a Marlboro. The moment suddenly felt more like an actor's interview than a potential one-night stand. He leaned back deep into the crook between his seat and the inside of his car door, settling in for a performance.

Amber went into it. Practically all in one breath, she told him all about Steely, about Fiji, about Uncle Brian and Chicago and the girl who stabbed Johnny in the belly. When she was finished, the lighter popped out and she lit up. She breathed in, heaving her bosom, and all Garry could think was, *this girl is the perfect Gretchen to seduce William Hurt. She's perfect.*

THE WEEK WENT BY IN a whirl of "Quiet on the set!" and warm towels after each "Cut!" because Amber's first big scene with William was supposed to be in the rain. Mornings brought early hair and makeup calls, bagels (toasted bagels) and memorizing new rewrites. The afternoons brought coffee and

M&Ms, Holly's funny text messages, flirting with the grips, winks and thumbs-ups from Greg to keep her confidence up. Evenings brought wine and chats and the near-impossible task of trying to wind down to get some sleep.

Amber never wanted it to end.

Chapter 25

A ARON
"We've managed to eradicate certain regions of the hemorrhaged varices at this point, but there are a couple that are really giving us a hard time. The cirrhosis is causing a major traffic jam inside your circulatory system and it can no longer handle more than around, oh, say forty percent flow. I didn't like what I saw in there today. Not good. Your whole system is backing up. Not good," the guy sounded like a mechanic discussing a car repair, "We'll get you going with a shunt as soon as you've recovered from today, and you'll need to continue procedures ongoing about every other month so we can keep an eye on them. I wish I could get in there every month, but we're too high a risk with the bleeding, and your anemia is becoming problematic."

Aaron stared at his bruised arms. His right wrist looked almost twice the size around as his left. He would've dropped a guitar pick if he'd had to hold one this week. His right thumb throbbed as he tried to toggle it. He shuddered. Was it a law that hospital rooms had to be freezing? He looked down at his bony knees, noticing as he hunched down how tight his underpants felt squeezed around his bloated waist.

The doctor read something from two now-empty and disconnected bags hanging next to Aaron's bed and wrote something in his folder. He flipped through some papers. Aaron felt like he had just flunked a test or something. He could feel some gas coming on also but tried not to embarrass himself. A few moments later, he regretted it, because the gas seemed to have gone the other way and was now cramping up his whole midsection. He refused to moan and shifted his weight from one bun to the other. The doctor was still bloody talking, "Yada, yada, even five more years, yada, yada—"

"What?"

His doctor looked up, seemingly annoyed to have his monologue interrupted. "What?"

"What was that about five years?"

"I said I doubted your liver function would be viable for five more years on the outside."

"And the inside?" Which was the inside, Aaron thought? Did that mean least? Focus, Aaron thought as he looked directly into the doctor's almost black eyes, gotta hear what this bloke is saying. The room seemed to suddenly smell heavy with ammonia and isopropyl alcohol. Aaron felt light-headed. Kinda nauseous.

"These things aren't an exact science, you know."

The doctor crinkled his brow as if he were a high school student figuring out a problem on a math quiz. "Oh, eighteen months, I suppose." He re-thought it. "Sometimes sooner."

Aaron's stomach dropped. The gas bubble in there would have plenty of room now.

"So, um…" Aaron trailed off.

"I'm talking about TIPS ASAP and your numbers will likely qualify you to get listed within the year."

"TIPS?" Aaron tried to remember the last time his doc had yada-yada'd something about it, "that's that crap thing where you shove some fecking tube thing in my guts and bypass the thing or something?"

"Mr. Spinnaker, you really are going to have to pay attention to the doctors when they explain things to you."

Aaron looked toward the soft voice that had just spoken from his doorway. He'd never been so happy to see his housekeeper Cindra before in his life. She looked cute, too, with a little corduroy cap over her blonde hair. Were those suede knee-high boots? Hot.

The doctor didn't look up from his notes.

When Cindra stepped beside him, Aaron gestured for her to sit. She leaned toward the bed, flushed slightly, then stiffened back to a stand. Her boss's shoes and street clothes were in a large clear baggie on a shelf next to the wall. Cindra decided now would be a good time to retrieve them.

The good doctor had already closed his folder and placed his pen into the breast pocket of his lab coat. He backed away from the area, practically mumbling, "We'll discuss the procedure in detail at my office next week when you come in. I'll see you then."

Cindra helped swing Aaron's feet over the side of his bed and step into his slippers. She could barely stabilize his thin frame against her own. Placing his clothes on the bedside, and stepping two feet back, she closed an orange-striped curtain in front of her while she waited. From behind it, she could hear faint grunts as her employer struggled into his clothes. Then she heard a quiet, flatulent sound, followed by a familiar-sounding Irish-accented mumble, "Such horse shite."

When Aaron opened the curtain again, Cindra settled him into a bright blue hospital wheelchair and pushed him squeakily down the hallway.

Chapter 26

UNCLE BRIAN

The horrid smell of burnt popcorn reached Brian's nose while he lay in the bathtub. It must've been pretty bad if the stink fought its way down the hall, under the door and past all the steam into his nose. He dunked under to rinse his hair. He was getting all pruney anyway.

After a quick stop over the toilet, Brian had very little to puke up. Just a teaspoon or two of bile. He rinsed his mouth with minty-fresh Scope and squinted into the mirror where he'd wiped steam off a face-sized circle. Brian didn't dare look at his emaciated abdomen. He was sure it looked fat, flabby and white. He spat once more in the sink for good measure before joining Gia in the living room.

Disgusted to find her eating charred corn from its blue-and-white paper bag, Brian flopped down next to his roommate on his leather couch. She didn't turn toward him, but gaped at the television, barely able to chew. Her left hand, still clutching a few kernels of popcorn, gestured wildly toward the screen.

A familiar-looking tree fairy stared at them with a huge face in a sideways close-up.

"Well, I'm refreshed," cooed the fairy, "Aren't you?"

AARON

Cindra paced through much of Mr. Spinnaker's nap. He often slept for three or four hours after these endoscopic procedures, but today he'd been out for almost six hours in the hospital before they woke him up and sent him home. He'd be up soon, and it was time to tell him.

She decided to show him instead. As Aaron took a mug of hot tea from his housekeeper's hand, she placed the TV remote next to him. She told him which channel to watch, then left him alone in his room.

Outside the door, Cindra said a silent prayer. "Dear God," she whispered, "Please show him that commercial."

AMBER

Carlos leaned into a two-inch-wide free space at the bar. If he wasn't going to get served for a while, he might as well get comfortable.

Holly and Amber had found two dance escorts for the evening, neither seeming to care which one went with which. Carlos thought the shorter guy was cuter, with longish brown hair that flipped in little waves around his ears. He could tell the guy was cut under his light blue and white striped button-up shirt, and the kid definitely had some moves. But the other dude was taller, which did count for something. Carlos presumed that Holly would be into him since the guy had a little salt-and-pepper around his temples. His tall shoulders rocked back and forth above the other three, and Carlos thought he seemed stiff. Maybe he was the DD and couldn't loosen up too much. Or maybe he was just so, so white.

Holly backed that thang up a little against tall-dude's crotch area. Amber saw it and laughed to herself.

"What's so funny?" Holly yelled to her, continuing to caboose the guy in his crotch.

Amber worked her way over to face Holly, bare shoulders shaking as she moved, "You're gonna castrate him if you're not careful!"

"What?" Holly doubled over, digging deeper into the guy, whose best option seemed to be pretending not to notice. He smiled a little.

Holly whirled around and grabbed his collar, pulling his face toward hers to the beat.

Amber found a comfortable position with cute short-guy's hands on her waist as she ground a little deeper with each measure of the music.

Carlos had discovered some flirty conversation with one of the waiters, but it only lasted a few minutes until the fellow had to get back to work. Carlos tried again to hail the bartender to no avail. He marched toward his slutty friends on the dance floor.

"This is so boring!" Carlos explained, grabbing one girl's wrist in each hand. The gentleman dance partners resisted, pulling the girls into themselves and amping up their dance moves.

Holly and Amber both looked at the whirling colorful room. Amber decided whoever could pull her hardest would win. Then she focused again on the beat. Carlos yanked them both a little harder and won. He led the two girls outside, where the night air immediately felt freezing. Holly put her hand on her belly and made an about-to-throw-up face. Carlos and Amber already found something outside to laugh hysterically about. They walked, arm in arm, toward Holly's car. Holly leaned over a short railing and called to them. Her yellow hair looked like a veil covering part of her face. Red lips pressed against each other bitterly. Before she could get a "Hey," out, Holly hurled. Amber laughed and pointed. Carlos sympathized a little more and went back to retrieve their girlfriend.

Amber stumbled as she tried to join them. Her ankle twisted, she laughed and decided she'd better not try walking just yet. Instead, she hopped up to sit on a high concrete planter, pulled a cigarette out of her handbag and lit it. She kicked her legs and surveyed the parking lot below from above.

A giant Cadillac Escalade pulled over in front of her. An older man in a valet uniform hustled over toward its passenger door, waited a moment and then opened it. A long dark brown leg came out first, followed by an absolutely gorgeous African American woman in a gold skirt and black one-shouldered top. Her hair looked like a slick tail of black silk. Every muscle flexed in her lean legs and arms as she moved. She wore a thin necklace that looked like a narrow-beaded scarf wrapped twice around her long, statuesque neck. Amber could smell a faint waft of expensive musky perfume. When the woman turned to retrieve her crystal-encrusted clutch purse from the car seat behind, she glanced past Amber as if she didn't exist. Amber might as well have been part of the overgrown palm plant behind her. Hell, she might as well have been some of the dirt it was planted in.

By the time the glamazon had fully unfolded her six-foot-tall figure, a handsome Black man had found his way beside her. His arm hid behind the thin small of her back as he led the woman past where Amber sat. Only as he walked by Amber, did he turn for a split-second to glance her way. Amber's legs may have been shorter and far less bronzed, but they were youthful and naked and sticking out of a denim micro-skirt right at the man's eye level.

As his eyes grazed over Amber's legs, she could see the shape of his face a little better underneath his LV-emblem hat brim. Suddenly, they locked eyes.

The man was A.J.

AARON

Curled up on his side, Aaron's body took up less than half of his white sofa. A handful of brown tufts, his hair stuck out from above his faux fur throw blanket like an oversized clump of lint. Breathing slow, long yet shallow breaths, Aaron's lack of movement gave an appearance as though he might well be dead. The almost-corpse faced the back of the sofa. Not a good vantage point to see the television, even had he been awake. Which Aaron was, most definitely, not.

Amber's fairy face finished her line, and the channel's programming cut back to its regularly scheduled sitcom rerun. Aaron's almost lifeless body didn't seem to care less. He was dreaming about childhood, anyway.

When Aaron had been just a wee lad, his mother used to take him to the local pub when she went once a week to help with their accounting paperwork. Aaron would sit on a tree trunk outside the back door, where the ground smelled like grass and piss. Aaron would find sticks and sword fight imaginary beasts. Then he would celebrate over their imaginary dead beast bodies by converting the sticks into air-guitars and strumming out a rock and roll victory anthem. The youngest waitress there would come out for a smoke, and tease him. Her shock of curly black hair contrasted with her pale face. Her lips, bright pink, curled around the end of her cigarette. Aaron would fantasize about them later, as a preteen, curled around something else.

Chapter 27

A ARON

"I'm telling you, it was her. I'm telling you, Aaron. It. Was. Her."

Aaron could hardly keep his voice stable as his stomach rolled and rumbled. He sputtered out, "Okay—" he wanted to add "thanks" or "man;" anything to sound a little more normal, but a small freight train seemed to be passing through his intestines at that moment, so Aaron just hung up.

A.J. stared at his phone. No, it hadn't dropped the call. Aaron hung up on him. This was getting to be a habit for the guy. A.J. shook his head and looked at the menu board behind the cute white counter waitress in front of him.

"I'll have a half ham and cheese with the tomato basil soup," he ordered, winking as was his habit. The cute girl turned toward a stack of various pastel ceramic bowls behind her. A.J. got a nice shot of her butt. Too-small pants. Nice. She reached above her head to grab an oversized saucer from the shelf above and A.J. could see an attractive flex in her back muscles through a gauzy-thin cream-colored T-shirt. She had a dancer's back.

The door opened to his right and a woman closer to his age swept in, bringing a wave of musky vanilla perfume in with her. A.J. guessed she must be forty-ish. Very sexy hair framed a pair of Prada sunglasses. Thick burgundy lips lined a half-open mouth as she removed the glasses. A fan of gorgeous eyelashes opened upward as the woman searched for the chalkboard wall-menu above A.J. and the cute waitress's head. He turned around again to retrieve his order and drop a ten into her little jar beside a huge brass cash register. Checking to make sure the hot lady saw his decent tip, which she did, A.J. headed up a quirky set of winding stairs to the plush cigar lounge upstairs. He felt a set of sexy-lashed eyes follow his ass upstairs. At least he hoped so.

AARON DRY HEAVED INTO his toilet. Something about gripping the edge of a clean white toilet seat felt strangely homey and familiar to his arms. The cold fresh porcelain comforted his cheek. Its cool caress smooth and oddly feminine. Cindra cleaned with this delicate lavender-pine soap, and it reminded him of his mother.

He would play in the grassy yard behind their neighborhood. There would have been a patch of lavender bushes chock-full of bees, all cute and busy with their silly work, work, work. Aaron would recline on a green pillow of silky lawn, staring up at puffy white clouds. He'd glance at his own bicep where it bent upward to support his head, proud that small muscles had begun to plump out his physique in a manly way. He'd smell his own scent and think, "I'm growing up to be pretty goddamn sexy, I am..." A song might come to him as he got himself caught up in the romance of changing cloud patterns.

He'd wonder where his Dad might be, what sexy woman might be with him and what pub he'd be going to tonight to spend whatever money he'd win playing cards that evening. He'd be proud of the machismo his Dad might be spraying all over the town, while glad that his mom got to remain innocent, albeit somewhat guarded and saddened by his absence.

Then, his mum would call his name, "Aaaaaron" in a descending minor third. He wouldn't answer right away because he liked the sound of her call. He'd listen, and lose himself as long as he could, finishing a new poetic stanza in his head before hopping up, all energy, bounding toward home and the smell of wonderful cooking.

Then they'd eat and ask each other about their days, make simple plans for the night, and move toward them. Mum would settle into a knitting-and-purling position in front of the TV set. Aaron would journal and dream, or play outside to find windows to break or graves to defile with boyhood mates and lassies.

Another wave of retching came up. He wished he could call his mum, but he couldn't. Even if she had been living, he wouldn't ever tell her any bad news, no matter what.

Steely remembered the last day of her life. She'd kissed him goodnight, he'd squirmed away, the way teenage boys did. He wasn't supposed to like her kisses at that age; he didn't even think about whether he did or not. He'd opened the window a crack, smoked a ciggy, waved the smell outside and laid down to sleep.

He didn't know what woke him at first. A faint sound must've been the thing that did it. The soft, small sound of a mug gently thudding on the yarn rug in the center of their tiny, tidy family room. A few tablespoons of cold tea had leaked out onto the rug.

Mum sat, slumped a bit. One hand rested on a Bible in her lap atop a bunched-up bit of half-knitted afghan. A ball of bluish-green yarn had rolled onto the floor and traveled a few feet to come to a stop beneath their small end table which held a softly-glowing lamp. Mum sat, slumped a bit. Her mouth had opened a wee space, and a small bit of drool had come out onto her chin. Otherwise, her eyes closed behind her glasses. Her right hand rested on the armrest, fingers open where the mug had last been before it fell. Mum sat, slumped a bit, and Aaron sat quietly on their sofa across from her. Their time alone had ended, and he didn't want to say goodbye quite yet, so he sat, slumped a bit, facing the body that used to be his sweet, sweet mum.

Chapter 28

A MBER
   "This is fecking bullshit," Aaron's voice said in Amber's message. "This is motherfucking, fucking goddamn bullshit. You call me. You fucking call me back, or, or—" The message cut off.

Amber's bowels dropped. She felt a tightness in her chest that seemed as if extra ribs had grown out of her sternum, creating a thick shield of bone which restricted her breathing. Amber's stomach went sour and she slumped in her chair, hair spilling into her face. Tears came out of her eyes in a sudden rush, but no sound. Amber couldn't breathe. With her right hand, she punched her own chest, suddenly. A noise came out. An awful, animal noise.

After sitting out on the deck staring at the tops of a nearby line of palm trees for what seemed like hours, Amber crawled into bed and fell asleep before she could even pull up her covers.

Holly came home, tossing her keys into a terracotta bowl that looked much like a shallow flowerpot. The word "HOLLY" was carved into it and filled with bright yellow glaze. Her key chain smushed onto the end-piece of a joint that hadn't been there before she left for her boyfriend's house. The condo didn't smell, but her sliding-glass door was open a little. A breeze moved a couple of pink zinnias she'd had in a vase near it. Holly's boyfriend sent her flowers once a week. She was so going to marry him. As soon as he asked her.

"Amber!" She yelled, opening the fridge with one hand and dumping out her old Starbucks cup into the sink with the other. "Amber! You home?" She took out a container of orange juice and poured herself a few ounces into a stemmed glass. "Ambershambler!!!" She took down a second glass and opened a cupboard to retrieve a bottle of Absolut. "You wanna little screwdriver? It's after five!"

From around the corner came a very sleepy-looking brunette roommate. Her eyes looked red and puffy like little slits surrounded by smudged makeup. She stopped in the walkway and leaned against it; hands placed on each thigh as she slid down the wall. Holly worried for a moment that Amber might fall all the way to the floor, but she seemed to stick there, halfway down, like a statue beginning to grow into the wall behind her back. Or out of it. She wore a white T-shirt and gray cut-off sweat shorts. One of her feet was bare and the other had a low light blue sock on it. Her arms had deep pink grooves slanting across them at different angles where a sheet had been pressing into them. She bit her upper lip with her lower teeth.

Holly took this all in and poured her friend some vodka before adding a small splash of orange juice. Sipping her own glass from her right hand, Holly held the other one toward Amber, who shook her head. "Come on, honey, you look like you need this." Holly held it up again, shaking it a little like a carrot toward a bunny. She tapped Amber's bare ankle with the tip of her own white sandal. "Aw, come on, it's happy hour and I don't want to drink alone."

Amber held up one very straight finger. "It is NOT happy hour," she said. However, after holding the finger up an extra beat, she re-shaped her hand to reach for the glass.

"Outside, you." Holly led the way toward the open patio door and pulled a chair close to her friend. She nudged a white metal café table with a colorful mosaic tiled top in the design of a peacock between them and set her glass down. Almost sitting down, she thought again and ran into the house once more.

Moments later, Holly returned with their terracotta ashtray and a fresh-rolled joint to share. The two sat quietly, enjoying the ritual of lighting the thing, taking a couple of drags and watching palm fronds wave overhead. By the time Amber's arms had returned to normal flesh-colored, Holly snuffed out the marijuana. Amber hadn't taken a sip from her glass, but Holly continued enjoying her own. She reclined back and put a sandal up on the table.

"Okay, girl. Spill."

Amber breathed in and spent the next half-hour telling Holly her whole story, from meeting Steely right up to playing Aaron's message for her.

Then they turned their chairs to one side of the patio deck and watched the sun settle low into the sky, sending gorgeous California oranges and yellows overhead like a happy-face umbrella. The relaxing whoosh sound of wind high up in the palm fronds seemed to cleanse everything ugly about her story from the air. Amber felt more relieved than she could remember, ever.

A thought flashed for a moment of Uncle Brian, and how maybe she could face calling him in the morning. It might be a good test to see if Holly didn't seem to hate her by tomorrow, after sleeping on all that unflattering information.

For now, they still felt like best girlfriends, warm and cheek-flushed from the contents of their now-empty glasses on the peacock table. As the sky faded from dark orange to blue, Holly shook her head, quietly saying, almost to herself, "Mrs. Steel Fingers Wildboy," she giggled, "that, I would not have guessed."

Amber breathed a single quiet chuckle, too.

"Is there anything else that you're not telling me?" Holly asked.

"Just one more," Amber replied.

"Okay, you might as well tell me that, too."

"Okay. But you won't believe me. Today was the first time I ever tried weed. I took it out of your drawer."

"Are you serious?" Holly's eyes widened.

Amber nodded and pulled down the oversized beach towel from the back of her chair. She snuggled into it, tucking her legs underneath her on the seat. "Yup."

AARON'S EMAIL INBOX was stuffed. A.J., A.J., A.J., spam, spam, other blokes, bitches, spam, A.J., A.J.... Amber. What? Was that Amber's email address bold and unread on the list? Aaron nodded toward Cindra as he took a cup of tea from her hand. It tasted like honey and mint. He scrolled down and clicked.

The font was standard, the message short:

I'm so sorry. Too scared to call you.
Want you to come to a film premiere next month.

Will you?
—Your Amber

Aaron shook his head and breathed a quick exhale out his nose, a maneuver his abdominal muscles didn't like so much. He stabilized himself by leaning against the edge of his desk. Her words read like an oldie-time telegram. *I'm so sorry*. STOP. *Too scared to call you*. STOP. Aaron's heart sped up. He felt love. Totally stupid, but he felt love.

He typed a reply:

Yes. Will be there. Send details.
—Your Aaron

Close enough to the Enter key to feel its warmth, Aaron recoiled, deleted *Your* and clicked SEND.
STOP.

AMBER SPILLED COFFEE all over Holly's adorable desk accouterments. Pink post-it notes shaped like a dress on a hanger, fuzz-coated rainbow-striped pen, pale orange desktop calendar with notations of recent auditions, all slightly antiqued now with warped brown watermarks across them. Amber jumped up, "Shit!" She looked around. Holly was still getting ready in the bathroom.

Amber herself should be in there ASAP. She had a meeting for Greg to introduce her to one of his old friends, an agent, this morning. There was even talk of a new part she might be right to play. Slamming shut Holly's laptop (which thank God had not gotten splashed with coffee), Amber hustled to the kitchen area behind her. Zooming around its center island, she grabbed a roll of paper towels with little printed caterpillars all over and dabbed handfuls all over the desk.

Tossing the wad into the trash as she turned toward the hall, Amber knocked on the door.

Holly opened it, revealing a full face of flawless makeup framed by a few remaining pink and blue rollers. Passing by her as she dropped a crumpled T-shirt on the floor, Amber hopped naked into the shower and turned it on. She stuck out her head.

"Please don't hate me, okay?"

Holly whirled around with a sour expression. Through pursed lips and with raised eyebrows, she asked, "What did you do, young lady?"

Amber laughed. "I kind of fucked up your saccharine utopia of desktop cuteness. With coffee just now."

"Oh, why?" Holly whined, pulling the last blue roller off the top of her head so a cascade of golden bangs could cover her forehead.

"When you hear why, I swear you won't be mad at me," Amber yelled from the other side of the frosted glass.

Holly pressed her hand against the shower door. "Ooo, juicy? Tell me!"

"Can't! No time!"

"Grr." Holly opened the door a couple inches and wiggled her strawberry-tipped fingernail inside. "We shall confer on this over happy hour this evening, missy." With that, she grabbed a tube of lipstick from the counter and was off.

"SUCH A BAD PLAN," GREG was saying as he made a left turn with his Jeep.

"Why?" Amber sulked. "It's the best way. If he's gonna break my heart, I would think my first premiere party would take off the sting, don't you think?"

"Break your heart? You're the one who ditched *him*."

Greg's GPS interrupted them. "Turn Right on Laurel Canyon Boulevard."

"Like I don't know that," Greg said with great sass to the computer voice, pressing a button to turn it off.

"It's complicated," Amber said.

Greg chuckled and flipped his bushy hair. "Okay, Drama Queen."

"Fuck you."

"Gee, it's only 9:15 in the morning and already I'm getting a Fuck You." He spotted a Coffee Bean. "Want anything?"

"Aren't we having a breakfast meeting?" Amber asked, staring out the window.

"It's in Santa Monica that could take an hour from here at this time of day."

"God, how much caffeine do you people need?" Amber poked his arm. "I would like a cigarette, though."

"You're right," Greg said tenderly, "I forgot you must be getting nervous."

"Thanks. Is that why I'm feeling so bitchy?"

"No, that's just you."

"Get ready... You're about to get Fuck-you Number Two!"

Greg laughed again. Ah, young people. He loved it. People his age never cracked jokes before noon. Over forty it seemed like nobody cracked jokes after noon either. Greg's energy soared. His agent friend, Helen, was going to love Amber, and he owed her a favor. Good karma all around. And his partner Garry was pleased with him. Always a bonus.

He turned on the radio and found a great Simon and Garfunkel song.

What a dream I had
Kissed with organdy
I felt your honey hair—

"Is this The Beatles?" Amber asked. Greg glared at her from behind his glasses.

"It's Simon and Garfunkel, child."

Amber laughed, slapping her bare knee where it stuck out from under an ivory pencil skirt she'd borrowed from Holly. "I know who Simon and Garfunkel are, you dork!"

Greg socked her gently in the arm. "Fuck you," he said.

They both cracked up and turned up the radio.

HOLLY JUMPED AT EVERY sound, thinking it would be Amber coming home. She had the cocktail ingredients all set up. They would have strawberry daiquiris. The blender stood as her companion beside where she sat at the center island on a high stool, kicking one crossed leg to the music she had playing. It was a Steel Fingers Wildboy song, one of her favorites. She kind of hoped Amber would come home with it still on.

Seven minutes later, the door did open. Amber tossed her condo key into the key bowl and walked toward the bedroom hallway, apparently not seeing Holly where she sat. Suddenly stopping, she turned around, throwing her arms up in the air touchdown style.

Moments later the two were screeching and jumping all over the kitchen, Amber singing, "I got signed, I got signed, I'm in Hollywood and I got signed!"

"You got signed, you got signed, look out, Hollywood, she got signed!"

They partied well into the wee hours at a club later, Carlos seething with jealousy, yet hugging Amber every five minutes. Amber didn't have the heart to tell him she'd also gotten a reading for the eighteen-year-old daughter of a famous comedian's new sitcom. When she booked it, she would put in a word for him and hopefully Carlos could afford to stop taking the bus to work.

Then, after that, Amber decided she would run for president and work on the cure for cancer.

Chapter 29

ARON

Aaron found his way down the hall, despite a sharp pain in his left side. He knew it was just internal stitching and was getting familiar with the way it felt. Best not to turn his head too much, just keep it straight.

Cindra's bedroom was down this hall, and he didn't want to disturb her. He wanted to find the photo album in a closet back here from his and Amber's wedding. He'd asked her to stash it where he wouldn't find it right after Amber left and he had been so pissed. But tonight, he didn't think it would hurt to take a peek. He couldn't think where else she would've hidden it.

Walking down the hall in his slippers, Cindra didn't hear Aaron coming closer to her domicile. Her door was open just a crack, in case he called her, and she started undressing for her nightly shower.

Aaron saw a slit of light around the door and breathed slower to make sure his housemaid wouldn't hear as his path forced him to walk by. Beside the ajar door, he turned his head a little—ouch—and peeked inside. He saw a golden silhouette of her skin against soft lighting. Cindra was bending over, and he couldn't help but linger as she did so. Such a graceful body, he thought, remembering that was of course one of the reasons he'd hired her.

A.J.'s voice came into his memory, "Now you want your house to be a party pad, awwright? Sexy maids and shit. But classy, though. You know, European and with accents and stuff." Aaron marveled at how far he and A.J. had come together since then.

Cindra stood up and turned profile as she leaned down toward the bed to pick up a towel. Aaron could see her upper thigh's shape silhouetted against a lamp in the background. He felt himself getting aroused. He wanted to nudge the door open just a little bit more.

Cindra bent over to pull a pair of flip-flops from under the foot of her bed. When she did, Aaron looked right between her legs. He saw pink and couldn't help but move his hand toward the crotch of his pants. He sighed.

Cindra stood up quickly at the sound, like an antelope when it senses a predator on the prowl. She turned her head toward the door. Aaron quickly stepped aside. Too quick. He lost his balance and reached for the wall as he fell backward onto the floor, hitting with a thud and a curse.

At the doorway, with one hand crossing her breasts, Cindra stuck her head out sideways at her boss. He was trying to get up, but all he'd managed so far was to sit up, propped with one arm. Both legs stuck out straight in front of him the way a five-year-old might sit. Aaron looked down in shame.

His housekeeper quickly retrieved her robe and lifted the frail man to his feet. She helped him back down the hall and settled him into his own bedroom, making sure the man had anything he might need before excusing herself again for the night.

Back in her room, Cindra dialed her mother's number and told her about the latest news with her rich and famous boss. Cindra's mom shook her head and tsk-tsk-tsked in all the right places. They both said they'd pray for him before hanging up.

Aaron jerked off for a couple of minutes before going to sleep. It didn't take much, and it didn't do much for him either. He wanted a glass of whiskey more than anything but would have to settle for a Kleenex and a sip of hot chicken broth left next to his bed by his dear maid.

Chapter 30

BRIAN
    Dino glanced at his watch for the third time. Its long hand had passed by ten more minutes since the last time he'd checked. Ten plus twenty plus however long the first one was... Well, it all equaled just plain old too darn long for that fellow to be in the bathroom. He wondered if he should check on him.

The diner looked dismal this morning. One of the fluorescent lights near the door had kicked down a notch in brightness when he turned them on at 6 a.m. and now it flickered. The day was depressing enough with its overcast cloud coverage and imminent storm. Adding a flickering light made it downright morbid.

Dino always got in a bad mood when Sharon was out of town. Her mother had fallen and hurt her hip for the second time so there hadn't been much choice. After dropping his wife off at Detroit Metro last night, Dino and Barney didn't feel so much like swingin' bachelors as lonely sailors since she'd gone. This morning he kept checking his phone for a message, but she must not have gotten a chance yet. Hopefully, she'd landed safely in Kentucky by now and was enjoying her sister's company and blessing her mom with the visit. Ugh.

Five more minutes had passed and Dino decided to check up on one of their favorite regular customers who'd been in the bathroom now for what must be going on nearly an hour. No one else had come or gone in there. The restaurant had only two occupied tables and one lone trucker at the counter, so he figured he could sneak away for a minute to check up on the situation. Opening the door, he was in for a shock.

One stall was locked, but obviously Brian had passed out. His legs stuck out from under the door, one pant leg scooched up to reveal a frighteningly bony white lower leg. Dino had to force the door open by lifting it from the bottom and pushing hard. Thank goodness he didn't hit Brian where he lay. It was clear from the blood on the toilet seat, streaming down its side and pooling to the floor, that Brian had been puking into it when he'd passed out. Dino suspected as much; it wasn't the first time he'd noticed Brian's strange bathroom habits.

CLAIRE AND NADINE WERE incorrigible. If Claire spotted a cute guy in the waiting room, Nadine would inevitably flirt with him by coming around the outside of the check-in counter, pointing out the specific columns of the sign-in form with bright pink and white acrylic nails. If Nadine had spotted him first, Claire would lean over the counter to purposely give the guy a shot of both cleavage and a warm wafting of Victoria's Secret Angel as she leaned over the counter to assist him. Either way, the guy was usually screwed. Two gorgeously dark-haired, eye-lined Chaldean gals weren't easy to ignore, even against a backdrop of hospital gray-and-white decor.

Dino got the Claire treatment. She was a head taller than Nadine and therefore at an unfair advantage. Claire had met her match, though. Dino spoke pretty much non-stop on his cell phone as he filled out the idiot-proof sign-in form with what information he knew about Brian.

"Yeah, he's in there now. If nothing else, he's going to need some stitches in his head. I'm telling you; he was not himself, Sharon. He kept trying to make jokes the whole time in the car, but he was barely awake and his head kept dropping down."

Dino paused, flashing a blue-white smile at Nadine as she glared in Claire's direction. Nadine blushed and poked her coworker friend in the butt with her pen under the counter. Claire swatted her hand like it was a fly and leaned lower toward the countertop.

"What's Brian's phone number, do you know?" Dino fumbled with the chain pen, trying to shove it into the hole on the fake wood grain counter. Claire helped with both hands, being sure to touch his wrist a little as she did so. As Dino nodded, Claire did her best to lock in eye contact. She didn't succeed, however, which elicited a quiet snort from Nadine, followed by a headshake of her long, shiny mane. Dino nodded in the gals' general direction and found himself an empty seat to plunk into. He leaned forward on two muscular thighs with his tan, buff forearms and continued speaking with his wife.

BRIAN'S NURSE POKED a syringe into the crook of his elbow, holding a rubber wrap around his pathetic bicep with the other free hand. The nurse smiled weakly as the vein wouldn't yield a flow.

"So sorry," the nurse muttered, trying again to feel around with an index finger.

Brian stared at his nurse's fingertips. They had a deep tan hue and a gentle, nimble way of moving around his own pale white arm. His nurse had closely shaved hair, almost bald, and appeared to be a young Chinese kid of barely five and a half feet tall. Brian felt old in front of him and tried not to think about how awful he must look to the kid. He had a blood-encrusted bandage haphazardly taped to his right temple and across his forehead. His glasses had to be put on crooked to accommodate all the extra tape.

As Brian watched the nurse go about his work, he kept thinking how sweet it was that some people decided to become nurses. Here he was, feeling like a worthless lump, and this young man stood on his feet all day for who knows how many hours poking total strangers in the arm over and over with his warm nice fingers. This cute kid, who could probably be out doing anything in the world he wanted, had already devoted who knows how many hours toward helping random people and maybe even saving lives.

Brian fixed computers, watched television and tried to get skinny enough so he could finally someday live a normal life. Who cared? Now he would probably get all bloated and fat from that huge bag of sugar drip they'd had him on for the last hour. Brian wished he was dead. And also, not gay, to boot. That would be nice. Dead and straight. Or just straight. Or at least just dead. A deep sigh overtook him, causing a chill. Brian shuddered.

Thanh kept probing his patient's pale, tissue-like skin and prayed silently inside his head for his heavenly father to please help one of this man's veins to give him enough to fill two and a half vials. Of course, being originally from Vietnam, Thanh prayed in Vietnamese.

THE BREAK ROOM BOASTED a yellow cake with white frosting, mostly torn to pieces on a foil-covered cardboard mat. Every month the company put up for a cake to represent anyone with a birthday that month. Brian could smell its sweet artificial vanilla as he brushed against the serving table, reaching for a newspaper on a wall rack behind it.

"Hey, IT Guy!" exploded a voice behind him which belonged to Phil Galveston, one of the salesmen. Phil nudged Brian with a chubby hip as he reached over his shoulder for an Auto Trader from the same rack.

"It's Brian, actually."

"Yeah, yeah, I knew it started with a B. So, did you hear what happened to Stan while you were on vacation?"

"I wasn't actually on a vaca—"

"Yeah, it was so sad. The guy broke up with his boyfriend—is that what I'm supposed to say, boyfriend?"

Brian flushed. Luckily Phil was already directing the conversation past him and toward Marcy, one of the assistants, who had just entered the break room with two other people in tow.

"I think it's 'partner,'" Marcy replied.

"Yeah, it's 'partner,' right, Tom?" Phil asked, snorting loudly. Tom, a tall forty-something with curly brown hair, leaned against the corner of the cake table. Marcy nudged past Brian, reaching for a paper plate and napkin.

Tom started cutting off a piece of cake to serve her. "Don't ask me," he punched Phil lightly on the arm and winked at Marcy at the same time. "I'm married."

Phil busted out in a loud sound that barely passed as laughter, "Yeah, don't ask Tom, his wife is pregnant!"

All burst out laughing, including Brian, who didn't know what was funny.

"So, what happened?" Brian asked after the peals died down.

Phil put his arm around Brian's neck. His yellow shirt felt like sandpaper. "Yeah, Brent here was on vacation."

"I wasn't—"

Marcy cut him off, "Huh, I always thought your name was Brett... Well, Stan broke up with his partner or live-in lover or whatever and when he came into work Monday, he looked awful—you know he always dresses so nice, usually—Well, he looked like he hadn't slept all night. His shirt was all wrinkly and not tucked in or anything. So, he wasn't here more than an hour or so before he starts crying right out loud in his cubicle."

One of the other assistants spoke. Her name was Wendy and she was a new hire. Brian knew this because he'd sent Oliver over to set up her new passwords a couple weeks ago. Wendy Blossom. She wore a purple shirt tucked into a gray pencil skirt. "My desk is across from his and he was like, wailing. I mean I thought he was going to hyperventilate, so I went over to ask him if he wanted water—"

Tom piped in, "Is this when he threw something?"

Marcy: "Yes, he hauls out and throws his pencil right at Wendy!"

Wendy: "Well, actually he just kind of threw it down, but it bounced off his keyboard drawer thing and it's a good thing I wear glasses because I think it would've totally hit me in the eye."

Phil glanced toward Brian and lingered an extra moment, probably because he wore glasses too. It seemed for a moment as if Phil noticed the white gauze and bandage on Brian's temple, half-hidden by the way he combed his bangs forward. But he said nothing and looked away.

Tom: "So then, is this where you called security?"

Wendy: "No way, somebody else must've done that. I tried to calm him down but he went crazy! He just started yelling at me to get out of his cubicle."

Phil: "I heard that! He was all, 'Get OUT of my cubicle. Get AWAY from my cubicle.' Security had to escort him out. It was hilarious!"

Marcy touched Phil's arm, "No, it's kind of sad because he just lost—"

Phil raised his eyebrows, "Lost his shiiii—" He raised his voice in sing-song glee. Tom laughed softly and looked at the floor.

Wendy turned toward Brian, grabbing his newspaper for emphasis, "No, I mean it turns out he lost his cat!"

Everyone's eyes widened.

Brian remembered about Stan's cat. He'd always had tons of photos up on his cubicle since the cat was a kitten, and whenever anyone in the break room talked about kids, or pets or pretty much anything, Stan would find a way to bring up something utterly silly that his cat had done recently. He had to admit some stories were kind of cute, like one time the kitten had curled up inside the crescent of a banana and Stan emailed everyone a photo of it. Brian's head throbbed. He wanted to sit down.

The group made their way to one of the round ugly Formica tables and sat, pulling in an extra chair from another table for Brian. Tom took the honor of wrapping up the story.

"So, it turns out his life partner or whatever either took the cat or let it go outside because when Stan got home from someplace the cat was gone and so was all the other guy's stuff." He finished by nodding about a dozen times.

After the obligatory group head nods, Brian tried to read the paper, sipping lukewarm low-sodium chicken broth from a thermos. The rest of the group bantered on, occasionally including him by asking something like, "So did you have a good vacation?" or "What's the deal with that Oliver guy, anyway?" Brian glanced at his watch and waited for the longest twenty minutes of all time to pass. Finally, it was time for them all to get up and go back to work.

As they stood up, Marcy gasped with the greatest idea in human history, "Hey, you guys, we should all get a card and sign it for Stan, don't you think?"

Wendy made a loud whiny sound that was probably supposed to sound sympathetic, "That is such an awesome idea! Marcy, you are so thoughtful."

Tom and Phil followed them out the door with nodding heads. Just as Phil had disappeared through the doorway, he patted the edge of the door jamb one last time, tossing behind him the words, "Later, Brett."

SHARON WHEELED A RED suitcase with a black duffel bag on top through her doorway. Barney's paws clicked toward the door, his tail wagging so hard she feared he might knock something over. She patted his head with her left hand and squished his chin with the right, breathlessly cooing that he was a good dog and he missed her, right? Once satisfied, Barney padded away down the hardwood hall and parked his furry body into position over a knotted sock.

Sharon wheeled the suitcase to the bottom of the stairs and felt the weird energy of being home. Dino must not be around to greet her, she thought, noting that after a shower she would head over to the diner. Crossing past the front room, she suddenly stopped short.

A man was sleeping on her couch.

GIA WANDERED THROUGH Brian's apartment, slapping one hand along the countertop as she called for her roommate. He hadn't been there when she got home from her liquor store night job four days in a row. Five in the morning, where the fuck was he? Did he take up jogging to burn even more calories he didn't eat? Psycho. She peeked in his bedroom. Immaculate, as usual.

From her officially designated drawer in the kitchen, she fumbled for a half-empty pack of cigarettes. Pulling one out between pursed lips, she remembered the rule about smoking inside. Gia started toward the door, stopped, said "Fuck it" out loud and parked her skirt-covered fanny on Brian's sofa. Lighting the cigarette with a red Bic from her hip pocket, she suddenly stood up with a "shit" and ran into the kitchen to grab a small plate for the ashes before it was too late.

Leaning her head against the cool black leather again, Gia closed her eyes. She imagined Brian in a police station, waiting to nark her out for stabbing that asshole. Police in her mind bustled all around Brian, carrying Dixie cups and manila file folders; sleeves rolled up above watch-wrapped wrists. Brian would lift an index finger once in a while, peeping a barely audible, "excuse me" toward no one.

This vision haunted her since the first time she'd moved in. Luckily, when it came to Brian, her trust issues faded and the vision dissipated into fuzzy colors and darkness as sleep crept in.

With her last moments of lucidity, Gia smiled at how a designated drawer sure beat a cardboard box or a grocery cart and this sofa sure felt softer than the concrete outside or the back seat of an abandoned vehicle. Brian was her bestie now, and she was gonna have to trust his tightly puckered ass. But where the heck was her tight-assed friend?

SHARON MADE COFFEE for Brian and handed him the cup. He sat on one of their barstools at the kitchen island while she leaned over the stainless-steel sink.

"We're worried about you, Brian. Dino and I talked on the phone when you went into the hospital, and we don't want to see you keep going on like this. Dino didn't think you should be alone, but hanging around here can't be good for you. You need to be with experts, honey. Don't you want to get better? Don't you want to go home? What did you think we were going to do, just set you up on the couch and pretend nothing happened?"

"I'm sorry, Sharon," Brian stared into the dark brown liquid. With his thumb, he traced the outline of a painted owl on the stoneware mug. He stood up, leaving the full coffee on the countertop.

"Hey, where are you going?" Sharon called behind him. Barney stood up as if he too echoed the question.

"To work."

"You're going to work?" Sharon wanted to ask, "Are you nuts?" But decided against it. Instead, she came from around the island, beckoning Brian back to his seat. "You can't go to work like this. Look at yourself, hon."

Brian looked down at his body, searching for whatever Sharon meant. It made him dizzy. His knees almost buckled as he grabbed the stool for support. Sharon helped him sit.

"Hmm," was all Brian could say.

"I'll tell you one thing. I am going to touch base with Dino, and then I'm coming back here. We're pulling out the yellow papers and figuring this thing out." She grabbed her purse and plunked a floppy hat over her red curls as she made her way toward the front door. "And you better be here when I get back, Mister!" With that, the door opened and shut again.

OLIVER CALLED HIS MANAGER'S extension with one hand while the other pulled a tootsie roll out of his front hanging file. He pulled out a red one, put it back, and retrieved a brown one.

As the phone rang, he tucked the receiver into the crook of his neck, using both hands to twist the candy open. No one picked up.

"Thish ish sho shtupid," Oliver hung up.

Immediately the phone rang. It was his boss. "What is it? Oliver, you have to stop bothering me on Fridays. Fridays are my busiest days. This better be an emergency."

Oliver tried to chew and swallow fast so he could talk. "I jusht wanted to let you know that Brian ... ish taking another pershonal day."

Long pause. His manager spoke through crunching sounds, "Whatever, Oliver. I don't care."

Oliver started to say goodbye, but his manager spoke again.

"I thought he was on vacation anyway—"

Oliver rolled his eyes and sighed. He was tired of covering for Brian, who didn't even have the courtesy to call him. But technically his IT partner outranked him in seniority and would be the one filling out his evaluation at the end of the year.

"Yeah, I'm sorry I forgot. He came in yesterday, but he'sh shtill on vacation for the resht of the week at leasht."

Another pause for crunching. "So, you're saying he's on vacation today but he came in yesterday." Pause. "Why?"

"Um, we had a lot to do." Oliver scooped out the red tootsie roll, wishing he hadn't made the call in the first place.

"Good. Good, then. Very good. Now can I get back to work? I'm leaving early for golf."

Oliver swallowed hard again, nearly choking as he said goodbye. It didn't matter, though, because his manager had already hung up.

Chapter 31

A MBER
Some women take hours of preparation to look glamorously disheveled. Some women take hours to look not disheveled. Amber's experience had included neither the time nor the resources to pull off either. Most days, she found herself pretty pleased if she at least managed to not smell like the night before.

Holly also belonged to neither the former nor the latter group of women, but for a different reason. She serendipitously belonged to the set that always looked glamorous, disheveled or no. She smelled great whether the day's activities called for a light, ocean fragrance or a heavier vanilla musk. Her dresser looked as if it belonged in a black and white movie to Amber, with a large mirrored tray reflecting up at bottles of all shapes and sizes. The classic parfums, like Chanel and Guerlain, lined the front ledge of the tray while less recognizable eaux de toilette created a modern art of their own in a collage of colors and shapes behind the organized front row. Everything Holly touched seemed to create the perfect balance between composed and free-spirited.

This Saturday, she stood facing a sink of dirty dishes, wearing pink rubber gloves that converged just short of the elbow into flared white vinyl cuffs dotted with tiny pairs of cherries. Her hair swept back and upward into a French-looking swirl which seemed to disappear seamlessly into pale gold and nearly white highlights. Layered tendrils trickled down her smooth pink cheekbones ending in bouncy little curls. All this was held together by what appeared to be a single pencil.

Amber didn't know how Holly did it. She couldn't even keep her gritty hair up in a clip at the moment. Half of it kept falling out. She pulled the toothed contraption out of the other half of her hair and chucked it across the room where it landed as if by design into a small silver trash bin. In her bedroom with both closet doors slid open and clothes thrown all around every surface, she sighed deeper with every "No," as she tossed more clothes about. Finally, this last sigh was deep and loud enough to sound much like a moan of agony, summoning Holly's head to peek into the doorway.

Amber stood before one mirrored door holding a white miniskirt in front of herself. It looked like a tennis skirt to Holly, and shamelessly (or shamefully, depending on your point of view) short. On the top, her mousy roommate seemed to entertain a notion of pairing the skirt with a little black polo shirt that incorporated a vinyl white belt at its tiny waist.

"Can you even fit into that?" Holly asked.

Amber glared. "I don't know whether to say fuck you or to cry."

"Aww, sorry." Holly made a puppy dog face. "I only meant with your hugemangous knockers."

That got a giggle out of her, and Amber did say, "Fuck you," but it sounded kind of nice through laughter.

"There, now. That's better." Holly came in and sat down on a corner of the bed, scooting something floral out of the way first.

"If I tell you I can in fact squeeze my giant boobs into this, will you tell me it's good enough?" Amber held the two pieces a little higher.

"Um, you mean for going out tonight?" Holly drew a hopeful breath.

"No, I mean for the—"

"Don't you dare!"

"Why?" Amber whined, "What's wrong with it?"

Holly found herself on her feet. "You might as well ask what's right with it. And then I would say, um, nothing. Nothing is right with this at all. First of all, your shirt's got a collar." She looked at Amber for some sign of understanding. Holly sighed and put a hand on her hip, gesturing wildly with the other hand. "The only women wearing a collar to the premiere will be old ladies, lesbians, or maybe a seeing-eye dog."

Amber sniffed. "What? I like collared shirts," Amber defended in a whiny near whisper.

"Sweetie, how do you not see that's the neckline equivalent of orthopedic shoes?" She sighed and changed gears from the disaster of a top. "And good god, this skirt is so short. You'd better not drop anything. Or sit. Plus, tennis, anyone? Not to mention, what the heck is this belt made out of?" She touched it. "Pure plastic? Ouch, it's sharp!" She pulled the white belt out of its two little loops attached to the black shirt. "Loops, Amber? Are you kidding me?" She looked closer at the belt, which was about a quarter-inch wide and upon further inspection had deep cracks on its edges as well as signs of yellowing. "Oh, my god, how old is this thing?"

Suddenly she snatched both pieces. "Okay. You are not wearing this. And you are not wearing anything black and white, okay? You want to stand out, right? We have to get you in a color! Do you want to fade into the background with the valet guys? Not to mention, this shirt is *cotton*. And the only thing worse than that for a film premiere—" She paused for emphasis on the last two words, "is the somewhat crunchy polyester content in this skirt!" With that, she tossed both pieces onto the bed next to where Amber had sat down during her lecture.

Amber stared down at them, her hair creating a straight and stringy veil of brown in front of her. When she looked up, Holly could tell her eyes had filled up with tears. Holly covered her mouth, gasping, "Oh my god, I'm so sorry! Oh, I suck. I am such a bitch. I am so sorry."

She sat next to her friend and put an arm around her neck. Amber's voice, practically a whisper, said, "Am I beyond hope?"

Holly rocked her a little, genuinely thinking over the question. She started to speak, but couldn't think what to say.

Amber's voice went up high, "Oh shit! You do think I'm hopeless!?" She laid back onto the bed into a pile of clothes and kicked her legs like a little kid.

Holly stood up, speaking loudly over Amber's whiny noises. "You are NOT hopeless. You have hope. And her name is Holly." She stood like a superhero, pointing at her own chest with a thumb. Amber barely raised her head to peek up at her. She lay back down again and rolled into a fetal position.

Holly took large bold steps around the messy room. She picked up garments one at a time, glancing at each for less than a second. Whenever she lifted a new piece, her face looked as if she expected cockroaches to scurry out from underneath. A few times her face looked as if she actually did see cockroaches there. Within five minutes she determined the clothing cupboard to be bare and gathered items into a thick fabric bundle across her forearm.

Tossing the heavy stack right next to Amber's head, she said, "Get up and get some clothes on. Any of these will do." Holly headed for the door. "Then put on some walkin' shoes because, girl, you and I are going shopping!"

CARLOS RESTED HIS FEET on the plush olive-green velvet chaise lounge, waiting for his girlfriends to join him in the spa's common room. He tried his best to calm the nervous energy pent up within his chest. Sipping some cucumber-and-lime-infused water, the dark-haired new spa client glanced casually at the few other guests in the room. Light streamed in thin slits across the back of one woman's white robe. She seemed to leaf through a magazine; Carlos could tell by the way her right elbow moved in and back out across the armrest of her wicker white chair. Another rather scrawny looking older man flexed his toes inward as he stared out at an ethereal gauze-filtered view of some gardens outside the window. The silence became deafening, but Carlos vowed to relax regardless of his overwhelming desire to jump on the chaise lounge and burst into a crazy leprechaun jig.

The day had cost $400, and Amber had just hooked him up with this birthday gift. That, and this weekend, he would see his own face on a giant silver screen. *What, what, what could be better?* He wanted to grab the other spa clients and start a conga line. *Nothing, that's what!*

Soon Amber and Holly ambled out from behind a tall bamboo wall screen. Holly looked fresher even than usual with her cheeks pink and all shiny. Amber seemed to be a few inches taller than when Carlos had met her. He checked her feet to see if she had heels on. Nope, just those bright blue disposable flip-flops, compliments of the spa. Amber served herself some ice water and plunked down next to Carlos, nearly sitting on his ankles before he could scoot them out of the way. She reached over and tenderly squeezed his knee, then turned to stare out the window. Holly had already finished her water and had just about fallen asleep in her own wing-backed wicker chair. Her right leg was tucked underneath her body on a lemon-yellow cushion and her other leg dangled gently toward the floor.

Just as Carlos himself began to relax into a near slumber, something woke him. Amber had reached silently around his backside and given him a quick goose on the rear. When he looked up, she was grinning ear to ear.

A CHUBBY DARK-HAIRED six-year-old wandered back and forth underneath black strap stanchions bordering a line of patrons waiting for the next bank teller to open. Amber stared at the electronic board where the next teller's number would soon appear with its accompanying arrow. The little girl looked up at her with wide eyes and one index finger slobbering around in her mouth. She didn't blink, and neither did Amber. Finally, Amber won the staring contest and the child began a very important new activity of bobbing up and down, trying to hit herself in the ponytail with the black strappy thing.

Amber clicked air in her teeth, trying to remember the last time she'd been inside a bank. She couldn't. All she recalled were disappointed and somewhat nerve-wracking trips to the outside ATM; keying in amounts such as $60, getting rejected for insufficient funds, lowering the amount to $40, getting rejected again, and finally on rare occasion being able to retrieve a fresh twenty-dollar bill from between the four little black rubber wheels inside the ATM's mouth.

Today, Amber didn't know what the balance would show, but Greg and Garry had told her to go and take a look at her most recent auto-deposit.

She'd watched the numbers climb from three digits to four, and then most recently to five digits over the last several weeks! First, she couldn't believe how much kept rolling in from the fairy commercial. It had aired like crazy and seemed to shoot out money with each airing like a little green geyser. Amber's second holding fee had been the first four-digit check she'd ever received in her life. Even writing out the few hundred bucks for her new agent, Helen, turned out to be a pleasure. Helen's 10% was more than her rent had been back in Detroit.

Amber thought of her old apartment there, the one Steely had basically gifted her before they'd married. At the time, she'd felt like a kept woman. Now that she had a five-digit bank balance herself, she realized what small change it must've been to Aaron; little more than a nice dinner out sans drinks or far less than one hotel party's worth stash of pot.

The teller's Drakkar Noir scent wafted straight through the little talking hole in the Plexiglas. Amber almost coughed from the shock of it, but within a moment or two, she actually liked it and noticed that the teller had smoky dark eyelashes and looked a little like Nick from old Chazzy's Saloon. She shook her head, recalling what an ass that guy had been, and how truly awful he was at sex. Like some kind of incredibly boring, methodical machine. For a second, she wondered what lucky new waitress he was screwing now, and muttered a quick *Thank God* in her head.

"Hey, sorry my printer is out of ink. Do you want me to handwrite your balance for you?" The teller pulled out a blank deposit slip and turned it over on the counter in front of him. He wore a silver ring on one finger with Celtic crosses all around it.

"Sure," Amber leaned toward the glass.

He pulled a green pen from his shirt pocket, clicked it, scribbled a few rings to test his ink, printed a dollar sign with two vertical lines, then wrote 85,068. He scooched the paper through the little trough under the glass.

"I'm sorry, what?" Amber stood, staring at the paper, frozen.

The teller had already pressed the button for his next customer, who was making his way to nudge Amber out of the spot where she was planted.

"I'm sorry," Amber said, noticing that her teeth were dry against her upper lip. "I'm sorry... Is this correct?" She shoved the yellow slip back underneath.

Customer number two lingered behind her—an extremely tall older woman whose perfume smelled like something between musk and mothballs. Too much frosted lipstick on a pursed, frustrated mouth. Amber stood her ground to double-check before leaving. The paper seemed blurry. *Did that say eighty-five thousand something?* She felt dizzy.

Amber put both hands on the narrow ledge, her side of the Plexiglas, waiting. The teller's eyelashes swooped downward as he double-checked the numbers. Suddenly, he pulled the pen out again.

"Oh, ma'am, I am so sorry," he said. Amber's heart sank a little, but did seem to resume a more natural rhythm.

He scribbled quickly and slid the paper back. Frosty Lips behind her huffed loudly.

Amber looked down, stunned. The teller had struck through the initial figure and rewritten it. The extra line wasn't part of the dollar sign at all. It was a one.

Holy shit. It said $185,068.

THE BUS TOOK FOREVER. Amber wasn't sure if she'd been pacing and muttering, "Oh my God, oh my God, oh my God," out loud or not. By the looks of the young teenage boy sitting on the aluminum bench staring at her, she may have been. She caught his eye and gave a shy smile. He looked unreassured and turned away.

Amber floated onto the bus steps and froze for a moment on the landing. The bus driver seemed to be saying something. Her hand did some stuff with change or something. Her legs found their way down the center of the bus and her fanny found its way into a seat. Her fingers found Holly's number on her cell phone and her voice managed to say something like, "Oh my God, oh my God, oh my God, are you gonna be home tonight?"

Holly's voice sounded either excited or confused. Amber decided she could figure that out later. Holly's voice said something. Amber cut her off, "Make Margaritas."

Holly muttered something about going to her boyfriend's tonight. Amber cut her off, "He can join us. I don't care. Call Carlos. Call the Gs. Make Margaritas. Lots of them."

Holly paused. Finally, she asked quietly, "Are you okay?"

Amber's body felt the stop of the bus. Her legs stood and carried her off at her stop. She could already see the two familiar palm trees that framed the entrance to their beautiful, wonderful apartment.

"Holly," she replied, "I am much, much more than okay."

Chapter 32

ARON

Cindra stepped out of Aaron's room, closing the door behind her. Aaron would try on the clothes she'd laid out, but she knew he'd be disappointed. Her boss had lost so much weight she could barely recognize him, yet his belly had bloated to a round balloon above the belt in his robe. She imagined he wouldn't be able to get his trousers up around it, let alone try to zip them up.

Inside the bedroom, Aaron discovered what his maid had been thinking. He'd already tried the trousers and now stood naked in front of a tall oval mirror, disgusted by what he saw. His silhouette looked like The Grinch Who Stole Christmas. He also noticed two salt-and-pepper areas of his hair around his temples looked a lot more like just plain salt than the last time he'd looked. His eyes had sunk in and showed deep dark brown shadows beneath them. His facial hair seemed to hang from gray tissue paper where there used to be flesh.

Aaron's legs had never been his manliest asset, but now he thought they looked decidedly similar to the legs of an ostrich. He would have buried his own head in the sand if he could. The room spun and within a few moments, Aaron's limp body fell to the floor with a thud.

Cindra quietly padded into the room, lifted the skin and bones onto a nearby white couch and covered him with his robe. She then put a blanket over him for extra modesty and shook the man awake. Barely audible, he asked for a glass of whiskey. His maid left the room and returned again a few moments later with a cup of tea. She set it down on the end table and tucked Aaron's blanket a little closer around his chin. He'd fallen fast asleep.

Chapter 33

B RIAN
Sharon laughed out loud at a few radio jokes on her way home from the diner. One DJ was trying out a list of lame pickup lines on the other one, who seemed to find a pun in each one. The two were laughing and seemed as if they'd been sharing a microphone for years. Sharon thought of Brian, sitting in her kitchen. She remembered how they used to finish each other's sentences and get into tickle fights. Both shy about their chubby bodies, they would grab each other's arms and fall into her pink and white gingham bedspread. Stuffed animals would fly around the room. Sharon's mom would yell from downstairs for them to pipe down, but Sharon could always hear a smile in Mom's voice as she yelled it. They'd hit each other with pillows and fall onto the floor. Brian's face would be red. Sharon would be sweaty. She'd feel his leg against the area between her legs and get turned on in her virginal teenage way. She'd nudge a little closer. Brian would notice then flush pink to red.

Sharon laughed out loud, shaking her head. How innocent she'd been, clueless that the guy was so blatantly, obviously gay. Even her mother must've known.

Pulling a hard left turn into the driveway, Sharon said a silent prayer that Brian would still be there waiting for her return. "Lord, please help him. Please let him be there and please let me help him," she whispered as she turned a key in the front door.

BRIAN RUMMAGED THROUGH Dino and Sharon's refrigerator. He couldn't find much there, as Sharon had been out of town and Dino got all he needed from the restaurant. The top shelf contained one half-empty tub of sour cream that had separated into a disgusting inch-deep layer of yellowish water atop a cracked whitish surface. Inside the door stood all the standard condiments, like soldiers in primary colors. The bottom shelf was lined with six different flavored coffee creamers. Two empty drawers sported a couple of dried-up stemmed leaves from what had likely been apples or pears at one time. The shallow center drawer contained a baggie of pinkish meat which Brian assumed was likely ham or smoked turkey, and one square of bright orange plastic-covered cheese food.

Brian decided the last bit would be his prize. He tried to find the plastic edge to unwrap the cheese, kicked the door closed with his foot and spun around to lean against the woodblock topped kitchen island. Spinning almost made him lose his balance, and when he steadied himself against the edge of the countertop, the cheese slice in his hand took the brunt of his weight. It dented evenly within the plastic. One corner stuck out where he'd already peeled it and Brian lifted the food to his mouth. Biting off the piece, he chewed. And chewed. It seemed to turn to sawdust in his mouth. Brian's forehead beaded sweat. His saliva tasted sour. The room spun again. Luckily, he was well wedged against the side of the island and didn't lose his footing this time.

The first bite still sloshing around in his dry mouth, Brian peeled a little more and bit off another bite. It crumbled against his teeth and tongue, joining the other bite like a couple pairs of socks in a dryer. Brian was getting sick of this game. His stomach made a gurgling sound followed by a loud whiny draining sound. He peeled the rest of the cheese and shoved it into his mouth.

Next thing Brian knew, he was lying on his side against the cold tile floor. His mouth tasted iron and his chin felt wet. Beginning to pass out, he noticed a puddle had formed near his face. It looked dark.

SHARON FOUND HER FRIEND on the floor, passed out beside a pool of bloody vomit. She called Dino, who was already in his truck on his way home. The couple helped the groggy patient into her vehicle and drove him to the hospital for the second time in one week.

GIA HOPED SHE WAS OVERREACTING. Maybe he really did come home while she was at work and she kept missing him? But her gut told her otherwise.

She rummaged through Brian's desk, finding very little to go on. This guy kept almost no paper around. Pushing a box of binder clips to the side, she lifted a forest green folder from its resting place on the bottom of an otherwise empty drawer. Across its front read "Canterly's Funeral Home" in gold embossed lettering.

Sitting on his black leather tall-backed desk chair, Gia leaned one elbow against the armrest. She placed the folder atop the closed laptop computer on Brian's desk. Opening it, she wasn't surprised to find it contained only a few pieces of paper.

One page described three price points for funeral services, from $13,500 down to $5500. One page showed several glossy photos of flower arrangements and their prices. On the opposite side, in the pocket was a typed letter. It read like a standard form letter, offering condolences and thanking Brian for his choice in "the grief-easing family professionals" of Canterly's Funeral Home. At the bottom of the page were a few blank lines filled in hastily with black pen. At "Name of Deceased" it read: Mr. & Mrs. S. Paige. Underneath that line, in smaller letters read the addition: & baby.

PHIL SHOVED ANOTHER bite of dry everything bagel into his mouth. It was a quiet morning and the sun seemed to have just peeked out after an all-night rain. The break room hissed gently from somewhere behind the fridge. Every few minutes Phil could hear a few new ice cubes fall into place within the freezer section. He hated quiet mornings. For some reason they made him think of his divorce; how loud and lively his ex-wife's house must be in the mornings, between his own two kids and her newly acquired stepson. His condo only sounded alive because Good Morning America was always on while he dressed for work. From down the hall, a little activity was coming nearer. *Thank God,* he thought, as Marcy and Wendy came chattering through the door.

"Phil!" Wendy cried out.

"You will not believe the scoop we just got from that fat IT guy," Marcy chirped.

"No, Marcy. He doesn't get any scoop from us! I'm talking about my bagel," Wendy pointed at the last few inches of carbs still in Phil's hand.

Marcy spun on her heel to face Phil. She shook her head, smirking. "Tsk, tsk, tsk, so you're the guilty one."

"Ha ha!" Wendy snatched the last bit from his hand.

"What?" Phil knew he was busted. "It's been in there like three or four days. I figured it was gonna go bad."

"Yoooou have been stealing my bagels every morning this week!" Wendy folded her arms across her royal blue silk blouse.

"And I bet you're the one who took my blueberry muffin," Marcy sat across from him, taking interrogation position.

Phil threw up both arms in a no-contest gesture. He leaned back in his red plastic chair. "What can I say, ladies? This is the way I roll."

Both women laughed and shook their fresh blowouts. Wendy's bangs brushed across her forehead while Marcy's bob bounced against her jawline. Their two versions of floral perfume mingled nicely together like a spring bouquet. Marcy stood up and pointed one long wine-colored fingernail toward her coworker. "You are bringing donuts tomorrow. That's your penance!"

Phil's face flushed pink from laughing. He nodded helplessly. "Guess I deserve that."

The three then sat down to exchange the latest gossip gleaned recently from Oliver, about how the other IT guy Brett or whatever was some kind of alcoholic or homicidal maniac or something and had to get put into rehab. Phil said he'd heard it was a spa clinic for anorexic people, but he'd only overheard someone telling someone else on the phone, so his source was probably less than reliable.

Conversation soon turned into whether or not their insurance covered rehabilitation services. Wendy offered information regarding the "Total Health Benefits" package, which covered psychological issues. Marcy recalled hearing about some guy who got hooked on painkillers after a hernia operation. He got to take almost a whole year off with worker's comp. Phil said that was him because he threw his groin out late one night when he was trying to steal the refrigerator. The ladies giggled again. More floral bouquets wafted into the air. Phil drummed his fingers on the table with glee.

Just then, Oliver came slothing into the break room carrying a waxy white paper sack full of pastries. For the first time ever, he received an invitation to sit with them. Grinning, Oliver passed out napkins and almond bear claws to his two new lady friends. Phil, who wasn't that hungry anymore, took a lemon-filled donut for himself. Oliver then proceeded to answer questions and clarify facts for the peanut gallery.

Eight minutes later, satisfied both in bellies and in curiosity, Phil, Marcy and Wendy stood. As if on cue, they pushed their chairs back into place and marched in procession back to their respective offices. Oliver nodded and waved goodbye to their backsides as his new best friends took leave. Then he ate two éclairs, crumpled the bag, tossed it toward the trash can and missed.

Chapter 34

A MBER
"I know but I thought you were kidding!" Amber punched Garry's arm, falling toward him a little due to the effects of tequila.

"One thing you should know about me, kiddo," Garry exchanged a look over Amber's head toward his boyfriend Greg, who winked back, "I do not joke about money."

"He does not joke about money," Greg chimed in on cue, slurring his speech, appropriate to the occasion and toasting the air.

Amber turned toward Garry, and leaning her back against Greg with alcohol-abandon, she giggled and soon found she could not stop. Holly found her way toward the laughter the way a cartoon toucan could follow the smell of colorful cereal, and joined in without hesitation. Moments later, the girls' small kitchen was full of bodies, doubled over and laughing. Hands rose up, holding glasses full of yellow-and-green frozen margaritas. Heads bobbed to lively music piping in from the living room side of the apartment. Holly's boyfriend found her waist and pulled her against him, rocking and laughing. His tanned wrist showed off a stunning silver watch against her flat stomach. Amber's tendrils of hair stuck to her sweaty face.

It was a good night.

MORNING SHONE THROUGH yellow curtains above the kitchen counter, where Holly had already begun to wipe clean every surface with lemon-scented soap. Toasted wheat slices popped up, were set onto a white porcelain plate, and covered with orange marmalade. A green-tinted margarita glass stood full of fresh iced tea. A white mug of coffee steamed next to it.

"Amber!" Holly called her roommate awake. Moments later, she came stumbling in, barefoot and wearing a matched set of a tank top and underwear in pink. Both pieces read, "Property of the Groom," in black across the front. She plunked down in front of the breakfast on one of two rattan stools. Holly leaned across from her, lifting her own coffee mug to take a sip.

"You look like hell."

Amber scoffed and bit into a corner of toast.

"You're nuts, you know that?"

Amber nodded, chewing.

"You're going to look terrible tonight, you know."

Amber swallowed. A tear sprang to her eye, but she managed to push it down. After finishing a few more bites, she spoke, "Do you think there is any way in hell I would have been able to sleep last night anyway?" She pushed the plate away. It still held one and a half slices of toast. Amber jumped up, screaming, "AAAhhhh! Girl, I am soooo nervous!!!"

Holly almost spat her coffee out, cracking up. Amber grabbed the sides of her hair and held them up like Pippi Longstockings as she twirled in a circle and jumped up and down. "Aaahh! I don't know what to do, I am so so so nervous!!!"

Holly came around the other side of her, calming Amber enough to get her seated again. She pulled the plate back in front of her and picked up the half-slice of toast. Holding it near Amber's mouth, she said, "Bite."

Amber bit.

"Now chew."

Amber chewed.

"Swallow."

The two girls got Amber fed between them. She drank her iced tea but couldn't do much with the coffee. Soon Holly got her into the shower, and into some jean shorts and white T-shirt. She told her friend to clip up her hair while she would get dressed herself. Returning to meet her roommate in the front room again, Holly looked her up and down to evaluate her work.

"Okay, darling. We're going to the spa."

Thankfully for Amber, the spa day did seem to calm her down. Later, as she started dressing in her bedroom, she looked in the mirror. She had to admit she hardly recognized the glowing, dewy-looking stunner that smiled back at her.

Her skin shone; her eyes sparkled. Even her hair seemed glossier. Her natural color had long since grown out and suited her again. Turning, she noticed her back was completely blemish-free and would look fantastic in the backless deep teal gown she and Holly had picked out together for the premiere.

Amber turned on her bedside clock radio and found a station with a lively song. Within ten seconds, she realized why she liked it so much. It was one of Steely's classics. Her eyes got wet almost immediately. She sat on the edge of her new light-green satin bedspread, feeling the white piping with the tips of her fingers. With her left thumb, she felt the soft underside of her ring finger where she should have been wearing a wedding band. A tear swelled just enough to fill her left eye and spill down her cheek. Of course, she remembered Holly's advice to *blot, not wipe*—the moment she wiped. Can't blot now that one eye looked like a raccoon. Reaching for a tissue, Amber changed the radio station quick before another tear came out. Too late.

Twenty minutes later, Amber emerged from the bathroom, face washed and shining again. Holly clucked at her when she came out of her own bedroom, already dressed, and found her roommate still standing around in her underwear.

Once again, like a fairy godmother spinning a magical cloud of stardust, Holly worked a whirlwind of beauty around her roommate. Stepping back from her creation, Holly took in a sudden breath. Her turn had come for watery eyes. Amber looked like a bona fide movie star. When Holly removed her hand from her gaping mouth, she spoke three classic words, "Damn, I'm good."

FROM AN AERIAL VIEW, human beings can look a lot like confetti. Various hair colors, clothing choices and random movements seem to climb and fall all over themselves, creating a swirling cloud of shapes and festivity. Tonight, adjacent to the beating throng of human activity, a red path to one side of the bodies traced a path alongside a huge concrete building, around a corner, up an enormous and ostentatious staircase and into the building's giant open doors. On the other side of this bold red line stood a white screen covered with blue-and-black lettering. Charity acronyms, production company names and icons of various public-relation fodder had been spaced perfectly on this backdrop with hopes to be viewed behind a close-up shot of a handsome tuxedo lapel or beside a glittering movie star's handbag.

Cameramen hoisted equipment on their hefty shoulders, spokesmodels stood in glaring spotlights with microphones, and grips shuffled about taping down anything that moved with sticky strips of gray, black, and blue. Some women at a table passed out gift bags. Police officers stood next to shiny motorcycles, holding helmets on the seats. Two huge beefcakes stood next to brass-topped stanchions where limousines dropped off leggy young women and their tall, handsome dates. A throng of around twenty plastic surgery addicts stood, wearing platform stilettos, hoping to be pulled in to pose for a shot with some older B-list actor or another by one of the many photographers. Two were being used at this very moment, in fact, flanking an elderly-looking thin Japanese man who sported a gray and white feathered fedora. The man's wife, wearing a white pants suit and carrying a black patent-leather clutch purse, looked on, offering notes and pose ideas to her husband. She appeared miniature next to a huge square lighting fixture with a bright yellow filter above her tiny head. Soon the old actor left the fake-breasted twenty-somethings without exchanging one word, took his wife's hand in the crook of his bony elbow and continued down the carpet.

Amber looked out her own limousine window and wondered what the event was all about. More than that, she hoped it wouldn't overshadow her own premiere night. Greg sat beside her, with one friendly hand on her knee. His palm sweated, so she pushed it aside before it could make a damp impression on the satin fabric of her gown. Garry, on her other side, smiled and told her for the tenth time how beautiful she looked. His eyes lingered on her cleavage, just below a diamond and pearl necklace she wore on a silver chain.

The necklace belonged to Holly. Earlier, she'd said, "Here. Something borrowed." Amber had joked that the event wasn't a wedding, catching her breath as she'd realized suddenly Aaron would be meeting her tonight. She'd touched the necklace with one hand and thanked her friend sincerely. They'd hugged, Holly left with her beau, and Amber had waited only a few more minutes after her departure before Garry came to walk her toward their waiting limo.

"Hey, I thought you weren't into boobs—" Amber kidded her director-slash-date. He laughed. "I'm bi, you idiot. That means I'm into everything."

Amber appreciated the joking. It seemed to distract her nerves. She couldn't decide if she was more nervous about the photo-ops, seeing herself on a large screen or meeting up with her estranged husband. She decided that she would rather not decide, or she may actually have a heart attack and miss the whole thing anyway. Looking out the window at the colorful mob of people, she took a deep breath. Suddenly, the car stopped and her door opened.

There she sat, looking a giant bouncer in the eye. She froze. He offered a huge pudgy hand toward her. Amber felt a sudden panic. She didn't want to miss the beginning of her film! Most of all, she didn't want to be late for Aaron.

"What's going on? Why are we stopping here?" she asked the strange man.

Garry leaned to her ear and shook his head. "Amber, this is the premiere."

Amber turned again toward the enormous man, noticing he had one of those clear coiled cords coming up from his collar and tucked behind an ear. The crowd noise was deafening. She could barely make out what Garry had said, but he seemed to have mouthed something about the premiere.

Now the security man seemed to say something. He shook his hand toward her a little, and said it again, "Mrs. Spinnaker."

Amber's stomach flipped over. She felt dizzy. *How did he know that?* Her hand took hold of the giant's, and the next thing she knew, she seemed to be standing up, facing Garry as he climbed out of the car after her. Greg, Amber and Garry trickled out from the vehicle like a string of pearls.

Crowd noise increased. She knew she was smiling. It felt as if the noise carried her like a buoyant sound wave that actually had mass. She felt as if she was floating on this wave, and it seemed to know where to take her next. The wave flowed from photographer to photographer. It carried her arm to her hip and her shoes to the tape marks on the carpet. The sound caused the thick shiny curls of her hair to flow behind her, and her purse to lift her hand into a pretty shape that gently showed off her delicate fingers. The wave smiled. It cheered; it seemed to actually emit love.

Amber spoke witty words to spokesmodels with microphones. She exchanged air-kisses with cast-members she hadn't seen in a few weeks. Everyone smiled from ear to ear and smelled wonderful. Her love interest from the film looked more handsome and boyish in smile than she'd remembered. His wife touched her arm warmly as if they'd been sorority sisters. Someone asked someone else about her and they gushed with compliments. Someone said the words, "Oscar nod." Amber beamed.

She could see Holly coming down the carpet several yards behind her. A plastic-surgery groupie flirted with her fiancé. He looked gorgeous with floppy sun-drenched hair and wearing a gray linen suit. Holly looked like a Barbie doll. Malibu Barbie, to be specific. Amber suddenly noticed how many people seemed to know the two of them, and in sudden revelation she observed that Holly's fiancé, from an outsider looking in, was clearly some kind of mogul people knew about.

Garry got bombarded with attention, but kept one hand on Amber's arm most of the time. He kept gesturing toward her as if she were a prize on The Price Is Right. He waved toward a cluster of preteen girls who were holding up rag papers with a photo of Amber on the cover. It was a full close up shot of her grinning face in full bridal gear from Clerkenwell. *How did they get those?* Every detail seemed to flutter and whiz by, on fast forward and slow motion at the same time.

Greg cradled her into his side like a protective big brother. Garry pulled their little chain this way and that, and when he got close, his face smelled faintly of expensive tobacco. She breathed it all in until she could hardly breathe anymore. Luckily, by that time, they were passing through the threshold of the building. Inside, the foyer ceiling seemed higher than the outside sky had been, and with more twinkling stars.

Escorts led Amber and Garry on high-speed down a tight side hall, beside huge arteries of electrical cords taped to the floor and bulging from walls in various colors. They popped into the theater from a low position near the front and beelined to some empty seats, front and center. The two suddenly fabulous VIPs gave little waves towards Greg and Holly who got smaller and smaller until they disappeared into another stream of bodies. Amber could faintly see the reflection of Greg's round glasses as he circled his way back around to the other entrance. Holly had faded from sight.

Seemingly miles away, Greg was making progress en route to sit adjacent to them via the other side. A chaos of bodies ebbed and flowed; each shifted the balance, like an entire school of fish, every time an individual tried to make an autonomous move.

Their row plus five rows behind them were roped off with velvet purple. Behind that were tables straddling the next couple of rows. On these tables stood light and soundboards with jet black cords weaving all over themselves in coils and piles. Behind the tables sat men and a few women wearing all black clothes, hats and headsets with yet more cords dangling from their necks.

Behind them, a row or two appeared empty but for a few people in suits with clipboards and bright yellow lanyards with laminated badges. Further still behind them and in a mezzanine above, dark round heads appeared in lines that went back into pitch-black shadows. Above the mezzanine, Amber couldn't tell for certain, but there seemed to be yet another balcony filled with people. Either that or it was decorated to look like another balcony. The theater ceiling loomed so high above her head that Amber could hardly believe all this could fit inside the building at all.

She felt vertigo looking up when suddenly Greg and his circular glasses popped up beside her again. He was pulling her arm by this time to sit down anyway, while Garry puffed up his director status to rebuff an apologetic security usher for almost refusing his boyfriend a seat next to them.

The evening began with a few words from a man in a tux who seemed very important. Then a comedian stepped forward to make a few jokes and introduce Garry, who stood up, waved, then upon further beckoning from the comedian along with audience encouragement, he went to the podium and said a few words. The Director thanked the cast, and particularly Amber for her hard work. When he said that part, he looked right at Amber and winked. After pausing for applause, he launched into a few more boring details, mentioning his own agent and some public relations people at his production company who had gone above the call of duty bringing this evening together, blah, blah, blah and without further ado, he hoped they would all enjoy the film.

Soon the emcee cracked a couple more witticisms, lights dimmed, and Amber transcended into her dream world for two hours. By the end, when the credits rolled with her name at the top, she realized the audience had become a frenzied mob of standing excitement. Greg hadn't looked away from the screen, but she saw wet streams coming down his face from behind his glasses. She touched her own cheek and realized that she also had been crying. The young woman on screen had walked away from a gravestone, head held high and jaw set toward an unsure yet decidedly noble new future, and everyone in the building had been moved by that silent final scene. Orchestra music swelled. The comedian had nothing funny to say. Instead, he gestured toward where Amber sat, surrounded by a standing ovation.

Once again, a bubble of energy and sound, accompanied by a helpful hand from Garry carried Amber to her feet, past the standing bodies of fellow primary cast members who shared her row, and out into the aisle. Amber's arm waved toward her much older and more famous co-star to join her on the small lifted stage with the comedian's podium. The two held hands and bowed slightly while the audience swelled once again into fresh applause. Amber knew her face kept smiling on its own. William patted her back a few times and winked at her presentationally. Soon she found eye contact with Holly who was crying and jumping up and down in the aisle amongst other crying and smiling faces. She then found Carlos, who struck a pose and shot two pointed index fingers in her direction.

A quick scan of the rest of the audience came up short. Aaron was nowhere to be found. Nor could she find Uncle Brian.

When her partner held her arm up and squeezed her hand one more time, Amber felt a fresh wave of her own tears fall, which were not ones of joy. On display beside this gracious fellow actor, supported by this delightful comedic emcee, surrounded by these unexpected adoring colleagues, friends and sudden fans, Amber had never felt this deeply, piercingly alone.

Chapter 35

HOLLYWOOD

Paparazzi almost kept the SUV from entering the hospital parking lot. Cindra put on her sunglasses and stepped out of her boss's vehicle, handing a valet the keys. He exchanged them for a blue ticket and accompanied the tall blonde woman toward the front door. Paparazzi, seeing she was nobody famous, turned away and convened again on the lawn nearest the street. Cindra thought they looked like grazing sheep as they milled around the lawn.

Inside, she gave her name to a large woman behind a dark wood reception desk and took a seat near a pillar. She reached for a six-month-old copy of Martha Stewart magazine and leafed through it until the receptionist called her name. Following a short young man in blue scrubs, Cindra arrived at the private hospital room door, whispered a polite thank you, and sat quietly beside her boss, who slept. She noted to herself that using an apple corer to cut out the center of a radish was a new idea she would like to try next time she picked some up at the farmers' market. Looking around, she almost tore out the recipe from the hospital's magazine but decided against it. She folded the corner of the page over and set the magazine next to an untouched tray of food on a hi-lo table beside Aaron's bed. She would have to copy the recipe down later.

Aaron stirred only once when a nurse came to trade out one of his saline bags. He winced as the IV inline tugged against his skin. It looked like bright pink tissue paper where the tape pulled against it. Cindra patted the area and rubbed it gently until his expression softened and he drifted off again to sleep.

The door opened.

In walked a young starlet with shiny brown hair and thick black sunglasses. She wore a navy-blue visor pulled down over the glasses and a long ponytail hanging down the back of her head. Amber glanced in Cindra's direction, dragged an empty chair across the floor to a stop beside Aaron's knees, threw herself into it and slumped face down into the blankets, bawling.

Cindra stood up silently and backed away from the scene, pulling a striped curtain closed in front of her. She exited the room, took the elevator down to the parking garage, handed a man her blue valet ticket, and left.

Amber did not stop crying for thirty minutes.

Chapter 36

BRIAN—DETROIT

Gia hated the yellow and orange waiting room in this place. You couldn't smoke. All the magazines were old and weird, like "Guideposts" and "Angels Among Us." People in here looked homely and depressed. The Muzak was worse than silence. Even the water from those little paper cones tasted stale and yucky.

She squirmed in her bright orange vinyl chair, wishing she'd worn jeans instead of a skirt. The skin on the back of her knees sweated where it touched the seat. Her shins felt itchy inside her tall boots. This place smelled like elementary school.

Brian came out from behind a heavy beige door. He smiled weakly. His eyes looked kind of sunken, but Gia thought he looked a lot better than last week. She jumped up and hugged him, probably a little too hard.

"How's my bestie?" Gia fawned over him, giving Brian her chair and pulling up a low table to sit across from him. An old lady behind a desk cleared her throat and pulled down her bifocals to glare at Gia over the top of the frames. Gia sighed and stood up from the table. She plunked loudly onto a sofa kitty-corner to Brian's chair. It seemed to be upholstered with straw. Gia shifted in her seat and gave the woman a quiet raspberry the moment the old lady looked away. Brian chuckled.

They stared at the floor for a few moments. Brian glanced out the window. Gia sighed and traced the pattern of brown and yellow mushrooms on the arm of the sofa. Man, this was some hideous fabric. She pressed her palms against her knees. Brian tapped his fingers against the thighs of his khakis.

They spoke at the same time: "So, how are you?" Gia said, just as Brian said, "Thanks for coming again." Gia leaned over and put her hand on Brian's armrest. He put his on hers. His eyes filled and he sniffed. Gia patted the seat next to hers on the sofa. Brian pulled his hand away and leaned forward, resting his elbows on his knees. He stared at the floor. She did the same. Several minutes seemed to pass.

Finally, Gia took a deep breath and said, "I remember once when I was living above this guy's garage. He was way older than me and he said I could stay there as long as I wanted to. Actually, it was more like I could stay there as long as I wanted to keep giving him head whenever he wanted, but I was only like fifteen or something, and I didn't want to go back to my dad's 'cause he was a creep and I didn't mind giving this guy what he wanted since he didn't even try to have sex with me or anything and he never really *forced* anything on me or whatever so I stayed for a while and there was this hole in the wall by the floor up there. So, I used to lie down by the hole and smoke out of it because the guy was a real anti-smoking freak—kinda like you," she laughed before continuing, "so there was this dog that lived in the house next to his. A real scrappy thing, maybe part like a little border collie or something because he would just run in crazy circles all night long. I mean this thing like never got tired. So, I would just lay there and smoke and stare and I'd think I was like that dog, ya know, just running in circles and not really going anywhere, but as long as I kept moving, I wouldn't have to really ever know it. You know, like, I wouldn't have to think about how I wasn't really going anywhere, I could like trick myself if I just kept running, you know?"

Brian waited while she paused and stared at him for some kind of acknowledgment. "No, I guess I don't really know what you mean."

Gia sighed and leaned back in her scratchy sofa.

Brian cocked his head. "Well, I mean, I guess I get it about not wanting to really think about things. I mean, I hate talking about stuff here in group. It's like everyone has all these problems—"

"Exactly!" Gia interrupted. "That's what I'm saying. I'd be like, I know my Dad's got problems, you know. Like he's the one with problems and this older guy letting a kid stay in his garage for blowjobs. You know, I mean I was just a kid but I knew *he* had issues, *I* didn't, ya know? I mean I was just trying to make my way, ya know?"

"But then you find out one day that you have issues," Brian's head slumped toward his chest, defeated. Gia thought for a couple moments. It would've been nice to light up a cigarette.

"Yeah, but honey," she leaned in and touched his knee, "Honey, you've maybe been through some shit that wasn't your fault, you know? I mean, I didn't ask for any of the shit that my fucked-up life brought me, for my Dad to be some creepo perv or for the school to kick me out for showing my tits to the janitor or whatever—" She checked for his reaction; Brian didn't flinch. "I was like that dog for so long, you know? But now," Gia stopped and breathed heavily for a minute. Her forehead scrunched up as she started to cry. A little boy stopped playing with some wooden beads on a wire to look at her for a second. The old lady at the desk looked up, then back down again quickly.

"I just wanted to tell you that I don't really feel like that anymore, you know, since I met you and stuff. It's like I'm not scared anymore."

Brian looked up, suddenly. He couldn't imagine Gia fearing anything. Suddenly, she looked so small. Brian realized she must've been even smaller when she was fifteen. He'd been big and weighed a lot at that age; he could've probably protected her. Now here he sat, skinny and still lots taller than his little Italian friend.

She was now full-on crying and talking through tears, "You're my best friend I ever had. And when Sharon and Dino came by and said something had happened to you, I just didn't know what I was gonna do. I didn't even think about where I would go or anything. I just wanted you to be okay. I just—"

Realizing other people had begun to shift uncomfortably, Gia quieted herself. She put her face in her hands and sobbed. Brian joined her on the couch and put his arm around her neck. Suddenly, he felt strong and tall.

"Gia. I'm going to promise you something. I'm going to get better and I promise you, I am going to get out of here. Soon."

Gia melted into his chest. Brian felt her warm tears soak through his shirt. He made eye contact with the receptionist, who had lost all sense of etiquette and didn't even try to hide the fact that she was staring. Brian patted his friend's hair with his left hand and gave the lady a little wave with his right. He nodded a little as if to say, "It's okay. I got this."

FOURTEEN DAYS LATER, Gia picked him up from the front entrance. Brian wheeled his suitcase out, lifted it without even so much as a grunt, and tossed it into the trunk. He then took the keys from his best friend and roommate, took his place behind the steering wheel and drove them both home.

Chapter 37

AMBER
Amber held Aaron's hand, feeling his wedding band tap against her own. She squeezed it a little before removing his ring and placing it on her own right thumb. Jewelry wasn't permitted in the OR.

Steely—Aaron Spinnaker on the chart clipped to the foot of his bed—was getting silly. His anesthesia hadn't yet kicked in to put him to sleep, but whatever they'd just pushed into his IV line was already showing him a good time. "Finally, some fecking deeerugs!" he joked. "Now just show me your titties and this will officially be my best day this year." Amber put his hand on her chest over her shirt. He squeezed weakly before his hand dropped limp on the bed sheet beside his hip. At least he smiled a little.

Cindra looked on, chuckling a little before looking out the window as if to give them some privacy. She knew she should probably leave the couple alone but somehow couldn't bring herself to step away. Who knew what results they would be hearing a few hours away? Who knew if she would see her kind, slightly idiotic, boss again after this morning? Besides, his young wife didn't seem to mind. Cindra convinced herself that she was being helpful as she'd insisted on holding Aaron's plastic bag of personal items. She waited to see if Amber would hand her the wedding band to place into the bag, along with his wallet, cell phone and handkerchief. She didn't.

"Aw, come on," Steely was whining, "Lemme see the old headlights before I go off to meet my maker."

Amber didn't like that comment. She pointed right in his face. "That is not even funny. Nobody is meeting anybody's maker. And that's all you get. A boob pat now and a full show when you come back out to me. It'll give you something to look forward to."

"Oh, so that's my reason to live now? Titties? Maybe I should be getting breast implants instead of a new liver?"

"Very funny."

"Aw, come on. One peek. It's not even for me. Cindra wants to see 'em. Right, Cindra?"

The maid closed her eyes and shook her head without turning it away from the window. Amber apologized for him. "The minute he goes to sleep, I'm giving you a bonus check."

Cindra laughed, shaking her head again.

"All this is quite nice, but I think I should at least get to see a boob before I die." Aaron's confidence and volume were rising by the moment. He started singing, "Doctor, doctor, gimme a show, of a very fine titty, before I go—"

Amber slapped his face lightly, and then grabbed his scruffy chin affectionately. "Hey, people have paid big bucks to see your wife's boobs!"

"Yeah, so they tell me," Aaron raised one eyebrow. "Rated R. For Roundness."

Amber shook her head, laughing, and lifted her shirt in a split-second flash. She bent down to kiss him on the mouth. "Sorry, I just had coffee," she said, smiling.

"Oh, that's nice, you little brat," Aaron smiled back.

Amber gestured toward Cindra to grab her purse from the windowsill. Looking down a moment, she rifled through it for a mint.

"You're my...ba...by..." Aaron was saying quietly.

Amber shoved an Altoid in her mouth and looked up at her husband. In an instant, he had fallen fast asleep. His mouth hung open. She gently pushed his chin up to close it, bent down and planted a minty kiss on his lips.

A quiet nurse peeked in. Seeing her patient asleep, she quickly stepped around Amber and wheeled Aaron's bed a few inches away from the wall. Two other nurses efficiently unplugged cords, unhooked bags, flipped switches and within moments the room was empty except for Cindra, where she leaned against a wall and Amber, standing in the center of the room clutching her purse with two hands.

———— ◦◯◦ ————

IT HAD BEEN A WHILE since this waiting room had seen so much activity. A forty-year-old woman in a teal scrub shirt and mom-jeans peeled clear tape off yet another box of individually wrapped Danish. She unloaded them into neat rows on the table in front of her. She noted to next replenish the trail mix, Nutter Butters and to refill her basket of mini water bottles. She gave the slotted donation box a happy little shake. Her daughter's basketball team fund would make money this week.

Outside, paparazzi buzzed like a swarm of bees. Reporters stood in the blazing heat, speaking into microphones. They turned their heads, calling out right and left as celebrities and semi-famous visitors whisked in and out through automatic doors. Long cars with tinted windows dropped off and picked up groups of twos and threes. Fabulous individuals wore their own miniature tinted eye-windows in the form of sunglasses. Some attempts to hide their identities from camera lenses worked, as certain people bolted in and out of the automatic door. Some didn't make it so easily and got stuck encircled by flashes while people yelled in their faces. Eventually, everyone who needed to get in, did.

Beefed up security checks at the door held steady and created a somewhat normal atmosphere once folks made it inside the glass-enclosed waiting area. Amber's recent friends joined Aaron's lifetime's worth of friends and other sycophants, associates and their well-behaved groupie guests and straggling entourage members.

In one corner, Amber sat between Carlos and Holly, who spoke no words but waited. A.J. stood near the OR door, glancing in every few minutes and jumping with nervous energy every time the door opened. Greg and Garry made small square laps around the area and chatted quietly, as though on a particularly sober early morning mall walk. Cindra kept folding and unfolding a cardigan on her lap.

Finally, a doctor came out and found a spot to stand in front of Amber's chair. Carlos politely rose and gestured for the doctor to sit down. He declined. Voices in the room quieted to a low hum. Amber listened to a few words, and nodded a couple of times. Once she put her hand to her mouth and gasped, but then nodded again and put her hand down again at her side. Holly held a tissue out toward her friend, but Amber was too engrossed with the doctor. Eventually, he left the waiting room and returned from whence he came, through wide OR doors. A.J. followed with his eyes until the doctor's image was no longer visible through the little wired window in the door. He paced a few times. When he could no longer stand his curiosity, he stepped over to where Amber sat again in her corner.

Chapter 38

MICHIGAN
"I don't care what you have to say about it, we're going!" Sharon unzipped her suitcase where it lay on their freshly made bedspread.

Dino rinsed shampoo out of his hair and yelled from the bathroom, "You're being unreasonable. Who would even watch the restaurant? I can't count on Danny right now. His wife is pregnant."

"What?" Sharon couldn't hear him from where she stood in their walk-in closet. She ran her hand along the tops of her blouses, settling on a white button-up that rarely showed wrinkles.

"Danny's wife is pregnant!" Dino yelled again.

Sharon tossed the blouse across the edge of her suitcase as she walked by on her way into the bathroom. She opened the door all the way and waved it to let some steam clear. Entering the steam, she sat down on the closed toilet lid. Dino shut off the water and reached out with a muscular forearm toward the towel rack. Sharon handed him a fluffy white towel. "Okay, so, what?"

"I said Wendy's pregnant. Danny just told me last night."

Sharon squealed. "Oh my god, that's so great! Good for them." She watched her wet husband step out of the shower onto a fresh white bath mat. His leg hair clung in wet streams over his muscular tan skin. Turning toward the mirror, Sharon fixed her own hair as she watched Dino's reflection.

"So, my point is we can't go to California because he won't be able to watch the diner."

"Why not? How far along is she?"

Dino scrubbed the towel on his thick hair. When he stopped it was all curly and going in every direction. Sharon couldn't help but notice he was adorable.

"Only a couple of weeks, but it's not that. She miscarried last year."

"Oh, how sad," Sharon stopped fixing her hair. "How old is she?" Her own head kept repeating her own age.

"I think late twenties. Danny's like thirty or so. She just got a job this year to get her mind off the whole thing and sure enough, now she's pregnant again already."

Sharon stood up and toweled off her husband's back. She reached around to his hip with her hand and squeezed the toned muscles there. Swinging around, Dino took his wife in his arms.

"Well, I did want to be there for Brian. He hasn't seen his niece in ages, you know. Plus, you know my cousin is just outside of L.A."

"I know honey," Dino kissed her nose, "But we can see your cousin's kids at Christmastime, and I really think Brian's doing great now. He does have Gia going."

"Yes, that's true. It's just so sad about his niece. I never really told you about their story, did I?"

Dino kissed his wife's right cheek. "Yes, actually you did. It is sad. But—" He kissed her left cheek.

"But it's not our life, right?" Sharon had heard this one before. Dino was right; she was rescuing again.

"Good girl." He wrapped his arms around her, picked her up and took his wife into the bedroom. Pushing the suitcase loudly off the bed, he laid her down in its place. Barney barked twice because the noise woke him up, but then seeing that nothing seemed out of the ordinary, the dog left the room.

"Dino?" Sharon asked as her husband unbuttoned the last few inches of her blouse. "When are we going to get pregnant, anyway?"

Dino looked into her eyes. "Well, if I don't give Danny a raise, we could probably afford it right now, actually."

Sharon reached up for both his shoulders in her hands. She wiggled underneath him and smiled. "Didn't you just give Danny a raise a few months ago?"

Dino's face melted into a slow smile. "Now that you mention it, yes, I did."

Sharon lifted her head and gave her husband a long, slow kiss. She reached around his hips with her legs and wrapped both arms around his neck.

"I think it's time, baby," Sharon whispered. Her husband, though, seemed to already have a head start.

GIA STOCKED THE LATEST rag mags in a rack below the front counter of the liquor store. At four-thirty in the morning, there was little else to do. Her only company at this hour was a faint whirring sound from a hot dog spinner, which sported one crinkly brown Italian sausage. A bright light reflection shined a straight line across the meat link as it spun.

a straight line across the meat link as it spun. Gia separated the magazines into stacks according to their titles. Two cheap ones featured stories about Brian's nephew-in-law. Was that what you'd call Steel Fingers Wildboy, she wondered? She thought it kind of funny since Aaron Spinnaker must've been at least a ton older than her best friend. Still in a squatted position, Gia flipped to the story page, which filled the centerfold. In bold capital letters across a two-page spread read the words, "Rock n' Roll's Newest Liver With a Side of Onions."

"Gross," Gia said to the page. Down its right margin displayed blurry photos of the front of a hospital, the back of someone's brunette hair (*presumably Amber's, or at least someone we're supposed to think is Amber,* Gia thought to herself) and a couple photos of blurry people in waiting room chairs mostly blocked by potted plants. An old photo of Steely on stage filled the upper left quarter of the story spread. He looked like a whitish blur against a backdrop of pyrotechnics and dancing girls in animal print hot pants. Gia chuckled and wondered if the photo might have been taken around the time she was a toddler. She read a few sentences full of cheesy puns and vague projections and closed the magazine. On purpose she put it on the rack backward, feeling suddenly protective toward her roommate's relatives whom she was planning to visit over the next few days.

Gia could hardly wait till after this shift. Her already packed suitcase awaited first use! A real suitcase! Hollywood! She checked her watch. Four thirty-two.

Standing up, Gia's knees cracked like loud knuckles. "Ugh," she grunted. She pulled a pair of sunglasses off a circular rack as she looped around the counter. Just as she put them on and checked her own reflection against the still-dark window, a guy wearing an orange camouflage baseball cap opened the front door. She had the glasses off by the time the door's little bell stopped clanging. He stepped across from her and asked how long that sausage had been sitting there. Gia replied, "Oh, just about forever."

He snorted and headed toward the refrigerator section. After scanning the inventory up and down, rubbing his round beer gut, the man returned with a pack of Snackables and a greenish banana. Gia rang him up and asked if he wanted the sausage on the house since she was gonna throw it away anyways. He glanced toward the heated container. "Nah," he replied, grabbing his stuff off the counter. Gia nudged closed the cash drawer with her hip as she said goodbye to the guy, then glanced at her watch. Four-thirty-seven, it read.

She put the sunglasses back on and grabbed the sausage off its spinner with her thumb and forefinger. Turning her back to a corner-mounted surveillance camera, which she doubted was even on anyway, Gia took a bite. She said "yuck," finished it, then wiped greasy fingers off on her jeans. Her watch read four thirty-nine. Looking at her reflection in the window, Gia told it, "This is gonna be one long-ass shift."

Chapter 39

HOLLYWOOD
"Hooooooray for Hollywood! Da da da da da da da, Hollywood, dah da da da da da da dum de dum dum, da dee da dum da da dum! Hooray for Ho-o-lly-wood!" Gia was being loud. Brian wanted to die. She held a sparkly water-filled globe up over her head and chased Brian around the gift shop. He would not run, however, so she had to keep backing away and running toward him to keep the game rolling. "There's no business like show business, la da la da da daa!"

"Oh, my God. I am going to have to kill you," Brian rolled his eyes until they hurt in their sockets. "I am actually going to have to drag you behind this building and kill you."

Gia held a huge pink T-shirt with Marilyn Monroe's face on it against her chest. At least it hid the edge of her tattoo sticking out from behind her overalls, Brian thought. At the bottom, the T-shirt looked so oversized that it completely covered her short shorts. All you could see were two skinny tan knees between the hem of pink and the tops of Gia's giant platform boots. She struck a pose and pretended to push down the bottom of the shirt between her legs. "Happy Birthday, Mister President," she was singing, badly. Brian couldn't help but laugh.

"If you're not careful, I'm going to buy you that hideous thing and make you wear it for the rest of the trip," Brian threatened.

"Really?!" Gia jumped up, gathering the shirt between her hands into a lump. "Oh my God, I will love you forever!" She flicked him with the fabric and headed straight for the checkout counter. Once the pink pile had been tossed atop the counter, she immediately rummaged through a container of water-filled pens, flipping them over to watch a tiny lady's bikini slide off and back on.

Brian dragged ass over to join her, pulling out his wallet. "How much is it?" he practically whined to the black-haired girl behind the counter.

"5.95," she smacked her gum. "But if you buy three, they're three for ten bucks."

This information caused Gia to squeal and run around the store again. Brian slapped a twenty on the counter. "Obviously," he said, "We'll be taking three."

AT AARON'S POOL LATER, Gia behaved no better. She insisted on wearing one of her new T-shirts into the pool. This one was cheap, white, paper-thin and when it got wet, Brian could see Gia's tattoo clearly through the fabric. The ink eagle stretched its wings above the words "LA Choppers" across the chest of the shirt, but rode a few inches below her breast line due to its XXL size and sopping current state.

Brian turned his head toward Holly in the chair next to him and said, "Well, at least she won't get a full sunburn."

"Eagles don't get sunburned," Holly chuckled, sipping iced tea from a bright green bendy straw.

Cindra refilled Brian's water glass. He thanked her and turned to watch Gia belly-flop into the pool. It splashed water all over his skinny white shins. Brian spread his legs apart and sat up, straddling his lounge chair. "What are you, five?" He asked.

Holly's fiancé was laughing and trying to pick Gia up to toss her into the deep end. Gia fought, laughing so loud it almost sounded as if she was getting hurt. Brian didn't like that but focused instead on the jazz music coming from an outdoor speaker behind a boxwood near his chair. The sun felt clean and warm. This really was quite nice.

Holly's cell phone chimed. "That's Amber," she said, recognizing the ring tone. After a short exchange, she pressed the off button and told the other three they were on their own for dinner. Amber would spend the night at the hospital again.

"Geez, I've barely even seen her," Brian complained.

Gia's body cast a shadow across his pale blue polo shirt. She was toweling off her face as she said, "I think we should all meet her there."

Holly jumped up. "That's a great idea."

Cindra spoke, a rare thing. "I could pack your dinner to bring there." She said. "I'll come too if zat's all right."

This didn't surprise Holly in the least. She walked over toward the patio door, placing a hand on Cindra's arm as she passed. "Yes, of course," she said, entering into the doorway's shadow.

Gia skipped behind them, wrapping her towel around her waist. Holly's beau was stepping into a pair of flip-flops close behind. His calves and bare ankles seemed to say, "I ski, play tennis and boat." Brian gathered up his and Holly's glasses and left the pool area last.

Inside, Cindra already had an open picnic basket set out on the kitchen counter. Holly stood behind an open refrigerator door. Wet footprints across the wood indicated that Gia had started toward her guest room. Brian grabbed a kitchen towel off the counter near the sink and bent down to wipe the water spots off the floor.

"I'll get zat," Cindra said, observing that Brian had already pretty much finished the job.

"You're nice," Holly said, taking the towel from his hand and folding it over the top of a lower cabinet door.

Brian smiled. "Almost as nice as you," he answered.

Holly's man called in through the open door from the deck, where he had paused just short of the doorway to answer a business call. "Hey, quit flirting with my woman!"

Brian flushed. That guy was so hot. "Sorry!" He yelled back.

Holly put her hand on Brian's shoulder. "So possessive," she whispered.

"I heard that!" called the sexy boyfriend from the door.

They all laughed and finished helping Cindra pack what was to be a simple yet ample al fresco dinner.

WATCHING AARON'S FINGERS labor to write was agonizing. Amber pretended not to notice the little grunting noises he made, nor the gurgly rattle of his nasal breathing. Poor guy had a tube that went up his nose and down the back of his throat to drain his stomach of bile and blood into a plastic container behind his head. Amber placed herself on the other side of the bed purposely, since the sight of it kind of grossed her out. With effort, she was trying to get used to it.

Aaron's stringy hair looked matted and oily now, but Amber didn't mind that much. She only felt glad he was recovering more quickly than doctors predicted. Only this morning, one specialist reported that his PT count seemed to be bouncing back, which meant liver function was already improving. Apparently, this meant his blood was beginning to clot normally, which helped quicken the healing process. Regardless, he would be laid up for some time and his general health would remain in question as doctors trained watchful observation on his recovery.

So far, Aaron had written two sentences. "Sorry I'm a shoddy mess. This is an important question."

Amber didn't move her hand from where it sat on his left shoulder. She looked into his yellowish eyes and mustered up a brave face. "Anything, babe. Whatever you want."

Aaron attempted to raise an index finger to indicate, "Wait a moment." When he did so, his weak hand lost grip on the blue pen and dropped it onto the bed. A split-second later his inclined blankets sent it rolling to the floor. Amber bent down to pick it up, started to hand it to Aaron but quickly thought otherwise. Aaron watched her movements, looking frustrated.

"Let me wash it off, babe."

He closed his eyes hard, in obvious irritation.

"You're not getting a dang infection from the grody floor in here, I'll tell you that," Amber called out loudly over the sound of the sink. She squirted some strong-smelling orange gel soap from a wall-mounted dispenser and scrubbed the sides of the pen with her hands. Reaching for a paper towel, she noticed how raw the skin on her hands was getting and made a mental note to pick up some lotion from the gift shop during Aaron's next nap.

Returning to his bedside, she pushed the notebook back into place, propped between a clump of blanket and his bed's side rail so Steely could see what he was writing. She patted the hair on top of his head, stroking it back. Poor darling, she thought, noticing how the littlest things were beginning to frustrate the hell out of him. It must be something like PMS—all sore, bloated, and cooped up in this shitty fluorescent lighting.

Aaron went to work again on his question. Instead, he wrote another statement: "I hope you answer Yes."

Amber thought for a moment, trying to imagine what he might ask her. She could tell from his straight eyebrows he wasn't setting up any jokes. Unless he was being deadpan? She searched his face again. No, definitely not.

Amber watched as her husband struggled to grip his pen and move it steadily across the paper into letter shapes. He stopped for a moment to hold up an index finger again, this time without dropping anything.

"I'll be patient, honey. Take your time." Amber patted his head some more. He shook it, tossing her hand off as best he could. The activity made him clench his gut muscles and flinch. Amber looked at the area on his abdomen where the white blanket got smooth because it covered a large padded bandage spot. *That much plastic taped to your skin must feel awful,* she thought. The flat area was so large, it looked as though some nurse had nudged his last lunch tray under there.

Lunch, she noted, consisted of a bowl of broth Aaron rarely touched and usually a tiny kindergarten-sized carton of grape or apple juice. *Funny how sick grown-ups become so much like kids. They seem not only helpless but innocent again.* Steely looked about four years old, fumbling with his pen like it was a chubby crayon.

Amber could tell Aaron was trying not to twist his body as he wrote. He had to make out the page peripherally, which took even longer, yet his perseverance impressed her. Steely had shaped up to be quite a trooper, above and beyond even rockstar expectations. She meant emotionally. Man, the dude could bounce back! She found this characteristic particularly sexy and fell in love with him more by the hour.

His capacity to forgive also amazed her, or so she hoped. Please, God, let him write something nice, she begged silently. Searching his face, the man did seem a bit angry. *Then again, who wouldn't be feisty with a new friggin' liver shoved all up in your guts?*

She tried not to imagine how his wound must look. *Was it huge? Did it have Frankenstein stitches all over it? Would his scar be straight or diagonal across his belly? Did it wrap around the back? How big was a liver anyway? Did it feel weird in there? What was its previous owner like? Did they like Steel Fingers Wildboy's music? Wouldn't it be crazy if this person had been listening to him on the radio when, boom, a sudden car accident and sure enough a few hours later their body was in a morgue and their liver was in a cooler getting carried into Steely's operating room? Or was that just how things happened in the movies?* She didn't dare bring any of these questions into the air, but every quiet moment seemed to fill her mind with these curiosities. Some would be answered soon, some later, and certain ponderances, she knew would never get satisfied.

Aaron had stopped writing for a moment, catching his breath. Amber didn't dare read it yet so she kept her face turned upwards, toward his. She prayed that "Divorce" was not one of the words he labored to write.

Her stomach felt queasy. She gripped the bedrail to keep the room from spinning. What if that's exactly what was happening next?

"You could take a little nap now and ask me later," Amber suggested.

Aaron shook his head, wincing even more along with an uncomfortable grunt. His wife decided she'd better let him get on with it. While he wrote more, she re-read the first couple of sentences. "Sorry I'm a shoddy mess. This is an important question."

Her eyes skipped the next blank inch and re-read the next part: "I hope you answer Yes." Yes to what? To divorce? She didn't want to think about it. Breathing slowly, she decided to say yes, no matter what he asked. She'd have to figure out how to face their reality sooner or later, whatever the possible or probable outcome would be. She wasn't going to risk his health by letting him get upset now.

Aaron pulled the notepad toward them. It flipped forward, falling face down on his own arm. He elbowed it in Amber's direction so she could pick it up. She braced herself and turned the pad over. Across the bottom section of the page, angling upward as the letters got smaller to make sure they fit within the margin's edge, Aaron had written, "I love you. Be here. Proper wife. Stay?" His eyes looked wide and wet and tired.

Tears stinging her own eyes, Amber grabbed the pen and paper. "Yes, I will," she said softly, sweeping her hand across his forehead before placing a kiss there. She pushed the notebook and pen down toward the foot of the bed. Between tiny kisses, she felt his tension release completely.

She, too, suddenly felt free. Like a rocket launch dropping empty, unnecessary fuel booster tanks. Finally finding lift.

Aaron's eyes were already closed. In his dream, neither of them was stuck in a hospital bed.

Chapter 40

Sharon peed on a stick. Negative. She slumped over her lap after waiting a few minutes on the edge of the bathtub.

Dino looked up at her in the mirror's reflection as he brushed his teeth. He spat and rinsed.

"I think you have to wait more than two hours after sex, silly," he laughed.

Chapter 41

Screams woke everyone in the house. Brian jumped out of bed too fast and hit his shin on the corner of its white-washed wooden frame. Jolted awake, Amber called out, "Aaron?" Cindra reached for her cell phone on her nightstand, opened it and held it to her ear for several seconds before noticing it hadn't rung.

More screams got everyone standing, pulling on robes and soon after, collecting in Gia's guest room, which also incidentally usually served as a pool room. Gia stood in red and white striped bikini bottoms, barefoot and topless with her hands held strategically over each boob. She looked much like a flamingo standing with one leg bent, foot pressed into the side of her other knee. Squeezed close next to the pool table for stability, she trembled, panting and continuing to make high-pitched whiny sounds.

"What the heck are you doing?" Brian took first place asking the obvious question. "Where's your hideous night-shirt?"

Cindra took a more sympathetic tact. Placing her long fingers on Gia's elbow to cradle it gently, she asked, "Where is your shirt, sweetheart?" Her "W"s sounded like soft "V"s. Gia tried her best to point with her forehead in the direction in front of her.

Amber joined Cindra's calm tone, "It's in the bathroom?" She walked toward the doorway. Gia screamed again, this time adding words to her sounds, "Not in there! Don't go in there!"

All three stopped short and became quiet. Brian tiptoed closer to his best friend. "What's going on? Is someone in there?"

Amber and Cindra stood straight like two deer listening for a predator. Each tightened her robe belt and drew the lapels closer over bare skin, tiptoeing forward.

"Okay, Gia, quit fucking around. Do you have somebody in the bathroom? Did you bring somebody here?"

Brian: "Who the hell is in there?"

Cindra had retrieved a pool cue from the wall rack and held it in front of herself like a bat, heavy end up. Amber followed suit. Brian folded his arms, annoyed. He squinted at Gia as he straightened his glasses.

Gia removed one hand from one boob to point toward the bathroom. Her other forearm had to do the job of covering both breasts. The eagle on her chest rose and fell rapidly with shallow breaths. "They're in there RIGHT NOW! I don't know how many there are. There might be three of them!" She backed toward the room's doorway, pulling the blanket off the bed as she passed near it. Once safely under the threshold, she wrapped the heavy fabric around her like a giant towel.

Cindra took a stance outside the bathroom door. Amber took the other side. Each held up their pool sticks. Brian did the yelling.

"Okay, you motherfuckers, come out of there with your hands up!"

Amber couldn't help but laugh, pretty sure that marked the first occasion of hearing her Uncle Brian curse. He emphasized the Rs and sounded so Michigan.

"Come on!" Brian called out again, this time from only a few feet in front of the bathroom opening.

Since Gia had stopped whimpering, the group could now hear some shuffling sounds emitting from the room. A towel made a loud flapping noise as if moved by a gust of wind. Something fell on the tile floor and made a metal rolling sound for a few clicks until it stopped. Cindra whispered, "Should vee call za police?"

Amber held her stick a little higher. "We're gonna call the police, you assholes."

"Mother-fuckers!" Brian said again, this time sounding a little more legitimately bad-ass, but not completely.

They all looked toward Gia, who had made her way half into the room again. She ducked down as if something might be about to fall from the ceiling. Her eyes hadn't blinked in a long time.

Suddenly, crashing sounds erupted inside the bathroom—flapping fabric, something metallic skittering on tile. Amber and Brian yelled at once. Gia gulped hard.

Amber shouted, "That's it, cocksuckers!" Cindra shivered and screamed in a startle. Brian screamed a few pitches higher. Gia went into a hysterical fit, covering her eyes with her hands as her elbows barely held up her blanket.

A seagull bolted out, wings out in full flight. Its wing clipped the side of the doorway, knocking it down to flip and fumble around on the floor, find its way to its feet and screech in fever pitch to its partner, who came strutting out, casual as a 1930s gangster.

Amber and Brian cracked up. Cindra sighed in relief, giggled, and immediately bent down to pick the first gull up a few inches off the floor, smoothing its wing. The bird seemed to like the attention. Satisfied it was okay, Cindra set the creature down, headed past the birds, past Amber, and opened a wide-paned doorwall which led out to a glass-surrounded large terrace balcony. Both gulls followed her, their heads bobbing as they cooed.

"How did zey get in here?" Cindra asked as she walked.

Gia had leaped onto the bed, cowering into a little ball on one pillow. She pressed herself against the headboard with her eyes squeezed as shut as possible. In answer to Cindra's question, she shrugged without moving away from her safe zone.

Brian looked at Gia, talking as best he could through his own laughter. "Did you leave the door-wall open last night?"

Gia shook her head. Brian sniffed the air. It smelled clean, like ozone and carpet fibers.

"Do you mean to say that you didn't have a smoke before you went to bed last night?"

Gia didn't move. Finally, she shrugged again.

"Gia," Brian teased, placing a hand on Amber's shoulder. "Gia, dear. Did you go out on the terrace and have a smoke last night?"

She paused, then nodded, barely.

"Then did you forget to close the door-wall after, maybe?"

Gia shrugged. Then she nodded.

"Then did you maybe get cold and close it last night later?"

Gia shrugged. Then nodded.

Amber nudged Brian, chuckling, "That means she slept in here for who knows how long while they were in here!"

Gia stiffened, eyes popping from their sockets.

Brian nodded, adding, "They could've been flying all around, walking on her face." He emitted his best Haunted House "Muahahaaa!"

"You shut your hole!" Gia was on the verge of not kidding. She rocked a little, still pressing her hand against the headboard.

"Okay," Brian caved a little.

"We're sorry," Amber apologized, "No more jokes, okay?"

Just as Brian and Amber's muffled laughter became difficult to contain and swelled again, each screamed suddenly. A third bird had quietly strolled out when they weren't looking and now suddenly took off into the air a couple feet in front of where they stood. It screeched just before continuing a flight pattern across the room, out the open doorway and above the silver railing which marked the top edge of the glass balcony wall. Bird number three had inspired the other two to exit the terrace, who replied with equally screechy excitement and lofted themselves into the air behind it. Cindra quickly ducked out of the way.

All three gulls now became a postcard; black-winged silhouettes against what no one had yet noticed was a glorious backdrop of dawn over the ocean. A million miles of sky blazed in vibrant dark red just above the waterline, became deep orange for a wide strip above that and broke into yellow that soon merged into blue. White stretchy clouds topped the picture like whipped cream and introduced shorter, puffier white cloud puffs yet higher overhead. The sun yawned behind the city due east with rays stretched in heavenly diagonals across the gorgeous setting.

Gia calmed down and tucked herself back into bed. Amber joined her and sat on the edge of it. She couldn't help but wish for a moment, how nice it would be if she could sit on Aaron's narrow bed like this at the hospital. *Due time*, she told herself.

Amber grinned at her houseguest, whose tan hands held the edge of her blanket across her mouth and nose. Her pretty dark eyes still looked mighty wide and round. "You don't like birds, I take it," Amber teased.

Brian planted in a comfy spot on an overstuffed wing chair. It sported burgundy leather and metal nailhead studs around the arm-fronts and in an arch above Brian's head. Other than the blue felt on the pool table, that chair marked the only thing in the room darker than the palest shade of gray.

"I fucking hate those bastard things," Gia muffled from behind her blanket.

Brian sniffed, nodding his head. "I'm learning a lot about you this trip," he said.

"Like that I hate filthy disgusting creatures that smell like rotten fish and crap?" Gia pulled the blanket completely over her head, shuddering. She kicked her legs and let out a yell.

"And that you sleep topless."

"Shut up, homo."

"You shut up, lezzy boobs."

"Okay, okay," Amber stood up, suddenly parental. "First of all, Uncle Brian, you are tripping me out. I don't even know who the heck you are." She put her hand on her hip. "Who are you and what have you done with my uncle?"

Gia pulled the blanket from her face long enough to stick out her tongue in his general direction.

"And you," she twirled toward Gia's hidden blanket-face. "What happened to that tough broad I remember from Chazzy's? You're scared of birds?" She laughed, "I don't know if you realize this, but you have a tattoo of a gigantic bird across your whole chest!"

Brian and Amber laughed again. Even Cindra chuckled as she stepped in from the balcony, pulling shut the glass door behind her.

Gia was yelling from under her blanket, "That's a fucking EAGLE, you guys are both morons. Seagulls are like chickens. They're practically rats with wings! An eagle could kick a seagull's ass. You guys are so stupid. You're un-American!"

Brian commented about Ben Franklin's initial suggestion to make the wild turkey our national bird. Gia sat up, accidentally flashing her headlights before yanking the blanket up again. She glared at Brian, "You are a fucking liar. If our national bird was a goddamn turkey, I would go out there right now and swim my ass straight to Cuba!" Brian doubled over, slapping his knee. Gia got all flustered, "I mean Hawaii!" Brian's laugh only increased. "Cuba, Hawaii, the Bermuda fucking triangle, whatever! You're an asshole, anyway." She got quieter, mumbling the rest to herself, "Stupid moron. I might have to kick your ass after breakfast."

Amber followed Cindra, who had already left the room. "Guess I'll get in the shower. Visiting hours start at seven anyway."

Brian got up and squished Gia's foot under the blanket. "Okay, you can beat me up later," he said, heading toward the door. Right after that he stopped and turned to her in a spooky voice, "Unless the seagulls sneak in and get you fiiiirrrssstt..."

Gia threw a pillow after him. "I hate you!"

Chapter 42

Greg slammed a can of Pepsi on his slate-gray granite countertop. It fizzed all over the top and down the back of his hand. Amber suppressed a giggle. She'd never seen him angry before, and frankly, his frustrated heavy breathing puffing beneath a white-striped yellow polo shirt came across extra girly. Plus, he was wearing a white visor that pushed down his wiry strawberry blonde hair into little flip-curls around his temples. His angry face looked extra babyish despite being a little bit wrinkly. If he'd heard her thoughts, she feared Greg's hissy fit may increase. Mostly, though, she didn't want to think about his point, which was probably right.

"Well, if your answer is still no, I'm not going to call Helen for you. You want to tell her she's working her ass off getting you seen and you won't even take an amazing opportunity when it comes along? She's going to look you right in your pretty young face and tell you right where to go."

Amber almost said, "H.E. Double-toothpicks?" but thought otherwise. Time for maturity, not jokes. *Money means a shit-ton to these people who never slept on a bus,* she thought. Sure, he might have been right when Garry added, "Your ship may not come in again." But it all seemed overly dramatic to her. Amber looked down at her French pedicure and thought, if one movie was all she got to do before she did the right thing for once, so be it.

Amber visualized Spain for a moment. All her limited mind's eye could see was a faceless matador in a Mickey-Mouse hat and fancy red and gold bolero jacket. Tight black pants with little slits just below the knee. She saw the cover of a childhood book and heard a woman's voice for a moment reading something about Ferdinand, a gentle bull. Where did that come from? Was that her mother's voice she remembered?

Back to postcard images, Amber forced herself to picture tall beige buildings with ornate wrought-iron flower boxes. Bright red flowers billowed down and spilled over tiled arched door frames. She was sure she saw that picture on a puzzle box once. She pictured tall triangular-torsoed men with inky black hair combed back perfectly. Dark eyes and long eyelashes. Wine, probably. Why not? Filming there may have been dreamy and romantic, but Amber snapped herself back in line. She imagined a vacation there, later, with Steely. When he got better, she would ask him.

Anyway, maybe she'd get a nomination, like everyone kept saying, and parlay that. Later. Or maybe not. Ugh, why wouldn't anyone just let her say no and forget about it? It was bad enough to do the right thing without Greg and Helen getting all personal about it as if she was letting them down somehow. Helen's voice on the phone earlier that day rang in her ears: "You can't shun your public when they don't even love you yet, honey. You have to do some rounds. Talk shows. We have to get your face in their faces."

Amber knew whose face she needed to be in right now, and that was the guy who'd loved and forgiven her. Didn't anyone around here care about doing the right thing? She looked at Greg, then Garry, who seemed to have forgotten what it was like to be in love. Or maybe they were just so comfortable they could take it for granted.

She looked down at her pedicure again, then fixed her gaze on Greg and decided not to look away until he well understood she would not change her mind. He waved his hand in the air and turned away from the staredown, defeated.

Everybody would be all right. She would be all right. All Right. Righty-ho. It's just that she'd decided the moment she saw Aaron in a hospital bed. She was on full-time wife-duty until he was okay. Done-deal and no take-backs, so there.

She tried to soften Greg's icy stare. He looked down and exhaled through his nostrils. She tried to convey this explanation to Garry with her eyes, too, but he wouldn't look at either of them.

Instead, he got busy opening his shiny black fridge door and reaching for a fresh can of soda. Anything to not look at his naïve young friend. He was afraid he might cry. He was afraid he might slap her.

"Any idea how many people would kill to be you right now?" he asked.

"Guys," Amber reached across the countertop toward Greg's hand, which he promptly moved away. "You guys, you just have to understand. I just got him back. I just got *us* back." She turned to Garry who was pretending to reorganize items in the refrigerator door. "You lost somebody close to you once, you told me."

Greg glanced up at her for a moment with stinging eyes. Garry fussed with the fridge again, closed the door, clicked open an icy cold soda can.

Garry remembered his first lover's face in a dream flash that seemed a lifetime ago. He remembered pale gray skin, sunken around giant blue eyes, still beautiful but scared as hell. He remembered white flowers on a closed casket. An old anger swelled up and grabbed hold of his chest. Fucking AIDS. For a time and for so many it had felt like they'd lived in a war zone, never knowing where the GD HIV would strike next. He remembered feeling scared, ashamed, then later fortified, redeemed, loyal. Crazy, he observed, how he could put horrid things behind, and still move forward. Crazy how he could cherish the worst memories and somehow carry them in his chest all this time later, still proud and almost patriotic toward something ugly he'd lived through, something shared indirectly and directly with one he'd known and loved; with many he didn't know, yet loved. He remembered those years in a washed-out black and white vision, like blurry old photos that had survived a holocaust. You don't want to look at them, but you can't throw them away.

A shiver went through him for a second. *Shake it off,* he thought and turned his heart toward Amber again, this crazy girl who for some reason he'd loved as much as anyone since the day he first spotted her, bitching about a bagel.

Reaching for a glass from an upper cabinet to find an excuse not to look at her again, Garry formulated how he could explain how important this decision would be for Amber's future. She was turning down the biggest opportunity of her life, and he would not let her do it without a fight. When a person has mindfully forgotten exactly how many years he is over fifty, the one thing he cannot stand is watching a kid waste potential.

"Alas, youth is wasted on the young," he huffed, pouring Pepsi into a tilted glass. Greg took off his glasses and rubbed his eyes a few times.

Amber looked at her hands, twisting an antique diamond Claddagh ring around and around on her wedding finger. "You have no idea how much I have fucked up in my life," she said quietly.

"My point exactly, honey." Greg paused again to keep from shouting. "Please don't fuck up any more."

"He's my husband."

"Yes, and he was your husband before you told any of us, too. He was your husband when you ditched everything and—"

"Tried to make it on my own. I know." Amber cut him off with a raised hand. "Greg, Garry, I love you. Please don't make me have to walk out of here right now." She set her jaw.

They searched their protégé's soft features as she hardened into flawless marble. She didn't look as if she would cry. Amber's ability to go completely from hot to cold in an instant had blown everyone away throughout shooting the last picture. With barely a nudge from the first couple rehearsals, she could put up a wall and tear it down right there on her face within moments.

Then, once she'd discovered her own emotional control, her work became as beautiful a talent as it could be scary. It was as if she was made of wax and could sculpt herself any way you asked. And once you earned her trust, she'd give over to this malleability without hesitation, without question. Her instincts took her emotions to places before she even knew it, and she seemed to surprise herself on a ride of discovery right along with those watching it happen from the sidelines. From theater seats.

Garry knew this was why he and so many had reached out toward Amber almost immediately. She didn't just do this onscreen; she lived it all the time. One couldn't help oneself but to want to be around to see what happened next! What on earth, Garry couldn't imagine what, could give someone less than half his age so much courage? It took courage to expose or protect. Misplaced or no, he believed this took a courage few actors ever tapped into; few human beings ever tapped into.

He'd concluded one day a few weeks into their saturated shoot schedule that either Amber was always acting or never acting. After that, he tried to figure it out but really couldn't tell. He doubted she herself even could tell the difference between real life and acting. All the world was this girl's stage, he realized, corny as the old Shakespeare line sounded in his own head. He'd never met anyone who so thoroughly did whatever the hell she wanted whenever the hell she wanted to do it. Even today as she stood there all cool, turning down an enormous paycheck, pissing him off in those little white shorts and a pale orange tank top, Amber amazed him.

"He needs me," she was saying. "He's a fucking star. He's worked his ass off. He needs more than nurses, and he deserves more than nurses! He needs someone to love him and to need him back. I need that. I so need that. I can't explain it, but I can't keep running—"

She cut herself off, realizing that was all she wanted to say. Amber waltzed past Garry and opened his fridge, grabbing her own soda, a 7-up. She retraced his prior maneuvers to get her own glass and followed suit pouring it into a tilted glass to reduce its fizz. While guzzling a big drink, Amber kept both eyes on Greg. She didn't want to miss him when he finally decided to look up. With Garry, she already knew she'd won.

Now Greg glanced at her once or twice, meandered over to his window to check out the grand and decidedly expensive view looking south over Hollywood from its hills. He tapped the windowsill a few times before turning to lean against it. Greg took a long drink from his own glass, staring at a giant piece of pop-art that hung on the opposite wall. It looked like a graphic print of an octopus which somehow also evoked the shape of a chandelier. The print could best be appreciated from its front view, flanked on either side by silver cylindrical wall sconces.

Greg retraced their on-going conversation over the past week. He considered the few intense phone calls he'd had with her agent, Helen, too. He'd assured his old friend that he could convince her client to change her mind. He'd explained to Amber the importance of an actor's second film after the whopping success of a sudden break-out hit and fame. He'd used the word "parlay" enough times for the sound of it to almost lose meaning. He'd explained how deeply he believed that Aaron would not only understand but would encourage her to launch into working again right away. He'd lectured her, he'd nagged. He'd crunched the numbers for her. He'd made an analogy to surfing, riding a swell when it came because you never knew when and if the next one would arrive. How quickly the tide would change. He'd convinced her to think it over another few days. He'd asked Holly to get on her case about it. He'd even offered to ask Garry to get production to delay Amber's start date by two weeks so she could give Aaron a little more time before she'd have to go to Spain to begin shooting. He'd pulled out all the stops. There were no more stops to pull out.

Now, with Amber refusing to break eye contact and not speaking a word, Greg knew his efforts had failed. He hated failure and indicated this with a long, arduous sigh in her general direction.

Moments later, Amber was on him like a koala on a eucalyptus tree, kissing all over his face with 7-Up-scented lips. "I knew you'd understand! I just knew you would!" she cried out, jumping up and down.

The two spent the next hour discussing Greg's ideas for his next commercial set, cracking jokes and sharing a large bag of flax-seed infused tortilla chips with hummus. Garry hugged his buoyant friend goodbye and watched her walk to her new car, barefoot and carrying silver flip-flops in her left hand. She got in, fussed a minute and lit up a cigarette as the electric window opened all the way down. Then she laughed, all giddy with youth and naïve hopefulness, tossed the cigarette out onto his driveway and called to them both in an Irish accent, "What am I doin'? I don't need this shite anymore!" She held up the rest of her pack, squeezed it and tossed it out toward some pink rosebushes along his driveway. Barely audible over the sound of her red Jag XJS shifting into reverse, Amber laughed, "Your gardener can clean those up!"

Greg laughed and shook his head. Then he went out to pick up the little mess after she'd disappeared. Still shaking his head, yet unable to keep from smiling, he tossed the debris into an oversized stone garbage urn as the two men continued back toward their gorgeous house.

Chapter 43

Allison Paige wore her mousy hair in a long, wavy carefree mop that stopped in a thick wedge at the thinnest point on her waist. Her skin glowed with a fresh-scrubbed pinkness. Having her first child early in her twenties had agreed with her svelte physique, which naturally snapped back into shape by the time her baby son was only a few months old. Unfortunately, her mental state did not.

Steven Paige spent most evenings busily tapping out his Great American Novel, about a young idealist visionary excited to take his place in the newfound enthusiasm of the industrial age, yet trapped in tedium with a wife and new baby. Steven scrolled the carriage up an inch to read his most recent typo, corrected the mistake with white goop and clicked the carriage back down. He removed his horn-rimmed black glasses and rubbed his ruddy face, from furrowed brow down to auburn mutton chops and scruffy chin. Late nights had been the only times he could write lately, after Allison had put their colicky baby down and then fumed and vented, hurling postpartum complaints at her twenty-six-year-old husband until she wore herself out.

Steven glanced at the crumpled afghan across the olive-green couch in front of the long, shallow table where he sat. He intended to sleep there again tonight.

Had Steven known what the night would bring, he wouldn't have gone to sleep at all. He would have quietly tip-toed across the hall to his three-year-old daughter's room, picked her up, sneaked into his own bedroom, softly lifted his tiny son from his crib and maybe put the three of them all in his boxy brown Buick. He would likely have wanted to save them. But no one can know what someone would have done if they hadn't done what they did, and on that cool autumn evening in Lincoln Park, Michigan, Steven Paige did not retrieve his children, get in his Buick and leave. Instead, he happened to finish a long sentence, type a period, cue up the page, tap five spacebar indents for a new paragraph and stand up in front of his chair.

In the kitchen, he poured a sulfur-smelling glass of water from the faucet into a tall glass with Fred Flintstone on it. He drank about half of it, noting that he'd need to refresh salt in the water softener soon. He placed the glass on a mustard-yellow Formica countertop.

Then, Steven Paige headed for the couch, unfolding a brown and green crocheted afghan as he fluffed up a yarn-covered orange pillow. He sat quietly and began to turn his body into a lying position sideways across the couch. Before he was finished, on this particular night, Steven heard a quiet voice from the darkness of the hall. He hesitated, hoping it had been the sound of his wife, perhaps settling the baby back to sleep before he would begin a crying jag that would awaken the whole house. His thoughts were interrupted by a confusing sentence.

"Steven, I made the baby quiet."

Steven replied, in a tone he'd gotten used to using toward his wife over the last several weeks. He sounded somewhere between annoyed and exhausted, answering, "What is it, Allison? What did you say?"

Allison stepped forward. In her hand, she held up a gun. It was Steven's gun, a heavy silver revolver.

"Steven, I made the baby quiet."

Steven jumped up suddenly, barreling toward his wife. On second thought, he stopped short, holding a hand out and saying as calmly as he could, "What do you mean, you made the baby quiet?"

"He's quiet now. He won't disturb you."

Steven took a bolder tone, hand still up, "Allison. Where is the baby?"

"He won't disturb you and your precious fucking writing," she spat.

"Allison. Is the baby all right? Allison." Steven stepped closer. As he took a second step, she shot him.

Steven Paige didn't tiptoe into his children's bed chambers, collect them and save them. Instead, he happened to crumble in place on the floor a few inches from his wife. She shot him again as his body went down, seemingly in slow motion, and surprisingly quietly. She shot his head a moment after he hit the floor. His glasses cast a shadow on the hardwood which looked a little like two tiny windows, Allison thought.

She turned toward her daughter's room, shot once toward the lump on the bed, then screamed. She didn't stop screaming on her own; it was the bullet in her own head which suddenly rendered her silent.

Moments later, a child's hand emerged from the quiet. It gripped the top edge of a comforter and slowly pulled it down, just a few inches, to reveal two large round eyes, blinking in dim shadows cast from a Holly Hobbie nightlight. Her bangs shook gently across her three-year-old forehead as she turned from one side to the other. Her tiny brain evaluated the situation as best it could.

Amber's small body climbed down from the youth bed and padded softly past the body of her mother, as well as the gore that marked where her face should have been. She quickly waddled into her parents' bedroom and pressed her face against two wooden bars, staring at the unmoving body of a baby boy.

She must have stood there staring at someone who would have been her little brother for a long, long time.

Chapter 44

"You have got to be fucking kidding me," Gia sat with her mouth hanging open until it was almost dry. Then she popped a square-shaped pretzel snack into it and chewed. She stared out the window past Brian's head into white clouds.

Brian pressed the button on his airline armrest and pushed himself back a few degrees, lining it up with Gia's.

"This is not something I would kid about," he said after a long pause. Brian stared out the window, too. A grid of reddish-brown squares appeared below, between some clouds for a moment before the view changed back to total whiteness.

"Jesus," Gia hadn't blinked once through the whole story. "Jesus."

"I know," Brian had mixed feelings about having told her. He had mixed feelings about talking about it at all. In his mind, he pictured Allison's face, a color photo from her high school days on a funeral card. A guilty sense of betrayal flushed through him but didn't last when he saw the genuine emotion in Gia's face. She wiped her lower lids with her tiny square airline napkin, leaving thick black streaks from eyeliner.

"So, she was there for three whole days all by herself? That's insane! Where were the neighbors? What did she eat? Jesus, she could have died from dehydration or whatever. Does she remember it?"

"I really don't know. I mean, by the time she came to live with me she was older and I guess I figured..." The phrase, *Say what I mean and mean what I say*, from rehab popped into Brian's consciousness. He regrouped, answering, "I really don't know, but we never talked about it. I guess I didn't want to talk about it—" Brian paused to recall three caskets, two large and one small.

People's faces he didn't know all around. Old lady smells of heavy perfumes and ripe lilies. Suddenly, his chest seized up and all Brian could do was stare out the window.

Gia closed her eyes and turned to face him in her seat. She seemed to fit into the narrow position better than most people could. She put her hand up near her face against the back cushion and tapped a few times. "So, the police open the door and there's this little baby, a toddler, and three dead bodies all around. I wonder if she was crying, or real quiet, or if she found a snack or was by the door, or—"

"Gia?" Brian whispered without taking his gaze off the view. "Could you do me a favor?" He reached to his side and patted her knee. It was covered with the pink T-shirt Gia had tugged down over her folded legs.

"Yeah, I know, shut up, right?" Gia reached down and took Brian's hand. "Sorry, Brian."

With that, hands held, the two best friends nodded off to sleep.

Chapter 45

H olly gathered the last bundle of clothes from the last corner of her closet.
Turning to look at the empty white walls and carpeting, she could still
see four faint dimples where Amber's bed used to lie. Holly smoothed a plastic
dry-clean bag atop the stack of garments across her forearm. She smiled to
herself, remembering.

She'd intended to find a roommate for a few years, but never got around to
it, so when Amber showed up into her life, all disheveled and full of pent-up
ambition, Holly had welcomed the energy in the place. She remembered
bringing the stranger into her home for the first time.

Amber had plopped one ugly-looking duffel bag on the mattress, black
with red straps and a duct tape repair, next to Holly's adorable extra bedspread
folded into a rectangle with a stack of sheets and pillowcases. She'd also had a
black messenger bag that looked frayed and filthy on the bottom. Thankfully,
Amber had set that grubby thing on the floor.

Holly remembered proudly showing Amber the clean, bright room, then
leaving her alone to get acquainted with her new surroundings. She'd gone into
the kitchen to wash a few dishes, and upon her return found Amber's face red
and sweaty. Her new roommate straddled one corner of the bed with a foot up
on its white wooden footboard, grunting as she wrestled with the elastic fitted
sheet as if it was fighting back. Holly tried not to laugh out loud but made a
noise that stopped Amber for a moment. When Amber turned in frustration,
her face looked angry at first—almost scary—and Holly's heart rate spiked.
Who invites a total stranger to move in?

But before she could think again, Amber's expression quickly softened into
a puppy-dog look that drew Holly in to help her put the pink and white striped
sheet in place. Once they'd finished the bed, the two new roommates spent

their first evening munching microwave popcorn and watching tapes of Holly's old high school plays. That had been the first of many slumber party nights, and the two girls never looked back.

Now, the room empty but for a white wicker end table and matching dresser, Holly suddenly felt very grown-up. She glanced at her engagement ring, which reflected a bright spray of light flickers on the floor and bottom half of the dresser. Turning it to enjoy the disco-ball effect, Holly squinted as the glare caught part of the mirrored closet door.

After dropping off those last few formal gowns across the back seat of her PT Cruiser, Holly went into the apartment one last time for a final pass. When she returned to Amber's bedroom, she looked down at the closet floor and gasped. She'd almost forgotten to take her Tweety-Bird rug with her! Bending down to roll it up from one end, just for a moment, she considered leaving it behind. After all, she was supposed to be all grown up and getting hitched. Then Tweety looked right at her, though, with those big round cartoon eyes, and she just couldn't leave the little guy who'd been with her since junior high. Heck, Tweety could line the floor of the back of her car! That would be perfect.

Lifting the rug, Holly found something hidden there: a folded piece of newspaper in a Ziploc baggie. She knew it must have been Amber's because she'd never seen it before. Holly picked up the bag and carried it to the end table, where she sat down. She opened it and unfolded the paper. Suddenly, she felt awful. Her stomach dropped as her eyes saw the words:

Mother of Two Shoots Husband Then Self

Holly snapped the paper back into a fold and shoved it into the baggie. *This is none of my business,* she thought.

ONCE OUTSIDE, HOLLY placed the baggie on the car seat next to her, turned the key and headed for Amber and Aaron's house.

After a visit with the couple, when Amber seemed distracted getting out some of Aaron's prescription bottles, the friend excused herself to the bathroom. She quietly hid around the corner, nodded to Cindra as she walked by, and popped into their bedroom once the coast looked clear.

Aaron and Amber's bedroom seemed a vast space with no place to put anything. Holly noticed each bed stand had one shallow drawer in it, but otherwise the room contained only a sofa, coffee table and some chairs. She stood next to the bed, glad that Aaron was no longer stuck in it every day. His side seemed to be the one on the left, as that bedstand held a couple of prescription bottles and a sad little kidney-shaped pink basin from the hospital. Amber mentioned that sometimes Aaron's medicine made him nauseous, and Holly couldn't stand thinking of her rock star friend vomiting into that pathetic thing during the night.

"Holllyyy?" Amber called to her, "You want some coffee?"

Holly didn't dare yell back; her voice would come from the wrong side of the hallway. She grabbed the baggie from her back pocket and shoved it into the right-side drawer. Then she beelined out the door, zipped across the hall and flushed the toilet in the bathroom. Coming out, she called to Amber, "What? Sorry I couldn't hear you."

Amber stood in the center of their kitchen with one hand on her hip. Aaron sat at the table, a blanket wrapped around his shoulders and a magazine open in front of him.

"Coffee?"

Holly sat at one of the barstools across from her. "Yeah, coffee sounds good." Then she sighed a little louder than she'd intended.

AARON LOOKED AT HIS sleeping wife beside him in bed. She almost appeared not to breathe at all, a sign she had once again worn herself out taking care of him. Before he went to sleep, she'd handed him his barf bin. *Fecking disgusting,* he thought, glancing at the terrible thing. *Couldn't they use a normal bucket? A silver champagne bucket, perhaps?* Aaron pictured that, puking his lights out into a shiny champagne bucket. In his mind, he saw yellowish-brown liquid landing in splashes across little square pillows of ice. The image seemed more of a memory than imagination, and he remembered he'd certainly experienced puking into a hotel champagne bucket or two in his Wildboy days. He'd certainly hurled into plenty a hotel toilet, shower, floor, sink... *Disgusting,* he thought again.

He opened his bedside table drawer with his left hand and scooted the pink eyesore into the open drawer. Trying to close it, the awkward angle made him lean forward, an activity his scarred abdomen did not thank him for. Grunting, he tried to close the thing again. The drawer was too shallow for the basin. *Gotta be nice and deep for all the puke,* he thought morbidly. Aaron lifted the pink thing out again, tossed it toward the floor and shoved the drawer closed.

Double-checking that his little wifey still slept, Aaron winced as he positioned himself lower. He closed his eyes and began the slow breathing that would bring sleep around within a couple of minutes. Inside the drawer near Aaron's head, behind a thin veneer of pale-varnished wood, lay a Ziploc baggie with a secret past inside. Aaron himself would never see it.

NEXT MORNING, CINDRA bent down beside her patrons' unmade bed. She picked up a pink plastic hospital bin and placed it on top of Amber's side of the bed stand. Pretty much since day one her boss had made it clear he didn't like "that sick-old-man nonsense starin' in me face while I'm tryin' to sleep."

She began to make up the bed. When done, Cindra smoothed a last wrinkle out of the comforter and moved on to straighten the rest of the tabletop items. She noticed one bedside drawer slightly ajar with the corner of something sticking up so it wouldn't close all the way. She opened it, half-expecting to find an overflowed pile of cigarette butts on the ashtray Mr. Spinnaker had always kept in this drawer, beside a half-empty bottle of whiskey or few.

It had been a while now since her boss had lived that way, and Cindra had been there for most of it. Today, the drawer was full of crumpled tissues, an open packet of drying out wet-naps and a Ziploc baggie with a paper inside. Cindra shook her head, smiling to herself and thinking, "Men!" She gathered the yucky used tissues and threw them into the open waste bag she kept in the center of the room as she cleaned. She wiped the inside of the drawer with a disposable anti-bacterial cloth. Just as she was about to put the baggie back in place, she realized it might be one of those info packets the pharmacist always included when they handed out prescriptions. Instead, she opened the bag and took a peek at its contents.

"Mother of Two Shoots Husband Then Herself," she read. Looking both ways first, Cindra sat on the edge of the bed. About halfway through scanning the article, she looked up to see one of her patrons staring at her from the doorway.

Amber waved, "How ya doin', Cindra? Good morning."

Cindra stood up with a start. She smoothed her cleaning apron over her jeans, looking down at it longer than necessary. The paper had landed on the bed beside her. Amber walked toward her with a different piece of paper.

"I hope you didn't already go to the drug store yet, because I thought of a few extra things we need," Amber was saying, holding out a short list toward the maid. She noticed Cindra's eyes looked wet and her lips were pressed together hard. Her pretty face, which stood about a foot above Amber's, seemed upset.

"What's the matter?" Amber asked, sitting on the bed, patting a spot next to her there. She picked up a piece of newsprint from the bed to clear a place for Cindra to sit down. "Are you okay?"

Amber looked at the paper as Cindra sat quietly next to her. "Did you get some bad news? Mind if I read this?"

Cindra took the paper from Amber's hand, folded it again and shoved it into the plastic bag. She sealed it and handed it back to Amber. "So sorry. I didn't know," she said, cheeks flushed.

Amber's brow furrowed for a moment until the moment of confusion turned into recognition. She recognized that large plastic bag with its bluish plastic zipper and folded newsprint. Amber may have been confused about how it got there, but she recognized it just the same.

That paper had been one thing she'd kept around wherever she went; in a pocket of her bag, in a drawer under clothes at Uncle Brian's house, in a box under her bed in her Detroit apartment, under Holly's Tweety Bird... Ah, now she understood.

"Holly gave you this?"

Cindra began gathering up her garbage bag. "No."

Amber narrowed her eyes, flipping the baggie from one hand to the other. She bit her upper lip with her lower teeth.

Cindra stood in the center of the room with her garbage bag in one hand. She didn't seem to know what to do next. Certainly, she should say something, she thought. "So sorry," again was all she could come up with.

"Where did you get this?" Amber asked.

Cindra pointed to Aaron's side drawer.

Amber's brow crumpled again. She breathed in deeply, held it, then exhaled. Holly must've found the article, given it to Aaron, and he didn't want to bring it up. Amber breathed a couple more times while Cindra stood there, thinking about the paragraph she'd just read.

POLICE FOUND THE CHILD sleeping on the kitchen floor beside a few open packets of Instant Oatmeal. "When we woke her up, she started smiling right away," said Officer Hill, who was first on the scene, "That kid was a real survivor. Never seen anything like it." The three-year-old child was immediately taken to Henry Ford Hospital for observation.

"WELL," AMBER SAID, standing up, "I guess that's that." She wiped a single tear from one eye and stepped toward Cindra, holding out the article toward the garbage bag.

Cindra protested, "Please, you cannot throw zat away." The maid tightened her grip around the top of the bag.

Amber nudged it toward the garbage again. "I don't need this anymore," she said.

Cindra reached for the item with her other empty hand. "You cannot throw zis away. Paparazzi." Cindra, having worked for a famous rock star since well before Amber came along, knew best.

Amber put a hand on her hip and rocked a little, thinking. "They're bound to find out one way or another," she finally said. "They always do."

Cindra opened the baggie and took out the paper. She hated to do it since she herself hadn't gotten to finish the article, but she tore it in half, with a little smirk. "Yes, but vee don't vant to help zem along, do vee?" Cindra tore the halves in half, turned the paper and tore them again a few more times.

Amber's heart pounded as she watched the paper become tiny scraps of confetti. She struggled to breathe deep enough to get oxygen. Her head spun a little until she sat down in one of their eggshell-colored upholstered chairs.

One hand on each armrest, Amber watched Cindra place some scraps in her garbage bag. The blonde trotted over to another small garbage basket in the corner of the room, deposited more pieces, then headed for the bathroom with the last third of the article's shreddings. She returned from that room, dusting off both hands, then went to work on the Ziploc baggie. After ripping the baggie into a few squiggly-looking strips, mostly for dramatic emphasis, she bent down and shoved the pieces of clear plastic into her garbage bag as well. Lifting it from the floor, the maid began to exit the master bedroom.

She looked once more at Amber, who was staring out the glass door at the ocean view. "I go to zee drugstore now," she said. Amber nodded slowly without looking after her.

About three minutes later, Amber hopped out of the chair and turned on the intercom radio. Loud jazz filled the house, revitalizing each hollow room with fresh new energy.

Chapter 46

A.J.'s arm felt damp with sweat where Steely had been holding onto it for support. Both men felt relief when Steely transferred both hands onto a Lucite podium sitting on a small stage in front of Hard Rock Café's large curved bar. A.J. stepped back, folding huge hands in front of his two-button tan suit coat. Steely's shaking knees became stable beneath him as soon as the applause in front of him swelled up to a volume that felt familiar. Three young girls with asymmetrical haircuts jumped up and down in the front section of the large audience. The rest of the crowd seemed full of large long-haired men, all forms of beards and goatees, do-rags, women in leather jackets, fringe, boots, lots of hair dye and thick eye makeup. Some folks had kids on their shoulders who cheered like crazy, only because their parents were doing it. Amber stood near the front corner, beaming. Her uncle stood next to her, equally owning a piece of the pride. A glittery sign waving back and forth somewhere near the back read, "WILD 4 WILDBOY."

Two slutty women joined Steely on the platform, one holding up a framed silky shirt with long frilly cuffs. The other held up two black boots, one in each hand over her head. She had to hold them out because on her head she wore a black cowboy hat with a wide silver band. Each woman wore long black earrings, black leather bustiers laced up the front and denim mini-skirts. Enormous black over-the-knee boots made them tower beside Steel Fingers Wildboy, looking like two black columns framing a classic statue. Steely's presence, however, trumped both females, especially when he reached for the inside pocket of his tailored black pinstriped vest, retrieved a pair of sunglasses and put them on.

The crowd went nuts. Flashes blinked. Amber and Brian cheered. The three sideways-haired teenagers bounced like beach balls. A.J. smirked and scratched at one sideburn.

Steely spoke few words, thanking his fans, announcing his retirement, appreciating his wife, and then reaching his arms around the skinny waists of his sidekicks to pose for a few fabulous shots. Once the mic turned off, he greeted each woman, hugging them one at a time whispering, "Good job" and "Nicely done."

A.J. helped him maneuver stiffly from the stage and directed the retired rock and roll legend toward a long table with a guitar-shaped ice sculpture in its center. On either side, various items of Steely's paraphernalia had been positioned. Photographers gathered in a flashing frenzy as Aaron signed first the glass picture frame then the side of one boot with a silver paint pen. His illegible signature started with a capital "S" before flattening out into a straight line, followed by an "F," another straight line, then a huge, clear "W," a swirl and a loop. Each signature took about three seconds. More photos, photos with Amber, photos with A.J., then photos with everyone else took up the next forty-five minutes.

Amber looked over at her husband. His smile had lost some of its width, a telltale sign that his energy waned. She whispered to A.J. who whispered to an assistant, who told the restaurant manager, who called their driver. A long, black limo took them home, where one of America's all-time biggest rock-and-roll legends sat down in an easy chair and promptly fell asleep before 8:30 p.m.

Chapter 47

Dino slapped a knifefull of peanut butter across a slice of wheat toast. Shoving almost a third of it into his mouth, he planted a sloppy pucker in the general direction of his wife's cheek. It hit her nose as she turned toward him. He bolted out the door, grabbing his jacket off a hook on the way.

Once in his pickup truck, Dino turned the key and rolled down the window. His wife was running outside toward him, bare feet kicking dry leaves out of the way. He couldn't help but laugh as her face came close to his in the open window because her hair swirled all over the place in the wind. She looked like a friendly red-snaked Medusa; a cross between Strawberry Shortcake and an ancient seductress who could turn men into stone.

With a last chunk of peanut butter toast still sticking out of his mouth, Dino reached out to push some of her curly red locks from her eyes. Sharon tried to help by shaking her head, which only seemed to bring more hair into her face.

"I gotta go, babe," Dino said through a mouthful. He chewed and swallowed as she answered.

"K, Dad, see ya later."

Dino started the truck and backed out quickly. He glanced behind him, over his shoulder, stopping fast before almost hitting one of their big outside garbage cans. Garth Brooks was singing about Two Piña Coladas on the radio.

Turning the wheel, Dino took his foot off the gas suddenly. The truck crept slowly back toward the street on its own, curving into the drive lane against the curb. His wife still stood in the driveway, laughing. Her bathrobe had fallen open and he could see her cute leopard-printed flannel pajamas underneath. They had pink buttons shaped like hearts. Dino had given them to her last Christmas.

Sharon watched her husband's face change from confused to delighted in about fifteen seconds' time. He slammed one Timberland boot on the brake pedal, making the damp pads squeak. The vehicle jerked a little as he shoved the steering-column shifter into park, opened the door and came running out across the lawn. Another car pulled up behind the truck. Seeing it was not moving and the door hung open, its driver stopped honking and went around it. Otherwise, the morning got back to its misty, peaceful self.

Sharon felt herself being picked up into the air and spun around. The sky looked huge over a swirling picture of red, orange and yellow treetops. Maple, sumac, pine and black walnut twirled all around. She could smell it all at once, and the beauty of it overwhelmed her. Sharon looked down at her hunky husband's face, all white teeth and crinkled eyes. When he put her down, she felt dizzy for about a second before his mouth was on hers, kissing peanut butter all over her lips.

Suddenly, as quickly as he'd picked her up, he plunked her down again. "K, Mom," he called back, running toward the truck, "See ya later!" he shouted, climbing into the cab and taking off.

After opening the diner's register, unlocking doors, and unloading a few boxes of napkins and paper towels, Dino could no longer help himself. He called his manager to come in early to cover him and spent the rest of the morning with his wife at the mall, gawking at nursery furniture, strollers and drooling over the loot in Baby Gap.

Chapter 48

Garry couldn't help himself. Amber had gone to the store and left him sitting there, innocently minding his own business in a chair on her back terrace, staring at some seagulls along the waterfront. Garry hadn't called Aaron out there to join him. He just did. The husband of his young friend (and he liked to think, protégé) simply came waltzing out with a full glass of grapefruit juice and happened to sit down in the chair right next to his. What was he supposed to do, ignore the man?

Within short order, Garry blabbed away, spilling all kinds of beans about the picture he wanted to shoot in Spain, Amber's part in it, and his own disappointment that she'd turned it down. He talked about financing, storyline and the amazing composer they had lined up to do a fully orchestrated soundtrack. He gossiped about another young actress who wanted to play in it and how much his partner Greg couldn't stand her annoying entourage of catty debutantes. He could really weave a yarn, keeping Aaron interested in every twist, turn and opinion about the subject.

Aaron listened intently, occasionally sipping and taking moments to digest the words while staring at the ocean. Amber's friend (and mentor, as she'd called him more than once) Garry was impressive and convincing when he got to talking shop. It reminded Aaron of his own enthusiasm for songwriting. Once a few lines or a riff got into his head, there was no stopping Steely from getting a whole song down. He would obsess until the finished thing came out, good to go. The creative process was like giving birth. Once a seed was planted, it would gestate and grow until the time came to burst forth. Your creation would introduce itself to the world, on its own, one way or another. You could help ease it along or get out of its way.

Aaron watched Garry go on about his project, eyes twinkling and words tumbling out so fast that his mouth could hardly keep up. Aaron pictured Amber in Spain, spinning around in a full skirt, shoulders wrapped in black lace. He pictured her in a flamenco pose, hair pulled tightly back with a rose at her ear. He saw her on a movie poster; not her, but a painting of her. Oh, the girl would love it, Aaron knew.

His choice was made. Aaron leaned over toward Garry, a painful move he quickly regretted and straightened again. This sideways turning business was going to take a bit more time. He held out a hand, offering a handshake to this welcome guest on his terrace.

"Whatever it takes, I'll get that cailín to do your film."

Garry loved the way Aaron said "film" like "fill-um" as if it had two syllables. He had no idea what a "cailín" was but assumed it must've meant his wife. In actuality, Steely was being tongue in cheek. The word implied Amber was an average girl.

"She won't do it, I'm telling you—" Garry thought of his conversation with Amber, wondering if he'd betrayed a friend by bringing this up at all. She seemed hell-bent on playing the lead role of wife these days, and nothing else.

"She's just a wee babe, I swear," Aaron said.

"Yes, I know, but she thinks she's all grown up," Garry sat back against the green weatherproof cushion of his chair, "I remember when I thought you could only do one thing at a time to get anything done—"

Aaron laughed. "Aha, yes, the single-mindedness of youth."

"It's balance that we understand later," Garry added.

Aaron offered a knowing nod, "We must. Life makes us," he rested a hand across his abdomen. Suddenly he laughed out loud, "I always thought I could do two things at a time," he chuckled again, a little quieter and to himself mostly, "I wrote songs, I drank. I played songs, I drank. I got laid, I drank. I smoked, I drank."

Garry laughed out loud too, shaking his own head in remembrance. "Ah, the juggling act of life, adding one ball in the air at a time."

Aaron kept laughing, "Those were the balls I started with."

"Don't even ask me what I was doing with my balls back then!" Garry slapped Aaron's arm. He didn't wince much at all.

The two shared a quiet moment as their laughter petered out. Aaron finished his juice in a long gulp. Nodding slowly, he turned his gaze back toward the ocean. It lapped to and fro, as always.

"You've got my back, right Cin?" He tossed his voice behind him. Cindra had been taking an extra-long time watering potted plants along the edge of the terrace, eavesdropping. She looked down, embarrassed.

Garry finished his own beverage, a glass of water with a wedge of lime. Cindra came forward to collect their drink glasses. She stopped in front of Aaron as he spoke to her, "When Amber goes to Spain, you've got me back, right? All these meds and doctor's appointments, all that malarkey?"

Cindra nodded.

Aaron looked at Garry. "It's done."

Garry shook his head, not convinced. "I'm telling you, that girl is stubborn."

Aaron motioned his hands into air-guitar position and sang a few lines from one of his top hit songs, *"I am man of the house, king of my hill, I am man of the house, just lookin' for a thriiiilll..."*

Garry wasn't so sure, but he laughed anyway. He was never into Wildboy's music and to be honest, preferred Elton John, but Steely's lyrics did seem to apply. He just hoped Amber would agree.

Aaron kept singing, *"I am the man of the house, balls to the wall, call or don't call cuz I intend to have it aaallll..."* He moved into a complex guitar solo in the air, scatting sound effects and entertaining his guest as only a true performer knew how.

Chapter 49

Nighttime air from the ocean smelled like no other kind of air in the world. Amber's skin felt bracing cold, but she loved it. A breeze moved two large sheer curtains into the room, like angels dancing before an elegant backdrop of black night sky. Two candles burned on either side of the bed, spilling a bright energetic citrus scent into the otherwise dark room. Aaron's face looked healthy with a ruddy flush from making love. In the candlelight with thick wavy hair spilling toward the edges of his pillow, he looked handsome as ever.

She couldn't believe he was ready to do it. After a few initial moments of worrying she might hurt him, she found a sexy slow rhythm they both enjoyed immensely. Amber didn't take long. Aaron mirrored both her enthusiasm and her timing.

Looking down at his content face, Amber planted a few kisses on her husband's forehead. "You okay, babe?" she whispered, receiving only a happy moan and nod in reply.

Chapter 50

S PAIN
Amber scanned the Spanish horizon for some sign of sunshine. It came smiling a few moments later over a breathtaking view of terra cotta triangle rooftops. She sipped a glass of orange juice and took a bite of shaved ham with toasted cheese from a white plate on the balcony ledge in front of her.

What seemed painfully impossible several weeks ago suddenly appeared as full of hope and optimism as the ample basket of fruit and nuts on the table beside her. She breathed in the romantic scent of jasmine from lush plants clinging to walls behind where she stood.

Amber glanced at the call sheet slid under her hotel room door during the night before. They wanted her on set by eight, so she'd better hop in the tub and start getting makeup ready any moment.

Her cell phone buzzed in the pocket of her robe. She checked a text message which read, "hello wife."

"hola husband," she clicked back, "u ok?"

"grand. no worries." A pause. Then, "have fun."

Amber put the phone back inside her pocket and turned to lean against the balcony one breath more.

Then she twirled round and headed back into her hotel suite. A knock on the door brought a delivery of yellow roses from Garry and Greg. Amber smelled one flower and placed the bouquet vase on a table close to the window. She took off her robe and draped it gently across the bed.

Standing still for a moment, Amber noticed how quiet everything seemed. She thought she could hear a faint breeze outside; she could feel warm sunshine streaming in from the window. She heard a bird, a dog, a motorbike in the distance, her own heart beating.

It sounded just fine.

Don't miss out!

Visit the website below and you can sign up to receive emails whenever Melissa Sorrentino publishes a new book. There's no charge and no obligation.

https://books2read.com/r/B-A-IFKL-GOEHB

BOOKS 2 READ

Connecting independent readers to independent writers.

About the Author

Melissa Sorrentino is a compulsive writer and romance lover who lives to explore the depths and shallows of womanhood. She's drawn to humor, endearingly complicated relationships, and all those deliciously imperfect in-between moments of life. If her work moves you, a brief review or star rating helps others discover it, too.